Praise for *Dracula in London*

"Inventive." —*Publishers Weekly*

"Fans of the darkly fantastic character will definitely find a comfortable spot on their shelves for this anthology. Each story is delightful and stays quite true to the original text written by Bram Stoker and published in 1897. Over a century later this cultural icon comes forward as fresh as in his first appearance. Take after take, the character of Dracula comes alive once more . . . Having thoroughly enjoyed the read, my hat is off to the numerous authors . . . Their collaboration presents a seriously fun collection that would likely please Bram Stoker himself." —*The Green Man Review*

"The accounts range from tongue in cheek to scary . . . Vampire fans will appreciate the way this collection rounds out Dracula's character by showing him as more than a predator capable also of fatherly affection and an appreciation for the theatre." —*VOYA*

"This strong anthology should appeal to the large audience for vampire fiction." —*Library Journal*

"Dracula fans who don't mind a little tampering with the myth will appreciate these tales." —*Booklist*

"While he lived in Victorian England, Dracula became involved with other people and events that the author chose to ignore. Mr. Stoker left it to some of the most famous writers of horror tales to complete the full picture by contributing fantastic stories to this anthology . . . The entire collection is excellent as no one fails to hold up his or her weight. Mr. Stoker would have appreciated this anthology." —*Paranormal Romance Reviews*

"A strong anthology with good writing. Highly recommended." —*KLIATT*

"Well-written and engaging." —*The Vampire's Crypt*

"Darkly alluring. Most highly recommended." —*Hypathia's Hoard*

Ace Books by P. N. Elrod

The Vampire Files

Dracula in London

Edited by
P. N. Elrod

ACE BOOKS, NEW YORK

THE BERKLEY PUBLISHING GROUP
Published by the Penguin Group
Penguin Group (USA) Inc.
375 Hudson Street, New York, New York 10014, USA
Penguin Group (Canada), 10 Alcorn Avenue, Toronto,
Ontario M4V 3B2, Canada (a division of Pearson Penguin Canada Inc.)
Penguin Books Ltd., 80 Strand, London WC2R 0RL, England
Penguin Ireland, 25 St. Stephen's Green, Dublin 2,
Ireland (a division of Penguin Books Ltd.)
Penguin Group (Australia), 250 Camberwell Road, Camberwell, Victoria 3124,
Australia (a division of Pearson Australia Group Pty. Ltd.)
Penguin Books India Pvt. Ltd., 11 Community Centre, Panchsheel Park,
New Delhi—110 017, India
Penguin Group (NZ), Cnr. Airborne and Rosedale Roads, Albany,
Auckland 1310, New Zealand (a division of Pearson New Zealand Ltd.)
Penguin Books (South Africa) (Pty.) Ltd., 24 Sturdee Avenue,
Rosebank, Johannesburg 2196, South Africa

Penguin Books Ltd., Registered Offices: 80 Strand, London WC2R 0RL, England

This is a work of fiction. Names, characters, places, and incidents either are the product of the authors' imaginations or are used fictitiously, and any resemblance to actual persons, living or dead, business establishments, events, or locales is entirely coincidental.

DRACULA IN LONDON

An Ace Book / published by arrangement with the editor

PRINTING HISTORY
Ace trade paperback edition / November 2001
Ace mass market edition / October 2004

ISBN 0-441-01213-2

ACE®
Ace Books are published by The Berkley Publishing Group,
a division of Penguin Group (USA) Inc.,
375 Hudson Street, New York, New York 10014.
ACE and the "A" design
are trademarks belonging to Penguin Group (USA) Inc.

PRINTED IN THE UNITED STATES OF AMERICA

10 9 8 7 6 5 4 3 2 1

Contents

Introduction

Okay, I confess it—I love Dracula! He IS the man!

The first time I remember seeing him was in Universal's *House of Dracula* with elegant John Carradine in the role. I was instantly addicted. From then on, I couldn't get enough of all the variations out there, good and bad, sublime and silly. Umpteen years pass and it still gives me a charge!

Hence this book. I wanted to put together a collection of stories with the Count as the focus, not a mere cameo, and ask the question, "What ELSE was Dracula doing in London when he was not being chased by Van Helsing and company?"

I feel very fortunate that some of the best writers in the business decided to answer. To have the chance to read so many delightful variations on a theme has been a dream come true. My sincere thanks to all of you for contributing your time and imaginations to this project. It's been an honor.

*   *   *

In 1897 the original novel *Dracula* was published, bringing little note or notice to author Bram Stoker.

Writers hate when that happens.

But over the next century, as though to make up for it, Dracula turned into an honest-to-God cultural icon. You say the name nearly anywhere on the planet and you're bound to get a reaction of some sort. "What are the odds?" one might ask Mr. Stoker, who would likely be astonished. Or amused.

I like to think that somewhere he knows his tale eventually achieved an immortality greater than that which his character met in that dark and thrilling opus.

My hope is that he might well have enjoyed this "tip of the hat" collection of stories centered around his best-known creation.

—P. N. "Pat" Elrod

To Each His Own Kind

TANYA HUFF

London was everything the Count had imagined it to
be when he'd told Jonathan Harker of how he'd longed
to walk "through the crowded streets . . . to be in the
midst of the whirl and rush of humanity." *Although,*
he amended as he waited for a break in the evening
traffic that would allow him to cross Piccadilly, *a little
less whirl and rush would be preferable.*

He could see the house he'd purchased across the
street, but it might as well have been across the city
for all he could reach it. Yes, he'd wanted to move
about unnoticed but this, this was wearing at his patience. And he had never been considered a patient
man. Even as a man.

Finally, he'd been delayed for as long as he was
willing to endure. Sliding the smoked glasses down his
nose, he deliberately met the gaze of an approaching
horse. In his homeland, the effect would have been
felt between one heartbeat and the next. Terror. Panic.
Flight. This London carriage horse, however, seemed
to accept his presence almost phlegmatically.

Then the message actually made it through the city's patina to the equine brain.

Better, he thought and strode untouched through the resulting chaos. Ignoring the screams of injured men and horses both, he put the key into the lock and stepped inside.

He'd purchased the house furnished from the estate of Mr. Archibald Winter-Suffield. From the dead, as it were. That amused him.

His belongings were in the dining room at the back of the house.

"The dining room?" He sighed. His orders to the shipping company had only instructed that the precious cases be placed in the house. Apparently, here in this new country, he needed to be more specific. They would have to be moved to a place less conspicuous, but not now, not with London calling to him. He set his leather case upon the table and turned to go.

Stepping around a chair displaced by the boxes of earth, he brushed against the sideboard, smearing dust across his sleeve. Snarling, he brushed at it with his gloved hand but only succeeded in smearing it further. The coat was new. He'd sent his measurements to Peter Hawkins before he'd started his journey and had found clothing suitable for an English gentleman at journey's end. It was one of the last commissions Mr. Hawkins had fulfilled for him. One of the last he would fulfill for anyone, as it happened. The old man had been useful, but the necessity of frequent correspondence had left him knowing too much.

Opening the case, he pulled out a bundle of deeds—this was not the only house that English dead had provided—and another bundle of note paper, envelopes, and pens. As he set them down, he reminded himself to procure ink as soon as possible. He disliked being without it. Written communications allowed a certain degree of distance from those who did his bidding.

Finally, after some further rummaging, he found his clothing brush and removed the dust from his sleeve. Presentable at last, he tossed the brush down on the table and hurried for the street, suddenly impatient to begin savoring this new existence.

"... *to share its life, its change, its death, all that makes it what it is.*"

The crowd outside on Piccadilly surprised him and he stopped at the top of the stairs. The crowds he knew in turn knew better than to gather outside his home. When he realized that the people were taking no notice of him and had, in fact, gathered to watch the dead horse pulled up onto a wagon, he descended to the street.

He thrilled to his anonymity as he made his way among them. To walk through a great mass of Londoners unremarked—it was all he had dreamed it would be. To feel their lives surrounding him, unaware of their danger. To walk as a wolf among the unsuspecting lambs. To know that even should he declare himself, they would not believe. It was a freedom he had never thought to experience again.

Then a boy, no more than eight or ten, broke free of his minder and surged forward to get a clearer look. Crying, "Hey now!" a portly man stepped out of the child's way.

The pressure of the man's foot on his meant less than nothing but he hissed for the mark it made on his new shoes. And for the intrusion into his solitude.

The portly man turned at the sound, ruddy cheeks pale as he scanned the ground.

By the time he looked up, the Count had composed himself. It would not do to give himself away over so minor a thing.

"You aren't going to believe this," the man said without preamble, his accent most definitely not English, "but I could've sworn I heard a rattler." Then he smiled and extended his hand. "I do beg your pardon, sir, for treading on you as I did. Shall we consider my clumsiness an introduction? Charlie March, at your service."

The novelty of the situation prodded him to take the offered hand. "I am . . ." He paused for an instant and considered. Should he maintain the identity that went with the house? But no. The Count de Ville was a name that meant nothing; he would not surrender his lineage so easily. Straightening to his full height, he began again. "I am Dracula. Count Dracula."

The smile broadened. "A Count? Bless me. You're not from around these parts, are you?"

"No. I am only recently arrived."

"From the continent? I could tell. Your accent, you know. Very old world, very refined. Romania?"

The Count blinked and actually took a step back before he gained control of his reaction.

Charlie laughed. "I did some business with a chap from Romania last year. Bought some breeding stock off me. Lovely manners you lot have, lovely."

"Thank you." It was really the only thing he could think of to say.

"I'm not from around these parts myself." He continued before there was even a chance of a reply. "Me, I'm American. Got a big spread out west, the Double C—the missus's name is Charlotte, you see. She's the reason we came to England. She got tired of spending money in New York and wanted to spend some in London." His gaze flicked up, then down, then paused. "That's one hell of a diamond you've got stuck in your tie, if you don't mind my saying so."

"It has been in my family for a long time." He'd taken it from the finger of a Turk after he'd taken the finger from the Turk.

"Well, there's nothing like old money, that's what I always say." Again the smile, which had never entirely disappeared, broadened. "Unless it's new money. Have you plans for this evening, Count?"

"Plans?" He couldn't remember the last time he'd been so nonplused. In fact, he couldn't remember if he'd ever been so nonplused. "No."

"Then if you're willing, I'd like to make up for treading so impolitely on your foot. I'm heading to a sort of a soiree at a friend's." His eyelids dropped to a conspiratorial level. "You know, the sort of soiree you don't take your missus to. Oh, you needn't worry about the company," he added hurriedly. "They're your kind of people." He leaned a little closer and dropped his voice. "His Royal Highness will be there. You know, the Prince of Wales."

About to decline the most peculiar invitation he'd ever received, the Count paused. The Prince of Wales would be in attendance. The Prince of Wales. His kind of people. "I would be pleased to attend this soiree as your guest," he said. And smiled.

"Damn, but you've got some teeth on you."

"Thank you. They are a . . . family trait."

The party was being held in a house on St. James Square. Although only a short walk from his own London sanctuary, the buildings were significantly larger and the occupants of the buildings either very well born or very rich. Seldom both, as it happened. It was an area where by birth and power he deserved to live but where it would be impossible for him to remain hidden. Years of experience had taught him that the very rich and the very poor were equals in their thirst for gossip, but the strange and growing English phenomenon of middle class—well researched before he'd left his homeland—seemed willing to keep their attention on business rather than their neighbors.

He followed Charlie March up the stairs and paused at the door, wondering if so general an invitation would allow him to cross the threshold.

Two steps into the foyer, March turned with his

perpetual smile. "Well, come in, Count. No need to wait for an engraved invitation."

"No, of course not." He joined the American in removing his hat, coat, and gloves, handing them into the care of a liveried footman.

"I expect you'll want to meet His Highness first?"

"It would be proper to pay my immediate respects to the prince."

"Proper to pay your immediate respects," March repeated shaking his head. "Didn't I say you lot have lovely manners. Where would His Highness be then?" he asked the footman.

"The green salon, sir."

"Of course he is, the evening's young. I should have known. This way then." He took hold of the Count's arm to turn him toward the stairs. "Say, there's not a lot of meat on your bones is there? Now me, I think a little stoutness shows a man's place in the world."

"Indeed." He stared down at the fleshy fingers wrapped just above his elbow, too astonished at being so held to be enraged. Fortunately, he was released before the astonishment faded, for it would have been the height of rudeness to kill the man while they were both guests in another's home.

At the top of the stairs they crossed a broad landing toward an open doorway through which spilled the sounds of men . . . and women? He paused. He would not be anonymous in this crowd. He would be introduced and be expected to take part in social discourse. While he looked forward to the opportunity of testing his ability to walk unknown and unseen amongst the living, he also found himself strangely afraid. It had been a very, very long time since he had been a member of such a party and it would have been so much easier had the women not been there.

He had always had a weakness—no, say rather a fondness, for he did not admit weakness—for a pretty face.

"Problem, Count?" March paused in the doorway and beamed back at him.

On the other hand, if this man can move amongst the powerful of London and they do not see him *for what he is* . . . "No, not at all, Mr. March. Lead on."

There had been little imagination involved in the naming of the green salon, for the walls were covered in a brocaded green wallpaper that would have been overwhelming had it not been covered in turn by dozens of paintings. A few were surprisingly good, most were indifferent, and all had been placed within remarkably ugly frames. The furniture had been upholstered in a variety of green and gold and cream patterns and underfoot was a carpet predominantly consisting of green cabbage roses. Everything that could be gilded, had been. Suppressing a shudder, he was almost overcome by a sudden wave of longing for the bare stone and dark, heavy oak of home.

Small groups of people were clustered about the room, but his eyes were instantly drawn to the pair of facing settees where half a dozen beautiful women sat talking together, creamy shoulders and bare arms rising from silks and satins heavily corseted around impossibly tiny waists. How was it his newspapers had described the women to be found circling around the prince? Ah yes, as *"a flotilla of white swans, their long necks supporting delicate jeweled heads."* He had thought it excessively fanciful when he read it but now, now he saw that it was only beautifully accurate.

"We'll introduce you to the ladies later," March murmured, leading the way across the center of the room. "That's His Highness by the window."

Although he would have much preferred to take the less obvious route around the edges, the Count followed. As they passed the ladies, he glanced down. Most were so obviously looking away they could only have been staring at him the moment before, but one met his gaze. Her eyes widened and her lips parted but she did not look away. He could see the pulse beating in the soft column of her throat. *Later,* he promised, and moved on.

"Your Royal Highness, may I present a recent acquaintance of mine, Count-Dracula."

Even before March spoke, he had identified which of the stout, whiskered men smoking cigars by the open window was Edward, the Prince of Wales. Not from the newspaper photographs, for he found it difficult to see the living in such flat black and gray representations, but from the nearly visible aura of power that surrounded him. Like recognized like. Power recognized power. If the reports accompanying the photographs were true, the prince was not allowed much in the way of political power but he was clearly conscious of himself as a member of the royal caste.

He bowed, in the old way, body rigid, heels coming together. "I am honored to make your acquaintance, Your Highness."

The prince's heavy lids dropped slightly. "Count Dracula? This sounds familiar, yah? You are from where?"

"From the Carpathian Mountains, Highness," he replied in German. His concerns about sounding foreign had obviously been unnecessary. Edward sounded more like a German prince than an English one. "My family has been *boyers,* princes there since before we turned back the Turk many centuries ago. Princes still when we threw off the Hungarian yoke. Leaders in every war. But—" he sighed and spread his hands— "the warlike days are over and the glories of my great race are as a tale that is told."

"Well said, sir!" the prince exclaimed in the same language. "Although I am certain I have heard your name, I am afraid I do not know that area well—as familiar as I am with most of Europe." He smiled and added, "As related as I am to most of Europe. If you are not married, Dracula, I regret I have no sisters remaining."

The gathered men laughed with the prince, although the Count could see not all of them—and Mr. March was of that group—spoke German. "I am not married now, Your Highness, although I was in the past."

"Death takes so many," Edward agreed solemnly.

The Count bowed again. "My deepest sympathies on the death of your eldest son, Highness." The report of how the Duke of Clarence had unexpectedly died of pneumonia in early 1892 had been in one of the last newspaper bundles he'd received. As far as the Count was concerned, death should be unexpected, but he was perfectly capable of saying what others considered to be the right thing. If it suited his purposes.

"It was a most difficult time," Edward admitted. "And the wound still bleeds. I would have given my life for him." He stared intently at his cigar.

With predator patience, the Count absorbed the silence that followed as everyone but he and the prince shifted uncomfortably in place.

"Shall I tell you how I met the Count, your Highness?" March asked suddenly. "There was a bully smash up on Piccadilly."

"A bully smash up?" the prince repeated lifting his head and switching back to English. "Were you in it?"

"No, sir, I wasn't."

"Was the Count?"

"No, sir, he wasn't either. But we both saw it, didn't we, Count?"

The Count saw that the prince was amused by the American so, although he dearly wanted to put the man in his place, he said only, "Yes."

"And you consider this accident to be a gutt introduction to a Carpathian prince?" Edward asked, smiling.

If March had possessed a tail, the Count realized, he'd have been wagging it; he was so obviously pleased that he'd lifted the Prince of Wales's spirits. "Yes, sir, I did. Few things bring men together like disasters. Isn't that true, Count?"

That, he could wholeheartedly agree with. He was introduced in turn to Lord Nathan Rothschild, Sir Ernest Cassel, and Sir Thomas Lipton—current favorites of Prince Edward—and he silently thanked the English newspapers and magazines that had provided enough facts about these men for him to converse intelligently.

He was listening with interest to a discussion of the Greek–Turkish War when he became aware of Mr. March's scrutiny. Turning toward the American, he caught the pudgy man's gaze and held it. "Yes?"

March blinked, and the Count couldn't help thinking that even the horse on Piccadilly hadn't taken so long to recognize its danger. It wasn't that March was stupid—it seemed that old terrors had been forgotten in his new land.

"I was just wondering about your glasses, Count. Why do you keep those smoked lenses on inside?"

Because the prince was also listening, he explained. "My eyes are very sensitive to light and I am not used to so much interior illumination." He gestured at the gas lamps. "This is quite a marvel to me."

Prince Edward beamed. "You will find England at the very front of science and technology. This . . ." he echoed the Count's gesture, trailing smoke from his cigar, "is nothing. Before not much longer we will see electricity take the place of gas, motor cars take the place of horses, and actors and actresses . . ." his smile was answered by the most beautiful of the women seated across the room, "replaced by images on a screen. I, myself, have seen these images—have seen them move— right here in London. The British Empire shall lead the way into the new century!"

Those close enough to hear applauded, and March shouted an enthusiastic "Hurrah!"

The Count bowed a third time. "It is why I have come to London, Highness; to be led into the new century."

"Gutt man." A footman carrying a tray of full wine glasses appeared at the prince's elbow. "Please try the burgundy, it is a very gutt wine."

About to admit that he did not drink wine, the Count reconsidered. In order to remain un-noted, he must be seen to do as others did. "Thank you, Highness." It helped that the burgundy was a rich, dark red. While he didn't actually drink it, he appreciated the color.

When the clock on the mantle struck nine, Edward led the way to the card room, motioning that the Count should fall in beside him. "Have you seen much of my London?" he asked.

"Not yet, Highness. Although I was at the zoo only a few days past."

"The zoo? I have never been there, myself. Animals I am most fond of, I see through my sights." He mimed shooting a rifle and again his immediate circle, now walking two by two down the hall behind him, laughed.

"And he'd rather see a good race than govern, wouldn't you, Highness?" Directly behind Edward's shoulder, March leaned forward enough to come between the two princes. "Twenty-eight race meetings last year. I heard that's three more visits than he made to his House of Lords."

The Count felt the Prince of Wales stiffen beside him. Before the prince could speak, the Count turned and dipped his head just far enough to spear March over the edge of his glasses. "It is not wise," he said slowly, "to repeat everything one hears."

To his astonishment, March smiled. "I wouldn't repeat it outside this company."

"Don't," Edward advised.

"You betcha," March agreed. "Say, Count, your eyes are kind of red. My missus has some drops she puts in hers. I could find out what they are if you like."

Too taken aback to be angry, the Count shook his head. "No. Thank you."

Murmuring, "Lovely manners," in an approving tone, March stepped forward so that he could open the card room door for the prince.

"He is rough, like many Americans," Edward confided in low German as they entered. "But his heart is gutt and, more importantly, his wallet is deep."

"Then for your sake, Highness . . ."

The game in the card room was bridge and Prince Edward had a passion for it. After two hours of watching the prince move bits of painted card about, the Count understood the attraction no better than he had in the beginning.

Just after midnight, the prince gave his place to Sir Thomas.

"It was gutt to meet you, Count Dracula. I hope to see you again."

"You will, Highness."

Caught and held in the red gaze, the prince wet full lips and swallowed heavily.

One last time, the Count bowed and stepped back, breaking his hold.

Breathing heavily, Edward hurried from the room. A woman's laughter met him in the hall.

The Count turned to the table. "If you will excuse me, gentlemen, now that His Highness has taken his leave, I will follow. I am certain that I will see you *all* again."

In the foyer, only for the pleasure of watching terror blanch the boy's cheeks, he brushed the footman's hand with his as he took back his gloves.

He very nearly made it out the door.

"Say, Count! Hold up and I'll walk with you."

March fell into step beside him as he crossed the threshold back into the night. "It's close in those rooms, ain't it? September's a lot warmer here than it is back home. Where are you heading?"

"To the Thames."

"Going across to the fleshpots in Southwark?" the American asked archly.

"Fleshpots?" It took him a moment to understand. "No. I will not be crossing the river."

"Just taking a walk on the shore then? Count me in."

They walked in blessed silence for a few moments, along Pall Mall and down Cockspur Street.

"His Highness likes you, Count. I could tell. You have a real presence in a room, you know."

"The weight of history, Mr. March."

"Say what?"

He saw a rat watching him from the shadow, rat and shadow both in the midst of wealth and plenty, and he smiled. "It is not necessary you understand."

Silence reigned again until they reached the riverbank.

"You seemed to be having a good time tonight, Count." March leaned on the metal railings at the top of the embankment. "Didn't I tell you they were your kind of people?"

"Yes."

"So." A bit of loose stone went over the edge and into the water. "Did you want to go somewhere for a bite?"

"That won't be necessary." He removed his glasses and slid them carefully into an inside pocket. "Here is fine."

The body slid down the embankment and was swallowed almost silently by the dark water. Replete, the Count drew the back of one hand over his mouth then stared in annoyance at the dark smear across the back of his glove. These were his favorite gloves; they'd have to be washed.

He turned toward home, then he paused.

Why hurry?

The night was not exactly young, but morning would be hours still.

As he walked along the riverbank toward the distant sound of voices, he smiled. The late Charlie March had not been entirely correct. The prince and his company were not exactly his kind of people . . .

. . . yet.

Box Number Fifty

Fred Saberhagen

Carrie had been living on the London streets for a night and a day, plenty of time to learn that being taken in charge by the police was not the worst thing that could happen. But it would be bad enough. What she had heard of the conditions in which homeless children were confined made her ready to risk a lot in trying to stay free.

A huge dray drawn by two whipped and lathered horses rushed past, almost knocking her down, as she began to cross another street. Tightening her grip on the hand of nine-year-old Christopher as he stumbled in exhaustion, she struggled on through the London fog, wet air greasy with burning coal and wood. Around the children were a million strangers, all in a hurry amid an endless roar of traffic.

"Where we going to sleep tonight?" Her little brother sounded desperate, and no doubt he was. Last night they had had almost no sleep at all, huddled against the abutment of a railway bridge; but fortunately it had not been raining then as it was now. There had been only one episode of real adventure during the night, when Chris, on going a little way apart to answer a call of nature, had been set on and robbed of his shoes by several playful fellows not much bigger than he.

Their wanderings had brought them into Soho, where they attracted some unwelcome attention. Carrie thought that a pair of rough-looking youths had now begun to follow them.

She had to seek help somewhere, and none of the faces in her immediate vicinity looked promising. On impulse she turned from the pavement up a flight of stone steps to the front door of a house. It was a narrow building of gray stone, not particularly old or new, one of a row, wedged tightly against its neighbors on either side. Had Carrie been given time to think about it, she might have said that she chose this house because it bore a certain air of quiet and decency, in contrast to its neighbors, which at this early stage of evening were given to lights and raucous noise.

Across the street, a helmeted bobby was taking no interest in a girl and boy with nowhere to go. But he might at any moment. These were not true slums, not, by far, the worst part of London. Still, here and there, in out-of-the-way corners, a derelict or two lay drunk or dying.

Carrie went briskly up the steps to the front door, while her brother, following some impulse of his own, slipped down into the areaway where he was for the moment concealed from the street. Glancing quickly down at Christopher from the high steps, Carrie thought he was doing something to one of the cellar windows.

Giving a long pull on the bell, she heard a distant ringing somewhere inside. And at the same moment, she saw to her dismay that what she had thought was a modest light somewhere in the interior of the house was really only a reflection in one of the front windows.

There were curtains inside, but other than that the place had an uninhabited look and feel about it.

"Not a-goin' ter let yer in?" One of the youths following her had now stopped on the pavement at the foot of the steps, where he stood grinning up at her, while his fellow stood beside him, equally delighted.

"I know a house where you'd be welcome, dear," called the second one. He was older, meaner-looking. "I know some good girls who live there."

Turning her back on them both, she tried to project an air of confidence and respectability, as she persisted in pulling at the bell.

"My name's Vincent," came the deeper voice from behind her. "If maybe you need a friend, dearie, a little help—"

Carrie caught her breath at the sound of an answering fumble in the darkness on the other side of the barrier—and was mightily relieved a moment later when her brother opened the door from inside. In a moment she was in, and had closed and latched the door behind her.

She could picture the pair who had been heckling her from the pavement, balked for the moment, turning away.

It was so dark in the house that she could barely see Christopher's pale face at an arm's-length distance, but at least they were no longer standing in the rain.

"How'd you get in?" she whispered at him fiercely. Then, "Whose house is this?"

"Broken latch on a window down there," he whispered back. Then he added in a more normal voice, "It was awful dark in the cellar; I barked my shin on something trying to find the stair."

It was a good thing, Carrie congratulated herself in passing, that neither of them had ever been especially afraid of the dark. Already her eyes were growing accustomed to the deep gloom; enough light strayed in

from the street, around the fringes of curtain, to reveal
the fact that the front hall where they were standing
was hardly furnished at all, nor was the parlor, just
beyond a broad archway. More clearly than ever, the
house said *empty*.

"Let's try the gas," she whispered. Chris, fumbling
in the drawer of a built-in sideboard, soon came up
with some matches. Carrie, standing on tiptoe, was tall
enough to reach a fixture projecting from the wall. In
a moment more she had one of the gaslights lit.

"Is anyone here?" Now her voice too was up to
normal; the answer seemed to be no. The sideboard
drawer also contained a couple of short scraps of candle, and soon they had lights in hand to go exploring.

Front hall, with an old abandoned mirror still fastened to the wall beside a hat rack and a shelf. Just in
from the hall, a wooden stair, handrail carved with a
touch of elegance, went straight up to the next floor.
Not even a mouse stirred in the barren parlor. The
dining room was a desert also, no furniture at all. And
so, farther back, was the kitchen, except for a great
black stove and a sink whose bright new length of
metal pipe promised running water. An interior cellar
door had been left open by Chris in his hurried ascent,
and next to it a recently walled-off cubicle contained a
water closet. A kitchen window looked out on what
was no doubt a back garden, now invisible in gloom
and rain.

Carrie was ready to explore upstairs, but Christopher insisted on seeing the cellar first, curious as to
what object he had stumbled over. The culprit proved
to be a cheaply constructed crate, not quite wide or
long enough to be a coffin, containing only some scraps
of kindling wood. Otherwise the cellar—damp brick
walls; floor part pavement, part dry earth—was as
empty as the house above.

Now for the upstairs. Holding the candle tremulously high ahead of her, while dancing shadows beat

a wavering retreat, Carrie returned to the front hall, and thence up the carved wooden stair. Two bedrooms, as unused as the lower level of the house and as scantily furnished. The rear windows looked out over darkness, the front ones over the street—side walls were windowless, crammed as they were against the neighbors on either side.

From an angle in the hallway on the upper floor, a narrow service stair, white-painted, went up straight and steep to a trapdoor in the ceiling.

"What's up there?" she wondered aloud.

"Couldn't be nothin' but an attic." Only a short time on the street had begun to have a serious effect on Christopher's English, of which a certain Canadian schoolmaster had once been proud.

Carrie spotted fresh footprints in the thin layer of dust and soot that had accumulated on the white-painted stairs. A clear image of the heel of a man's boot. Only one set of footprints, coming down.

The trapdoor pushed up easily. The space above was more garret than attic; it might once have been furnished, maybe servants' quarters. The floor entirely solid, no rafters exposed, though now there were dust and spiderwebs in plenty. The broad panes of glass in the angled skylight, washed by rain on the outside, were still intact, and it was bolted firmly shut on the inside; if you stood tall enough inside, you could look out over a hilly range of slate roofs and chimney pots, with the towering dome of St. Paul's visible more than a mile to the east.

On one side of the gloomy space rested an old wardrobe, door slightly ajar to reveal a few hanging garments. But the most interesting object by far was a great wooden box, somewhat battered by much use or travel, which had been shoved against the north wall.

Chris thought it looked like a coffin, and said so.

"No. Built too strong for a poor man's coffin, not

elegant enough for a rich man's." What was it, though? There were two strong rope handles on each side, and a plain wooden lid, tightly fitted by some competent woodworker.

Christopher, ever curious, approached the box and tried the lid. To his surprise, and Carrie's, it slid back at once.

"Look here, Sis!"

"Why, it's full of dirt." She was aware of a vague disappointment in her observation, and not sure why. Only about half-full, actually, but that was no less odd. Stranger still was the fact that the neat joinings of the interior seemed to have been tarred with pitch, as if to make them waterproof. Of course so tight a seal would also serve to keep the soil from leaking out. But *why* would *anyone*—?

The earth was dry. When Carrie picked up a small handful and sifted it through her fingers, it gave off a faintly musty, almost spicy smell, with a suggestion of the alien about it.

Christopher was downstairs again, moving so silently on his bare feet that Carrie had not realized he was gone, until she heard him faintly calling her to come down. She slid the lid back onto the box, and carefully lowered the trapdoor into place behind her.

Her brother had turned on the gaslight in the kitchen and discovered some tins of sardines abandoned in the pantry. Presently they remembered the box of kindling in the cellar, and it was possible to get a wood fire started in the kitchen stove.

The sardines were soon gone. Brother and sister were still hungry, but at least they were out of the rain.

That night they slept in a house, behind locked doors, curled up in a dusty rug on the kitchen floor, where some of the stove's warmth reached them. Barely into October, and it was cold.

*　　*　　*

Next day, waking up in a foodless house and observing that the rain had stopped, they were soon out and about on the streets of London, trying to do something to earn some money, and keep out of trouble. But in each endeavor they had only limited success. Carrie was certain that the neighbors had begun to notice them, and not in any very friendly way. So had the bobby who walked the beat during the day.

There was one bright spot. On the sideboard, as if someone had left it there deliberately, they found a key which matched the locks on both front door and back.

Vincent still had his eye on them, too, or at least on Carrie. And "Don't see your parents about," one of the neighbors remarked as she came by. She answered with a smile, and hurried inside to share with Christopher the handful of biscuits she had just stolen from a shop.

Shortly after sunset, threatening trouble broke at last. The rain had stopped, and people were ready to get out and mind each other's business. One of the neighbors began it, another joined in, followed by the walrus-mustached policeman, who, when voices were raised, had decided it was his duty to take part.

And joined at a little distance by the nasty Vincent, who before the policeman arrived boldly put in a word, offering to place Carrie under his protection. He had some comments on her body that made her face flame with humiliation and anger.

Carrie could not slam the door on Vincent, because he had his foot pushed in to hold it open. He withdrew the foot as the bobby approached, but Carrie did not quite dare to close the door in the policeman's face.

"What's your name, girl?" he wanted to know, without preamble.

"Carrie. Carrie Martin. This's my brother Chris."

"Is the woman of the house in?" demanded the boldest neighbor, breaking in on the policeman's dramatic pause.

Carrie admitted the sad truth, that her mother was dead.

Another neighbor chimed in. "Your father about, then?"

The girl could feel herself being driven back, almost to the foot of the stairs. "He's very busy. He doesn't like to be disturbed."

Somehow three or four people were already inside the door. There was still enough daylight to reveal the shabbiness and scantiness of the furnishings, and of the children's clothes, once quite respectable.

"Looks like the maid has not come in as yet." That was said facetiously.

"Must be the butler's day off, too," chimed in another neighbor.

"You say your father's here, miss?" This was the policeman, slow and majestic, in the mode of a large and overbearing uncle. "I'd like to have a word with him, if I may."

"He doesn't like to be disturbed." Carrie could hear her own voice threatening to break into a childish squeal. For a little while, for a few hours, it had looked like they might be able to survive. But now . . .

"Where is he?"

"Upstairs. But—"

"Asleep, then, is he?"

"I—I—yes."

"How old are you?"

"Sixteen."

"Oh yes, you are, I *don't* think! See here, my girl, unless I have some evidence that you and the young 'un here are under some supervision, you'll both be charged with wandering, and not being under proper guardianship."

Carrie, standing at bay at the foot of the stair, gripping her brother by his shoulder, raised her voice in protest, but the voices of the others increased in volume, too. They seemed to be all talking at once, making accusations and demands—

Suddenly their voices cut off altogether. Their eyes that had been fixed on Carrie rose up to somewhere above her head, and behind her on the stair there was a creak of wood, as under a quiet but weighty tread.

She turned to see a tall, well-built, well-dressed man coming down with measured steps. Perfectly calm, as if he descended these stairs every day, a gentleman in his own house. His brownish hair, well-trimmed, was touched with gray at the temples, and an aquiline nose gave his face a forceful look. At the moment he was fussing with his cuffs, as if he had just put on his coat, and frowning in apparent puzzlement at the assembly below him.

Carrie had never seen him before in her life; nor had Christopher, to judge by the boy's awestruck expression as he watched from her side.

The newcomer's voice was strangely accented, low but forceful, suited to his appearance, as his gaze swept the little group gathered in his front hall. "What is the meaning of this intrusion? Officer? Carrie, what do these people want?"

Carrie could find no words at the moment. Not even when the man came to stand beside her in a fatherly attitude, resting one hand lightly on her back.

"Mr. Martin—?" The bobby's broad face wore a growing look of consternation. Already he had retreated half a step toward the door. Meanwhile the nosy neighbors, looking unhappy, were moving even faster in the same direction.

"Yes? Do you have official business with me, Officer?"

Vincent had disappeared.

The policeman recovered slightly, and stood upon official dignity; thought there might be some disturbance. Duty to investigate. But soon he too had given way under the cool gaze of the man from upstairs. In the space of a few more heartbeats the door had closed on the last of them.

The mysterious one stood regarding the door for a moment, hands clasped behind his back—they were pale hands, Carrie noted, strong-looking, and the nails tended to points. Then he reached over to the hat rack on the wall behind the door, and plucked from it a gentleman's top hat, a thing she could not for the life of her remember seeing there before. But of course she had scarcely looked. And then he turned, at ease, to regard her with a smile too faint to reveal anything of his teeth.

"I take it you are in fact the lady of the house? The only one I am likely to encounter on the premises?"

The children stared at him.

Gently he went on. "I am not given to eaves-dropping, but this afternoon my sleep was restless, and the talk I could hear below me grew ever and ever more interesting." The foreign accent was stronger now; but in Soho accents of all kinds were nothing out of the ordinary.

"Yes sir." Carrie stood with an arm around her brother. "Yes sir—that is, there is no other lady, er woman, girl, living here at present."

"That is good. It would seem superfluous to intro-duce myself, as you have already, in effect, introduced me to others. Mr. Martin I have become, and so I might as well remain. But when others are present, you, Carrie, and you, young sir, will address me as 'Fa-ther.' For however many days our joint tenancy of this dwelling may last. Understand, I do not seek to adopt you, but a temporary arrangement should be to our mutual advantage. A happy, close-knit family, yes, that is the face we present to the world. When it is neces-sary to present a face. Ah, you will kindly leave the upper regions of the house to me—if anyone should ask you, it is really my house, paid for in coin of the realm. In the name of Mr. de Ville."

"Yes sir," said Carrie, elbowing her brother until he echoed the two words.

"And now, my children." Mr. Martin, or de Ville, set his hat upon his head, and gave it a light tap with two pale fingers, as if to settle it exactly to his liking. Carrie noticed that as he did so, he ignored the old mirror on the wall beside the hat rack. And she could see why, or she imagined she could, because the small mirror did not show the man at all, but only the top hat, doing a neat half-somersault unsupported in the air, its reflected image disappearing utterly just as the hat itself came to rest on the head of the mysterious one.

"I am going out for the evening," he informed them. "I advise you to lock up for the night as solidly as possible. Do not expect to see me again until about this time tomorrow. Pleasant dreams. . . ."

On the verge of opening the door, he checked himself, frowning at them.

"The two of you have an undernourished and ill-clad look, which I find distasteful, and will only provoke more neighborly curiosity. Here." White fingers performed an economical toss; a small coin, glittering gold, spun through the air. Christopher's quick hand, like a hungry bird, snatched it in midflight.

That night brother and sister slept with full bellies, having gone out foraging amid the early evening crowds, to a nearby branch of the Aërated Bread Company. At a used furniture stall Carrie had also bought herself a nice frock, almost new, and a couple of pillows; it was awkward living in a house where there were no beds or chairs. And Christopher had found a secondhand pair of shoes that fit him well enough.

They were going to sleep on the kitchen floor again, but they were getting used to it.

"Where'd *he* sleep, is what I'd like to know," said Chris next day, climbing the stairs up from the parlor. The man had said he'd not be back till sunset, so now in midafternoon there was no harm in gratifying their curiosity, never mind that he'd said to keep below.

Both of the bedrooms were as desolate as ever, and the dust on their floors showed only their own footprints, one set shod, one five-toed, from the first night's exploration.

"And how'd he get into the house?" Carrie wanted to know. "Didn't come past us downstairs."

"You don't suppose—?"

"The *skylight?* Why'd a man do that?"

" 'Cause he don't want to be seen."

And they went up the narrow white stair, through the trapdoor.

The skylight was as snugly fastened as before. Out of persistent curiosity they approached the mysterious box again. The lid, once moved, fell clattering with shock and fright.

"Oh my God. He's in there!"

But none of this awakened Mr. Martin.

After initially recoiling, both children had to have a closer look. In urgent whispers they soon decided the man who lay so neatly and cleanly on the earth in his nice clothes was not dead. His open eyes moved faintly. In Carrie's experience, people sometimes got drunk, but never had even the drunkest of them looked like this. Some people also took strange drugs, and with that she had less familiarity.

A ring at the front door broke the spell and pulled them down the stairs. A solid workman stood on the step, cap in hand. In a thick Cockney accent he said he had come to inquire about a box, one that might have been delivered here "by mistake." Carrie, in a clean dress today, and with her face washed, denied all knowledge and briskly sent the questioner on his way.

"I don't think he believed me," Carrie muttered to her brother, when the door was closed again. "He'll be back. Or someone will."

"What'll we do? Don't want anyone bothering Mr. Martin. I like him," Chris decided.

Quickly the girl took thought. "I know!"

Within the hour the bell rang again. This man was much younger, and obviously of higher social status. Bright eyes, dark curly hair. "Excuse me, Miss? Are you the woman of the house?"

"Who wants her?"

"I'm George Harris, of Harris and Sons, moving and shipment." A large, clean hand with well-trimmed nails offered a business card. Carrie read the address: *Orange Master's Yard, Soho.*

"Oh. I suppose you're one of the sons."

"That's right, Miss. I'm looking about this neighborhood for a box that seems to have got misplaced. There's evidence it was brought to this house, some days ago. One of a large shipment, fifty in all, there's been a lot of hauling of 'em to and fro around London, one place and another. Ours not to reason why, as the poet says. But our firm feels a certain responsibility."

"What sort of box?"

George Harris had a good description, down to the rope handles. "Seen anything like that, Miss?" Meanwhile his eyes were probing the empty house behind her.

And Carrie was looking out past him, as a cab came galloping to a stop outside. Two well-dressed young gentlemen leaped out and climbed the steps. George Harris, who seemed to know them as respected clients, made introductions. Lord Godalming, no less, but called "Art" by his companion, Mr. Quincey Morris, who was carrying a carpetbag, and whose accent, though not at all the same as Mr. Martin's, also seemed uncommon even for Soho.

The new arrivals made nervous, garbled attempts at explaining their urgent search. There had been, it seemed, twenty-one boxes taken from some place called Carfax, and so forty-nine of fifty were somehow now accounted for. But this time, Lord Godalming or not, Carrie held her place firmly in the doorway, allowing no one in.

"If there is a large box on the premises, I must examine it." A commanding tone, as only one of his lordship's exalted rank could manage.

At that, Carrie gracefully gave way. "Very well, sir, my lord, there *is* a strange box here, and where it came from, I'm sure I don't know."

Three men came bustling into the house, ready for action, Morris actually, for some reason, beginning to pull a thick wooden stake out of his carpetbag—and three men were deflated, like burst balloons, when they beheld the thin-sided, commonplace container on the parlor floor.

"Our furniture has not arrived yet, as you can see." The lady of the house was socially apologetic.

Quincey Morris, muttering indelicate words, kicked off the scruffy lid, and indeed there was dirt inside, but only a few handfuls. And the two gentlemen hastily retreated to their waiting cab.

But George Harris lingered in the doorway, exchanging a few more words with Carrie. Until his lordship shouted at him to get a move on, there were other places to be examined. On with the search!

At sunset Carrie's and Christopher's cotenant came walking down the stairs into the parlor as before. There he paused, fussing with his cuffs as on the previous evening, But now his attention was caught by the rejected box. "And what is this? An attempt at furnishing?"

"You had some callers, Mr. Martin—de Ville—while you were asleep. I thought as maybe you didn't wish to be disturbed." And Carrie gave details.

"I see." His dark eyes glittered at her. "And this—?"

"The gentlemen said they were looking for a large box of earth. So I thought the easiest way was to show 'em one. Chris and I put some dirt in and dragged it up from the cellar. 'Course this one ain't nearly as big as yours. Not big enough for a tall man to lie down in. The gents were upset—this weren't at all the one they wanted to find."

There was a long pause, in which de Ville's eyes probed the children silently. Then he bowed. "It seems I am greatly in your debt, Miss Carrie. Very greatly. And in yours, Master Christopher."

Mr. de Ville seemed to sleep little the next day, or not at all, for the box in the garret held only earth. In the afternoon, Carrie by special invitation went with her new friend and his strange box to Doolittle's Wharf, where she watched the man and his box board the sailing ship *Czarina Catherine*. And she waited at dockside, wondering, until the Russian vessel cast off and dropped down seaward on the outgoing tide.

As she returned to the house, feeling once more alone and unprotected, she noted that the evil Vincent was openly watching her again.

He grew bolder when, after several days, it seemed that the man of the house was gone.

George Harris came back once, on some pretext, but obviously to see Carrie, and they talked for some time. She learned that he was seventeen, and admitted she was three years younger.

Five days, then six, had passed since *Czarina Catherine* sailed away.

George Harris came back again, this time wondering if he might have left his order book behind on his previous visit. Carrie made him tea, out of the newly restocked pantry. Mr. de Ville had left them what he called a token of his gratitude for their timely help, and sometimes Carrie was almost frightened when she counted up the golden coins. There was a bed in each bedroom now, and chairs and tables below.

Tonight Chris was in the house alone, curled up and reading by the fire, nursing a cough made worse by London air. Carrie was out alone in the London fog, walking through the greasy, smoky chill.

She heard the terrifying voice of Vincent, not far away, calling her name. There were footsteps in pursuit, hard confident strides, and in her fresh anxiety she took a wrong turning into a dead-end mews.

In another moment she was running in panic, on the verge of screaming, feeling in her bones that screaming would do no good.

Someone, some presence, was near her in the fog—but no, there was no one and nothing there.

Only her pursuer's footsteps, which came on steadily, slow and loud and confident—until they abruptly ceased.

Backed into a corner, she strained her ears, listening—nothing. Vincent must be playing cat and mouse with her. But at last a breath of wind stirred the heavy air, the gray curtain parted, and the way out of the mews seemed clear. Utterly deserted, only the body of some derelict, rolled into a corner.

No—someone was visible after all. Half a block ahead, a tall figure stood looking in Carrie's direction, as if he might be waiting for her.

With a surge of relief and astonishment she hurried forward. "Mr. de Ville!"

"My dear child. It is late for you to be abroad."

"I saw you board a ship for the Black Sea!"

His gaze searched the fog, sweeping back and forth over her head. "It is important that certain men believe I am still on that ship. And soon I really must depart from England. But I shall return to this sceptered isle one day."

Anxiously she looked over her shoulder. "There was a man—"

"Your former neighbor, who meant you harm." De Ville's forehead creased. His eyes probed shadows in the mews behind her. "It is sad to contemplate such wickedness." He sighed, put out a hand, patted her cheek. "But no matter. He will bother you no more. He told me—"

"You've seen him, sir?"

"Yes, just now—that he is leaving on a long journey—nay, has already left."

Carrie was puzzled. "Long journey—to where, sir? America?"

"Farther than that, my child. Oh, farther than that."

A man's voice was audible above the endless traffic rumble, calling her name through the night from blocks away. The voice of George Harris, calling, concerned, for Carrie.

Bidding Mr. de Ville a hasty good night, she started to go to the young man. Then, meaning to ask another question, she turned back—the street was empty, save for the rolling fog.

Wolf and Hound

NIGEL BENNETT AND P. N. ELROD

Sabra stood on the cliff overlooking the sea, scenting the rising wind for magic. She braced against cold updrafts buffeting her small body, her long hair torn free, whipping about like Medusa's snakes. She braced and let it come until she could determine if it was the simple spice of some minor weather-wizard or the dank reek of deeper sorcery.

As the church bells below tolled midnight the air abruptly went still, waiting. In the fields behind her she heard the dolourous bleating of sheep. In the town below a dog frantically barked warning. Then the storm itself burst upon sea and land. She could see the very color of its force on the wind, angry red streaks shot through with a violet so deep as to be black.

Spreading her arms wide, she sang into the night, her clear voice going out to the rocks below, then dancing across the wild gray waters of a harbour to a mist-hidden horizon. The returning echo against her soul confirmed her suspicion. The quickening wash of the gale had real spellwork behind it: old, dark, and dangerously powerful.

Blood magic it was.

Blood magic . . . and death.

Out there beyond the breakwater . . . a drifting schooner. *That* was the source. Did it carry plague such as she'd seen ravaging all the world in those short centuries past? If so, then there was little she could do to stop it. A rare stab of true horror pierced her, but only for an instant. Great would be that calamity, but it was part of the natural cycle of the earth. This was decidedly un-natural. Which brought it within her sphere of influence.

By miracle or curse, the ship found its way into the harbour, going aground, causing much activity among the locals who ran to its aid. She wondered if any of them marked the black shape of the huge wolf that leaped to shore from the deck. It charged straight for a sea cliff and the darkness of the churchyard above. The beast did not pause, but continued past the church, heading for the shelter of a broken abbey, heading directly toward Sabra.

The wolf found its way up the last steep rise, gaining level footing not five paces away.

Much larger than any she'd seen before, it was big as a calf, a match for any of the hounds of Annwyn. Raw hate gleamed from red eyes. Swinging its heavy head in her direction, long teeth bared in a growl, it advanced on her. She did not move, except to hold out her hand in a placating gesture. She spoke Words of Calming in the Old Tongue. The creature snapped in reaction, ears flat, hackles up as though she'd clubbed it instead. Beneath the thick fur, muscles bunched, and it leaped at her, its reeking jaws closing upon her throat, ripping flesh like paper. She fell backwards under the weight of its body and kept falling. Both of them launched spinning from the cliff, dropping into empty, roaring space. . . .

Sabra awoke fully from the dream.

She lay inert, eyes shut, only mildly aware of the

ornate bed in which she'd slept the day through, and tried to hold fast to the last shreds of the vision, seeking more details. Clearest of all was that picture of herself standing on the cliff overlooking Whitby Harbour. Sweet Cerridwen, but she'd not passed through Whitby in decades, why now?

Used to all sorts of nightmarish dreams, her gift of Sight was usually more forthcoming with meanings to explain the mesh of images, but not this time. Whether the wolf was a literal or symbolic danger she could not tell. Whatever was astir knew how to cloak itself, which meant a formidable magical skill. She could not ignore such a strong, if murky, portent and made the necessary arrangements for the long rail journey home.

Taking advantage of certain modes of this century's fashion, Sabra covered her pale skin in long gloves and a heavy cloak, and draped a dense black veil over a wide-brimmed bonnet. Warm for August, but it protected her from the burning sun and offered welcome isolation. She appeared to be a recently bereaved widow in deep mourning. None would question why she took no meals in the train's dining car. Those feedings she sought elsewhere from willing and forgetful companions. No more dreams of blood magic disturbed her day-sleeps, which was frustrating. She wanted more information.

It took days of travel to reach England from St. Petersburg where she'd been keeping an eye on Victoria's granddaughter, Alexandria. By then the storm Sabra had envisaged had come and gone, the mystery of it cold, though gossip was still rife. The macabre tale of a dead captain sailing his deserted ship into harbour confirmed to her that she'd done the right thing leaving the Russian court to investigate this. Whatever had been aboard boded ill for the realm she'd pledged to guard.

She spent a week in Whitby, sensing nothing useful, learning little of import except that the wolf had also been real enough, though all thought it to be only a large dog. According to a newspaper report, it had fled the ship following the same path she'd seen in her dream, vanishing into the night, perhaps to prowl the moors, alone and afraid.

Or so people assumed.

Shape-shifters were not unknown to her. Most were harmless, but this one was different, else its magic wouldn't have drawn her attention so strongly.

She sought and found information about the ship's cargo and its final destination, tracking it to Purfleet. Taking to the rails again, she followed the same route to King's Cross station, and ultimately to the badly aging mansion attached to old Carfax Abbey.

The place was deserted save for a number of boxes in the ruined chapel which proved to be filled with earth.

So . . . that was it. One of the European Breed come to settle in England. She had no objection to them, so long as they conducted themselves with wisdom and discretion. Thus far she was unimpressed. This one—if she drew the correct conclusion from the captain's log printed in the papers—had killed the entire crew of the ship on which he'd sailed. Why had he not simply cast his influence upon them to make them forget his presence? All those of undead blood had that talent, but this had been vicious and barbaric beyond reason.

Then there was the matter of the magic.

Whoever this newcomer might be, he commanded powers beyond those of his peers. The Europeans had sufficient supernatural strengths within their inherent natures, but to combine those with black sorcery made for a frightening potential. Before she could return to Russia, Sabra would have to determine their extent—and his intentions.

Still in the convenient isolation of widow's weeds, Sabra took rooms at a nearby hotel. In the days to

come she maintained a loose vigil on Carfax, primarily
after dark, as she judged it to be the most likely time
for him to return, but that proved a disappointment.
The only activity she marked was noting one night that
nearly half the boxes were gone, the signs left in the
thick dust indicating the invasion of a carting firm going
about its prosaic business.

Then there was the occasional excitement when one
of the lunatics from the sanitarium next door escaped.
He always came to Carfax, crying pitifully to gain entry
to be with his "Master."

The poor brute was touched by the moon all right,
his disturbed mind reacting badly to the European's
strong psychic trace. She visited the fellow once in the
late hours, speaking through his barred window in hope
of learning something useful. Alas, his madness was
something even her powers of influence could not
pierce. All she got was his insistence that "the Master
was here," to which she assigned its broader meaning.
If the European were on the immediate grounds, she'd
have sensed him.

Growing impatient with the wait—for August had
long vanished and September was nearly gone—Sabra
tried a scrying ceremony one night while the moon was
still at full. The results, as she stared hard into the
mirrored surface of a black bowl filled with water, were
mixed. She saw the delicate shadow of a young woman,
but nothing of her face or location. The shadow became less and less substantial, then vanished altogether.

Not good, Sabra thought grimly, then added a handful of earth taken from one of the boxes to the bowl.
She stirred it clockwise and waited for the water to
grow still again.

This time she saw *his* shadow. It stretched long and
solid in the moonlight, reaching far over city and field.
The shadow was not black, but blood red. No surprise
there. She sought to raise her view, to see the man
himself, but he kept drawing away from her. His

shadow suddenly changed shape, first into that of a wolf, then a bat, and finally dissolving into countless fly-specks that swirled away to vanish in the wind. She did not think he was aware of her; this was only part of his normal protective magic.

And probably strongest at night, she wryly concluded upon waking from her trance.

The next time she made an attempt was at the brightest hour of noon, closing her shutters and pulling the draperies close.

The visions were clear now, but dark: deaths and burials, images accompanied by vivid emotions. She was at last able to see the young woman. Dead now. There had been much unhappiness and suffering for her. Though she'd been hedged round with protections, they were not sufficient to keep *him* from sating his appetite for her. Poor lost child. She'd have had little idea what was happening to her, nor would she have known how to defend against it. There was much to be said for keeping alive old superstitions and wives' tales. The great dawning of science had helped many with its light, but there were yet things walking abroad who took advantage of the shifting shadows in the chasms between science and faith.

Dire change had already wrested the girl from her final sleep, too late to restore the balance there. However, Sabra had gotten a distinct clue to follow, a very clear vision of a churchyard with a marble mausoleum, and the impression that it was fairly close.

At dusk she set out searching for a specific building to match the one she carried in memory. London had hundreds of churches, but she had a scent to follow the right one. Death and sorrow leave their own unique spoor.

Not far from Hampstead Heath, she found the church and its attendant cemetery. There she got confirmation that the gods favored her presence, for she arrived in time to witness a most peculiar event. Four

men, one old, the rest young, were hoisting themselves
over the churchyard wall. With no small exertion they
eventually succeeded, albeit in a most undignified manner. They should have scouted the area first and made
use of a convenient overhanging tree but a few yards
along the wall. Sabra had the advantage of them with
her excellent night vision. Despite her skirts, she nim-
bly climbed the friendly branches to drop silently on
the other side.

Though stealthy as they threaded through the tomb-
stones to the mausoleum, they did not have the look
of grave robbers, being too well dressed. Medical men
seeking a corpse suitable for dissection? No, for one of
them produced a key to the structure. Mourners? They
were in for a wretched surprise. She hid behind a
shadow-steeped cypress, close enough to observe.

The older fellow, who had a Dutch accent, seemed
to be in charge, unlocking the mausoleum that they
might enter, then shutting them all inside. She stole
forward, listening through the door cracks as they la-
bouriously opened one of the coffins within . . . only
to find it empty. That did not sit well with the other
men, who all seemed connected to the young woman
who should have lain there. They demanded an explanation, and the old man, whom they addressed as "Professor," provided one. He was quite detailed.

Ah. So that was it. Hunters. He was trying to train
his acolytes in the mysteries of destroying Nosferatu.
With indifferent success, it seemed, though he managed
to convince his unhappy students that something odd
was afoot and that they should hold watch.

They soon quit the tomb, Sabra withdrew to the
cypress, and all save the professor settled in to wait.
He busied himself by working some sort of putty
around the door, explaining that the crumbled-up Host
he'd mixed into the stuff would prevent the Un-Dead
from entering through the cracks. This positively scan-
dalized Sabra. There were other, more respectful meth-

ods of sealing a place. Holy Water or a blessing would have done just as well. Perhaps he was trying to make a dramatic point with his students.

Sabra settled in, senses alert. She'd have had to wait anyway; this added company was merely an unexpected complication. It would be most interesting to question the professor, but later, when she could hypnotically control him.

If he survived the night. Even a young Nosferatu was a deadly opponent to ordinary mortals. Sabra hoped the men had armed themselves. And with the right weapons.

A distant clock struck the quarter-hours. Slowly, most slowly. She found no fault with the other guardians in their determination; it was a weary vigil and in such a place as to excite the morbid side of one's imagination. Cemeteries held no fear for her, but she did not approve of them, disliking the idea of all those bodies lying corrupt in the good earth.

The ancient Britons had sensibly exposed their dead, letting the elements and animals have their way with the flesh until naught remained but clean bones, which were then tidily interred. For a time they'd adapted the northern custom of burning the corpse, setting off a spectacular blaze none of the gods could miss, releasing the spirit to soar free from its clay prison.

Either way, there would be no doubt to anyone that the deceased, and any illness he or she carried, was indeed dead and would remain firmly, safely, and harmlessly on its *own* side of the veil. This relatively new custom of burying bodies in the ground or leaving them boxed up in mausoleums was indecent, not .to mention unhealthy. Far better to let the natural corruption of the flesh take place in the cleansing wash of open sky or by purifying fire than to hide it away to fester and rot in the airless dark.

Well, if one must have such dreary spots, best that

they be on holy ground, which was good for certain
numinous matters. But there were some types of magic
that ran beyond the bounds of the ordinary rituals of
faith. . . .

The clock struck two, and moments later she heard
the old man's hiss of warning. The group's whole attention riveted upon *something* coming up the yew-tree
avenue. Sabra ventured out a bit for a glimpse.

A young woman clad in filmy grave garments, the
same one from the scrying-vision. She walked slowly,
ghost-like, not yet aware of the men. There was no
mistaking what she'd become, but that dark bundle she
held close to her lithe body . . . a *child?* Sabra was
aghast at this cruel turn of appetite, and set herself to
leap forward and to intervene, devil take the
consequences.

But matters moved too swiftly; the instant of intervention passed when the men startled the girl, who cast
the child away. She should have fled, but instead turned
the full power of her charm upon one of them, apparently her husband. It was as though none of the others
existed for her. She'd have ensnared him on the spot,
but the professor stepped between, using a crucifix to
thwart her. Only then did the girl seem to realize her
danger and darted for the tomb—to be repulsed by the
Host. The change should *not* have left her vulnerable
to such holy objects; it was the corruption of the European's dark magics that had done that to her.

Sabra's heart sank. This was bad. Very bad.

The professor removed a portion of the putty so
the girl could slip inside the tomb, which she did, her
ability to do so adding to their consternation. He replaced it, then announced that they would return on
the morrow. They quickly left, taking the child.

What a terrible little drama, Sabra thought, *and alas
for the grieving husband.* He was the most shattered,
but then who would not be? To have a loved one die,
then return from the grave so hideously changed as to

turn that love into loathing would break the strongest heart and will. She trusted that his friends would see him through the worst of it; there was nothing she could do for him but seek the source of his loss: the European.

She left the cypress and tried the door of the tomb. Locked, and Sabra was not in the habit of carrying skeleton keys. On the other side she sensed the girl's roiling feelings: rage, frustration, confusion, pain, and terror, the mindless terror of an animal.

With as much reverence as she could summon, Sabra peeled away some of the putty, then pressed her hands flat against the cold stone of the tomb.

Come forth! she commanded.

Strong as she must be in her new state, the girl had no defense against such a Summoning. Within seconds she'd seeped through the thin opening and stood trembling on the grass. She'd been pretty in life; in the death-that-was-not-death she was radiant.

And from the look in her wide eyes, she was also quite mad.

Once a helpless innocent, now returned to prey upon the most helpless innocents of all. She had no restraints and no reason left in her addled brain. Little wonder she'd reacted so foolishly to the hunters, seeking sanctuary in a place no longer safe. She was like a child pulling a blanket overhead to keep out the monsters.

Sabra tried to fasten her attention with hypnosis, hoping to draw her from the darkness, but to no avail. What remained of the girl's mind was quicksilver elusive; she voiced only vague ramblings about being lonely and hungry. Her eyes focused once—on Sabra's throat—and she started eagerly forward, but Sabra put a stop to *that* with a rebuffing word and gesture, freezing her in place. The girl subsided, moaning miserably.

Most of the converted made the transition with little or no shock to the mind. Of course, it helped when their lovers took the trouble to acquaint them with what to expect. Sabra asked the girl for the European's name, but she didn't even know that much. Less than the poor lunatic from the asylum.

With no small disgust—for the European, not his pathetic victim—Sabra released the girl to return to her hiding place. She was malleable to some forms of suggestion, so Sabra took care to instruct her to sleep deeply for the next few days and nights. It would ease her sufferings. By then the old professor and his friends would have had time to return and deal with the wretch. She was entirely lost to insanity and the European's magic; death would at least free her spirit. A tragedy, but there was no other help for it.

As for the heartless bastard who had *done* this to her . . .

Sabra returned to her hotel, sleeping lightly until midmorning, when she donned her widow's weeds, paid the accounting, and set forth for Carfax, carrying a carpetbag of such items as she might need for an outdoor adventure. It would be only a slight rough-out for her; she'd camped in worse places in her varied travels. But, oh, the abbey was so filthy, the dust a foot deep in some places. Why were some men such pigs? She'd known wonderful exceptions over the centuries, but this European was not in their number.

She gathered wood, twigs, and vines and made a broom, the first to cross the threshold in several decades. She swept out an inner room of the house, banished its resident nest of rats, and blessed it to make it a place of power. Then she sat cross-legged in the middle of the circle she'd chalked on the floor. Before her was the scrying bowl, its water muddied by earth taken from the boxes. There she focused the whole of her concentration, trying to contact him through that link. The possibility existed he would go to ground, but from his vile treatment of the girl and the murder of the ship's crew, Sabra judged he would be more curious than cautious. If he was that arrogant he might think himself immune to harm—a weakness she could exploit.

Sabra lost track of time. She surfaced once, days later, drawn out one night by a strange commotion in the attached abbey. The hunters were there, apparently having followed the same trail of boxes as she, and busily opening them and blessing their contents. A convocation of rats turned up, one of the European's devisings meant to discourage burglars, but the men countered with some fierce terriers to chase them off, and continued with their work, placing pieces of the Host in each box. She smiled approval for their cleverness. It would not please their quarry.

Armed with this new advantage, Sabra later returned to her room with a fresh handful of reconsecrated soil and added it to the scrying water. When she sent her thoughts forth—*now and finally!*—she encountered *his* solid presence, and the jolt she sent him struck like an electrical shock. The returning echo carried his reaction: reflexive rage . . . and vast puzzlement.

Good. It was about time he noticed her.

He delayed answering. In all likelihood he'd never encountered one such as herself. Another few days passed before prudence surrendered to curiosity, and she sensed his approach to Carfax not at night, but at noon. Perhaps he thought that like his own, her unnatural powers would be at their lowest ebb in the sun, and preferred to keep things on a physical level where he would have the advantage.

She went down to the abbey to greet him, perching primly on one of the boxes, not so much to make a point, but because it wasn't layered with dust like the rest of the stinking sty.

The great door opened, and he paused on the threshold, allowing his eyes to adjust to the dimness within. It left him beautifully silhouetted. If Sabra had a crossbow in hand and been so minded, he'd have much regretted the error.

Tall and thin, with a cruel sensual face, and a fierce intellect alight in tiger green eyes . . . yes, that poor girl had stood no chance against him at all. Few would. There was a poisonous aura around him that boded ill to any who brushed against it, like a carrier of plague.

He came in slowly, his harsh, red-flecked gaze fixing on her like a fiery arrow. He took in the boxes, certainly aware that they'd all been interfered with, made useless to him.

"Did you do this, woman?" he demanded, his voice rumbling so deep with suppressed fury that it stirred a breeze around him. The place was in need of such; the air was unbreatheably thick with grave-stench.

"I'm not responsible," she replied, holding to an even tone. "But we must speak—"

"Who are you, woman?"

Well, she did *not* care for that contemptuous address. As though being a woman was a weakness. And she would never give him her true name. Names held power; he had quite enough already. "You may call me Miss Smith. And you?"

His red lips twitched. Amusement or scorn? Probably both. "I am the Count de Ville. I own this place. Why are you here?"

He had a sense of humor to go with his arrogance. With but a small shifting of accent one could pronounce it as "Devil." "Very well, Count de Ville. In the name of Queen Victoria I command and require that you give an explanation for your activities since you've come to this land."

His stare was priceless. *"What?"*

I've never been very good at presenting credentials, she thought. "I shall be brief, but you must listen and think most carefully. The evidence is that you committed murder on the high seas. The ship on which it occurred is still at Whitby Harbour, along with its logs.

The evidence is that you did seduce and willfully murder a young woman, but not before transforming her against her will to become one of your own breed, the motive as yet unknown. These are most serious crimes, Count de Ville, and they must be answered for."

Another long stare, then a roaring bark of laughter that filled the room. "You do not know with whom you are dealing."

Hm. Romanian accent. Probably one of those minor princes so used to having his own way that he'd forgotten how things were done in the outside world.

"I may also make the same observation," she responded. "I remind you that you are not in your homeland, but mine, and are answerable to her laws."

"English law?" He spat.

Older than that. Much older.

De Ville looked carefully around, scenting the heavy air.

"There are no others here, sir," she said. "You will find this to be a most singular court."

"You have me on trial?" He seemed ready to laugh again.

"Indeed, yes. Use your common sense and respect what it tells you about me."

He glared. She felt an icy hand caress her protective wards. His gaze turned inward as he concentrated, eyes rolling up in his head, palms out as he delved past surface appearance. "You have Knowledge. But it is not such as to help you here."

"Count de Ville, you are a man of great intelligence, yet you are ignoring some very important danger signs. I strongly suggest you heed them. Would I be here alone with you if I could not take care of myself? Would I have even been able to call you here if I did not have considerable skills at my disposal?"

He was silent, thinking. Past time for it, too.

"Now, sir, let us get to the business at hand. Explain yourself."

"I will not."

There were ways around that. She fixed him with her own gaze, tearing past the protective hedges now that he was close enough. What she found was revolting.

He was old, but not ancient, and another name was in his mind . . . Vlad, Son of Dracul, yes, that was it. She'd heard of him, quite the vicious devil against the Turks in his day—and his own people. He was decidedly savage to any who challenged his authority. She swiftly closed off a random vision of a forest of writhing bodies impaled on stakes and moved on to his present-day concerns. He had plans to establish himself in England. The British Empire, right or wrong, was the seat of real political influence for the world. He'd once been in the center of such a maelstrom in his distant land between the forests. He wanted to resume that sort of absolute control again, but on a much larger field. He had some very specific plans on how to do it, too. Sweet Goddess, if he ever got to the Queen or the Prince of Wales . . .

Frozen with surprise, he gave a start and tried to throw her from his mind. She withdrew at her own speed, leaving him panting from the effort of trying to hurry her.

"What *are* you?" he asked, when he'd recovered.

"You already have the answer, but *my* apprenticeship was very much elsewhere than in the hell-depths of the Scholomance."

"What know you of that?" His shock was such that he'd lapsed into Romanian. Still in tune with his mind, she was able to translate.

"I know much. I know that you are gifted with the Talent, but you do not see beyond the gratification of your own needs. You do not see forward to the consequences of your actions on yourself or others or the general balance of all things. That is blind and blatant irresponsibility. You've grown careless and foolish or you are simply mad. And your ambitions are such that I cannot allow you to continue unchecked."

"You have not the strength to stop me."

Damn. He possessed more arrogance than wisdom. She'd hoped to be spared the ordeal of her dream. "Sir, let it suffice to say that I am used to dealing with real monarchs, not some incognito lordling with delusions of his own importance. You are an invader here, I see that now, and, by the authority of the queen I serve, I command and require that you immediately leave and return to your homeland."

She did not remotely imagine he would go quietly. From her touch on his mind she understood there was only one way to deal with him, only one thing he would respect. And she also understood the play of her initial dream, why it had ended in that manner.

He reared to his full height, like a cobra preparing to strike. "Ah, but I see it now. Talent and power you do indeed possess, but as for delusions of importance . . . you are nothing more than an escapee from that ridiculous madhouse across the way. Unfortunate for you, young woman. But you are comely, and for that I shall make it pleasant."

The first wave of it stole suddenly over her like a heady perfume. Sweet, but that was meant to mask the underlying bitterness. It was most potent, though, and deeply compelling. Sabra felt her body willingly respond to his seduction, though her emotions recoiled. She could physically fight it, but it would do her no good, for he was bigger and stronger. She could magically fight it, and win, but he would have to die. She had no objection to killing, having done her share in the past, but her Sight told her his was a different destiny, entwined with that of the hunters. She knew better than to fight Fate.

He drew close, looming over her, eyes flaming with

hunger, desire, and triumph. She smiled dreamily, as that poor girl must have smiled, and waited as though enspelled for him to take her.

He did indeed make it pleasant, murmuring softly in his own tongue, tilting her head to one side with the light touch of a fingertip. His breath was warm on her bare throat, his kiss gentle. Under other circumstances she might have welcomed him as a lover, but they were too far apart in spirit for that.

Then he held her close and tight, and bit into her flesh. Though he did not rend it like the wolf in her dream, the effect was the same. She gasped from the sudden pain, felt her blood being strongly drawn away, as though he were taking life from her soul, not her body. Perhaps he fed on souls, enjoyed corrupting innocence. That would explain his lengthy torture of the girl.

Nothing like that for me, Sabra thought. He intended to drain her dry. He pressed hard upon her, drinking deep.

She allowed it, waiting.

He was not the only one adept at blood magic.

But . . . hers was far older.

All that was of the divine—no matter the faith— was his bane. He'd chosen his dark path and thus made it so. And if the Host repelled him then so would . . .

His strangled scream, when it came, made it all worth it.

He reeled away from her, hands clawing at his mouth and throat. Staggering, he crashed against one of the boxes and fell. She watched his sufferings, showing no expression, but with a great lifting in her heart. Sometimes justice could be most satisfying.

Vlad, son of Dracul, writhed in the dust, choking and groaning his agony. She'd seen such symptoms before, but then the effect had been from strychnine, the convulsions so strong that the victim broke his own bones from his thrashings.

"In my veins runs the chill doom of Annwyn's hounds," she explained, rubbing her throat as the flesh knitted up. "They will harry you forever, you bastard son of the Scholomance."

He shrieked, twisting.

"You feel also the holy fire of Cerridwen."

Another shriek, his back arching, then he abruptly collapsed and went still.

Sabra stood over him, taking in the ravages her blood had executed on what remained of his soul. He yet lived, but the fight had gone out of him. When he finally opened his eyes to her, they were suffused with terror.

"Return to your own land, dragon's son," she whispered. "This place is not for you."

*   *   *

Telegram from Mina Harker to Van Helsing:
"Look out for D. He has just now, 12.45, come from Carfax hurriedly and hastened towards the south. He seems to be going the round and may want to see you: Mina."

The Dark Downstairs

ROXANNE LONGSTREET CONRAD

Here, now, Nora, dry your eyes. I know it's a sad day, but we should all get about our duties now. She's in a better place.

What, you want to hear about Dracula? At a time like this? Go on with you, you must've heard the story a dozen times by now, what with Mr. and Mrs. Harker and all the rest of 'em in and out of the house—oh, I know, they don't gossip to servants, but still, who notices us? Stand just outside the parlor, ear to the door—I know the tricks, missy, don't think I don't.

Hush, now, keep your eyes on your work. There's Mrs. Bannock, she'll have the hide off of us if we don't finish these by teatime. What was we talking about? Dracula, indeed. Well, Nora, I never did see half what they say happened at Hillingham, and believe me, I was in the thick of it. No dogs, nor wolves, nor any of that foolishness. Dracula? Yes, I figure as I saw 'im, but believe you me, he weren't the worst of it. Not by a long chalk. *They'll* never tell that part of it, 'cause it doesn't concern the Quality.

Who does it concern? Us, of course. The down-stairs. The servants.

'Ere, you need that knife? Give it over. Now, where was I? No, I'm not telling about Dracula, I'm telling you about Elizabeth Gwydion.

First thing you have to know about Hillingham is that it's been in the Westenra family for centuries, a good old country house in Whitby, near the sea—the family come down from London every season for the summer. By July Mrs. Westenra and Miss Lucy had arrived, along with Miss Lucy's friend Mina Murray—yes, Mrs. Harker, but she was Mina Murray then—and they brought Rose with them as ladies' maid. In the house there was Mr. Gage, the butler, and Mrs. Ravenstock, the housekeeper, and Mrs. Brockham, the cook, and of course me upstairs, and Penny, and Jeannette the parlor maid and Alice the downstairs maid and Kate the tweeny, and Mary in the scullery, and Joseph the bootboy, and George the footman—

What do you mean, a large staff? Small enough, for the size of Hillingham, I can tell you. Up at five, bed at midnight; some things never change, eh? For all Dr. Van Helsing's such a kind man, still things have to be done, don't they?

Where was I? Oh, yes, the staff. Well, that was the staff at the start of July, but it didn't stay that way, 'cause of Rose, who got herself in trouble with a young man. Well, you can well imagine, Mr. Gage sent her packing without a reference. Poor Rose, she were crying something awful. Elizabeth Gwydion showed up the very afternoon, to Mrs. Ravenstock's relief—Welsh, they said, neat as a pin, a bit foreign-looking, skin like the finest, palest cream. Pretty? Oh, if you like. Too pretty, to my mind.

I was polishing the banister rail when she came sweeping up, head high, the way great ladies do; she was looking at those stairs as if she'd bought 'em whole. I knew she was going to be trouble—did you know, she wouldn't even let us call her Liz? No, it had to be *Elizabeth,* like the Queen herself. And Mrs. Ravenstock thought she hung the moon.

She had skills, I suppose. She was good with stains; when Miss Mina cut her finger and got blood on her best blue gown it was Elizabeth who took it away to clean it, wouldn't give it over to the laundry maid Gracie at all. 'Twas Gracie who carried the first tale about her, I suppose. She whispered to me as how she saw Elizabeth sucking the blood out of that dress, like a half-starved woman licking at spilled soup.

Poor Gracie. Dead two days later in her bed when I went to wake her, her skin blue and cold, her eyes staring up at the ceiling. No sign what killed her. Mrs. Ravenstock said it was her heart, but the poor little bint was only fifteen. Poison, I say. But as nobody sent for the constable, it'll never be proved.

With Gracie gone the work got harder. Soon enough we found we was washing the sheets as well as ironing them, and doing most of Elizabeth's work as well. Mrs. Ravenstock told us to stop our complaining. She took Elizabeth's part every time, no matter the cause; the way she looked at that girl fair gave me a turn. And Elizabeth looked at her like Mrs. Ravenstock was a cream pastry at afternoon tea.

Dracula? I told you, I'm *getting* to him. Now be quiet and listen, stop wiggling like a wet puppy. All right, now, where was I? Oh, yes, Gracie was dead, poor soul, and upstairs, Miss Lucy was having her own troubles. Sleepwalking, the way she used to as a child. Nothing to fret over, I said at the time, but of course I was quite wrong about that.

I made an enemy out of Elizabeth Gwydion about then. It was over a little thing, really, sounds ever so stupid. It was over me being Catholic. Mind you, now, the others tolerated it right enough. "Oh, Mary Margaret, she's heathen," they'd say cheerfully, though not

where the Mistress could hear. Mr. Gage knew I kept
to my faith, and he said nothing about it. I even wore
a crucifix, under the neck of my dress, of course. That
was what caused the trouble. I was bent over scrubbing
the floor and my crucifix must have slipped off, it fell
on the floor and I didn't notice it.

Well, Miss High-and-Mighty Elizabeth stepped on
it as she walked by, and screamed like she'd put her
foot on a nail. Hissed some foreign words at me and
all but slapped me, she did; kicked over my bucket,
water and soap everywhere, and flounced off with her
cap-ribbons bouncing. Well, naturally, I complained of
it to Mrs. Ravenstock, but she told me I must have
overset the bucket myself and to mop up the mess and
not to carry tales. The look in her eyes was like she'd
had herself an opium pipe. Well, I wasn't content to
be leaving it at that—after all, I'm not a clumsy cow,
and there was no call for Elizabeth to do such a thing.
The row brought Mr. Gage, who called Elizabeth
down.

She lied, of course, but Mr. Gage didn't believe it.
He gave her a dressing-down such as few of us had
ever heard, and when she looked at me there was a
smile on her lips, but murder in her eyes, and I knew
that wasn't the end of it.

The next morning there was broken glass scattered
on the floor next to my bed. I might've cut my feet
bad except that I got up on the wrong side to pick up
my Bible, which had fallen off the nightstand. When I
struck the candle I saw the glass glittering like ice, and
my skin crawled, I can tell you. I hadn't heard a thing,
not breaking glass, not someone creeping around in the
dark. I could well imagine Elizabeth Gwydion's pale
hands scattering that glass, her bloodless face bending
over me as I dreamed.

What do you mean, what did I do? Got a dustpan
and cleaned it up, of course. And smiled at her nice
when she passed in the hall as I was sweeping wet tea

leaves on the carpet to lay the dust. Smiled for all I was worth, I did. Confusion to the enemy!

The next day there was something in my tea. I barely touched it, but still it made me sick, sick enough that even Mrs. Ravenstock let me take an hour to lie down in the evening after supper. That was when I dreamed.

I dreamed there was an adder in the house. A black shining adder as glided from room to room, winding around the feet of the servants. An adder that wound itself around Mrs. Ravenstock's ankle and oozed up under her skirts. I fair screamed the house down in my dream, but nobody heeded. She went on with her mending, and all of a sudden her eyes flew open and she jerked hard, as if somebody had pushed her, and then she was lying on the floor and the adder was crawling away toward the stairs.

Mind you, my gran had dreams. She dreamed of a cave-in at the mine, and it happened just the way she said. I don't hold none with imagination, it's destructive to a woman's character, but I didn't imagine this. I dreamed it, and that's a different thing entirely.

Mrs. Ravenstock? Next day she was hale and well, except for that opium distance in her eyes. And doting on Elizabeth. But the day after *that* Mrs. Ravenstock caught her heel in her dress hem and fell down the service stairs, and broke her neck.

So. After Mrs. Ravenstock's death—which was accident, sure enough—you can well imagine things changed. For one thing, we were already short a laundry maid and now a housekeeper, and next thing you know the bootboy Joseph had given notice, and so had the scullery maid Mary. Now, you can't hardly run Hillingham on so few servants; Mr. Gage was fair desperate, I tell you. Meanwhile, things were bad upstairs, too. Miss Mina left to meet her fiancé Jonathan, and the whispers came round that Mrs. Westenra was in poor health. Miss Lucy's sleepwalking had gotten so bad it scared us half out of our wits. Yes, even me, though I don't hold with nonsense.

One morning as I came around the corner with my broom and tea leaves—mind you it was well before six in the morning—I saw a ghost floating white in the hall. I froze, my breath locked in my chest, and after a second or two I realized the floating white ghost was Miss Lucy.

She was dead asleep on her feet, her gown fluttering in a cold draft that poured out of her room, her fair hair lifting and twisting around her pale face. As I watched her, her head fell back, and her lips parted, and she spread her arms wide. She let out this long, low sigh that frightened me ever so much more than a scream—something immoral in that sigh, I can tell you. Desperate. She pressed herself against empty air, her whole body arching.

Well, it was indecent! And frightful! I tore my eyes away from her and saw that Elizabeth Gwydion was standing at the bottom of the stairs. Pale as something drawn with pen and ink, and her lips were stretched wide in what I couldn't have ever named a smile.

Well, the only thing I could think was *dear sweet Mary save us all.* So I did what any good Catholic girl would have done. I crossed myself.

Miss Lucy's eyes flew open, wide and blank as a winter's sky, and she collapsed to the carpet in a froth of wind-whipped gown. Downstairs, Elizabeth Gwydion shrieked; when I looked to her she was staring at me, and the hate of it fair burned me where I stood. Her eyes smoked, I tell you, and I thought she might strike me dead in my shoes.

Right then Mrs. Westenra came out of her bedroom, her hair still in night-braids, and cried out at the sight of her daughter spilled on the carpet. Poor dear lady, I remembered what Mr. Gage had said about her health; she looked fair to drop. But she got down on her knees and took Miss Lucy's pale hands in hers, and said, "Mary Margaret, fetch some brandy. Immediately."

Well, of course the brandy was locked up—you don't leave brandy lying where any servant could sneak a glass, do you? So I went for Mr. Gage, straight through the kitchen where Mrs. Brockham, red-faced, was bent over the pots and Jeannette, parlor maid or not, was whisking eggs with just enough force to be surly about it, straight to the closed door of the butler's pantry, where I knocked.

He didn't answer. Well, of course I knocked again, and said his name. Mrs. Brockham left off her stirring to stare at me. I knocked again, fair pounding this time.

"Here now." Mrs. Brockham frowned at me. "What's the trouble, Mary Margaret?"

"I need brandy for Miss Lucy!"

We went through a bit more knocking and rattling before she opened the door and went right in. And screamed, her hands flying to her mouth. I squeezed around her and saw Mr. Gage lying half across his desk, his eyes bulging and gray. Dead for hours, likely. I suppose I might've screamed, too. It brought Jeannette running, who dropped to the floor in a dead faint, and George, the footman, who as a man was too mindful of his dignity to faint, though he swayed a bit and looked very pale.

"Better tell the mistress," Mrs. Brockham said, voice gone all weak. "Get on with you, girl!"

I went, my shoes knocking on hard wood. Mr. Gage, dead? Butlers didn't die, at least not in service, not in that undignified way like they were no better than the rest of us. Up the stairs I went, my heart hammering in my chest.

Crouching there next to Miss Lucy and the mistress was Elizabeth Gwydion, with a glass of brandy in her hand that she held to Miss Lucy's lips.

I wasn't thinking, mind you. Not a bit of it. I

reached out and I slapped it out of her hand, sent it crashing against the polished wood of the wall.

Mrs. Westenra shot to her feet and snapped "Mary Margaret! Whatever has got into you? Stop this instant!"

I gulped down some air and tried to steady my voice, but I didn't take my eyes off of Elizabeth Gwydion. Behind me I heard the whisper of voices—Penny and Kate and Alice at the foot of the stairs, watching.

"I sent you for brandy," Mrs. Westenra continued coldly. "When you didn't return Elizabeth was good enough to fetch some. Now explain yourself."

"Mr. Gage," I managed to say. "Mr. Gage has passed, ma'am."

"Oh," Mrs. Westenra said faintly. "Oh my. That is most—distressing. How—"

"Don't know, ma'am."

"I see." Mrs. Westenra took a deep breath. "I've already sent for Dr. Seward about Lucy. When he arrives, I'll have him examine the body. I'll address the staff presently."

"Yes ma'am." I dropped a very small curtsy and turned to do what she'd ordered, but she stopped me one more time.

"Mary Margaret," she said. "Tell Cook to make it a cold breakfast."

Mind you, she wasn't a cruel woman, Mrs. Westenra; she was a good employer, never harsh, never unfair. But if you ever wanted to know the difference between upstairs and down, there it was in the one short command. Mr. Gage was *dead,* and all it meant was a cold breakfast instead of a hot one.

Do? What could I do? We ate our cold meal, waited for Dr. Seward to come and tell us it was Mr. Gage's heart, most unfortunate, but natural enough. Took him all of a minute to glance at the body and say so, and then he was off to Miss Lucy.

The minute he was out of sight, Alice began to cry, and Penny, too, both good for nothing the rest of the day because they were sure the house was doomed. Floors didn't get scrubbed, or the carpets swept, or the brasses polished. With Mr. Gage and Mrs. Ravenstock gone, Mrs. Brockham didn't have the heart to force us to it.

Jeannette run off that night, not even asking for a reference. That left me, Penny, Alice, Kate, Mrs. Brockham, and George.

And Elizabeth Gwydion, of course. Herself.

Poison? Oh, of course it was, Nora, whatever Dr. Seward might have said. Herself had tried to kill me already, and she'd done for Gracie and Mr. Gage and probably for Mrs. Ravenstock as well. If I'd had any sense I would have packed my carpetbag and followed Jeannette. But I never did have sense, everyone's said so.

I stayed, instead. And that night, I dreamed of Whitby Abbey.

In my dream I followed Elizabeth Gwydion there to those tumbled white stones, and in moonlight she was all marble and shadow. Mind you, the place is harmless enough in daylight—I'd climbed the place from one end to the other, as a girl. But this dream-abbey was drenched with black, and every shadow hid horror.

Dracula? Oh, aye, I'll give you Dracula, you silly bint, because that's who came to her there in the dark shattered ribs of the church. He poured himself out of the shadows, tall, he was, tall and cream-pale, with heavy foreign features—red, red lips the only touch of color to him.

The evil of him made my skin crawl, even as far away as I was. He looked like a man, but he wasn't, he was more, he was worse, and he stank of rotting blood.

Elizabeth dropped right to her knees in front of him, drowning herself in a thick puddle of fog.

"Well?" His soft, deep voice carried to me on a dream wind. "Is it done?"

"She is prepared for you, master," Elizabeth said, and she looked up at him with a slave's devotion, fair turned my stomach. That accent to her voice, the one she claimed was Welsh, it sounded thicker now, and I was dead certain it came from farther away than Cardiff.

"Excellent. I will go to her soon. The others?"

"Servants of no consequence." Elizabeth's face twisted in sudden distaste. "There's a meddling maid who deserves your personal attention."

"I do not stoop to battling servants," he said. "If you think she does not recognize her place, then show it to her, Elizabeth my beauty. Teach her the pleasure of obedience."

She groveled to him. She crawled to him, *crawled*. It made me sick to see anyone, even Elizabeth, stripped of dignity like that. He put a booted foot against her ribs and rolled her on her back.

The pleasure of obedience, indeed. I'd see him in hell first, and her, too. At that moment he—the *thing*—turned and met my eyes. Not surprised at seeing me—he'd known I was there the whole time.

It was like staring into the sun, all that blinding hunger. He drank me down like a bracing tot of hot gin.

"Well." He smiled slowly, those red lips parting like the edges of a new wound. "A *dreamer*."

He rushed at me, darkness and the stench of rotten blood, and I screamed myself awake.

Dr. Van Helsing had been in and out of the house by that time, though I'd had aught to do with him. He'd come back to do some terrible strange thing to Miss Lucy, taking blood from Mr. Holmwood and putting it in her veins. A Godless thing to do, I still say;

no good can come of a thing like that. Still, Dr. Van Helsing had a kind way about him, and I saw him cross himself once, when they were praying over Miss Lucy. So I knew it was likely we had a bit in common—and, anyway, he was foreign.

I made myself bold and talked to him uninvited.

Yes, of course I know it could have gotten me shown the door! Blessed Mary, well I know it! But I had to do something, so I spoke to him about the dreams, and Elizabeth Gwydion, and all the deaths below stairs. Which he hadn't heard, of course—the deaths of servants weren't worth mention, I suppose. And he was gravely worried about it. Did you know he smelled like caraway seeds even then? And a sharp mint he liked to chew. He was ever so nice to me, and he told me to watch Elizabeth Gwydion close, and tell him what she did. He'd be gone that night and the next day, going back to his home, but he'd receive my report on his return.

Mind you, the household was in chaos. No butler, no housekeeper—poor Mrs. Brockham wasn't up to the task. And the maids were in hysterics, terrified of losing their positions but even more terrified of leaving them. George, the footman, insisted nothing whatsoever was wrong, but then he was a dim sort, and as the only man in the house, I suppose he had to say it. So there was no one left to tell me that I couldn't stay with Miss Lucy. I sat up outside her room that night, and when Elizabeth Gwydion came to the door I told her right sharp to be on her way. Later that day, going down the stairs I'd traveled at least a thousand times, something wrenched hard at my foot and I fell. It was a fearful long fall, but I turned on my side, wrenched my shoulder, bruised something terrible—and I didn't break my neck, like poor Mrs. Ravenstock. Must have been a terrible disappointment for Miss High-and-Mighty Elizabeth.

After that, it was a quiet night. I suppose I fell asleep in the chair outside of Miss Lucy's room. I woke up in pitch darkness, and something cold was touching my throat.

Well, you might imagine, I drew breath to scream, but a hand clapped over my mouth, and I pushed, pushed hard, threw myself off of the chair and down to the carpet. This time I did scream, and loud enough to wake the dead. Wasn't more than a minute I suppose before light bloomed gold in Mrs. Westenra's doorway, and there she was staring at me, her face gone dead pale, her eyes big as saucers.

Lying half across me was Miss Lucy, her skin ice-cold, her color like ashes. She had two wounds in her neck, fresh drops of blood staining the white linen of her nightgown. Poor thing, she was like a breathing corpse. I got to my feet, and Mrs. Westenra bent down to help, but her color was almost as bad as Miss Lucy's. I couldn't *drag* the girl, it wasn't proper, but George was nowhere to be seen, nor any of the other servants.

Except Elizabeth Gwydion, coming up the steps with a candle. She was smiling.

"I'll help you," she said, and took Miss Lucy's feet. I hated the idea, but what choice did I have, then? We carried her into the bedroom and laid her in the disordered bed; I tucked her carefully in, added blankets from the wardrobe, and closed the open window.

All the garlic flowers Dr. Van Helsing had left around the room had been swept into a corner. The necklace he'd asked Miss Lucy to wear was broken on the floor.

I looked up and Elizabeth Gwydion was staring into me, digging her eyes in like claws. Smiling.

"Too late," she said.

"We'll see about that," I snapped, and saw that Penny had finally worked up enough courage to come down, and lurked like some hunted animal behind the doorframe, only her round pale face showing. "Penny! Get George and tell him to drive like Jehu for Dr. Seward. Go now!"

She went, her bare feet padding on the carpet. Elizabeth Gwydion never quit smiling.

"Mary Margaret—" Mrs. Westenra, who'd been standing quietly by my side, put a hand over mine as I straightened blankets atop Miss Lucy. "That will be all. I'll sit with my daughter."

Elizabeth Gwydion lost her smile. She didn't like that, didn't like it at all. She'd thought Mrs. Westenra defeated, I saw.

But she bobbed a curtsy and said, "Tea, ma'am?"

"Fine," Mrs. Westenra snapped. Elizabeth went.

"Ma'am—" It was terrible forward of me to say anything, but I had to. "Ma'am, best not to drink anything she brings you. Until Dr. Seward arrives."

She blinked and nodded. After a moment she looked at me again, and there was new strength in her eyes.

"You'll defend my daughter?" she asked. "Against anyone?"

"Yes ma'am."

She took her hand out of the pocket of her nightrobe. She was holding a shining silver paper knife, and she passed it to me and folded my fingers around the warm handle.

"Take it," she said. "Use it if you have to."

I left her and went downstairs to warn Cook that the battle was on.

But Cook was gone. Whether she'd run or been dragged away, we never knew; no trace of her was ever found. Penny had found George and sent him on his way, but as the day dawned, then dragged on, Dr. Seward didn't come. There was no telephone at Hillingham, though the Westenras had one in the London house; I missed it most sorely, because help was miles away. Still, Dr. Seward would come. Surely.

Towards five I sent Kate out to walk into Whitby and find help—the constable, if nothing else. She'd only been gone a few minutes when she came back, screaming like the house was afire, to tell me that George was lying dead, the carriage smashed, on the rocks at the turn of the road. After that I couldn't get any of them to go.

So night fell, and we were all alone. Four maids, two ladies, and Elizabeth Gwydion. But Dr. Van Helsing would be back early in the morning. All we had to do was see daylight again. So I told the others, and so it was.

But it was a terrible long night. Dead quiet outside, not even a breath of wind. Just the crash of the sea in the distance, and the sense that the whole house was holding its breath.

Mrs. Westenra dismissed Elizabeth. Oh, you should have seen the woman's face—cold, haughty, amazed. But Mrs. Westenra was too soft to make the woman leave the house in the dark; she settled for sending her to her room and telling Penny to watch the door.

It was close on midnight when I took Penny a cup of hot cocoa and found the chair outside of Elizabeth Gwydion's room sitting empty, though the seat of it was still warm. And the door open just a crack.

I pushed it to find poor dear Penny lying on the cold wood floor, struggling. She flung out a hand to me. Elizabeth Gwydion had hold of her feet, and stooped over her, like an evil black shadow—

Yes. *Him.* Dracula. He tore loose of Penny's throat and looked at me, parted bloody lips in a smile, and his teeth were sharp and white, and Elizabeth Gwydion let go of Penny and shot to her feet, grabbed hold of my arms. I cried out and tried to fight but she was horrible strong, and the stale smell of her, the rotting stench of *him,* made me faint and sick.

I suppose what saved me was the crucifix, which I'd mended and still had hung around my neck. It swung free and caught the light, sending Dracula reeling back.

Remember that I told you I never saw him make himself dog or wolf or bat? I saw him turn to a stinking black mist like flies that whipped away through the open window. At the time I thought he was afraid of me. Now I think it was just that he was impatient to be about his other business.

Elizabeth still had hold of me. She was fearful strong, but I had a lifetime of scrubbing and lifting and hard work behind me, and I threw her off—

—Out the open window. I rushed to it, hoping to see her crushed on the stone below, but she was clinging to the brick, clinging with needle-sharp nails. Her pale face grinned up at me, and I screamed; she laughed and scuttled away down the wall like a black-shelled beetle.

I ducked back in and slammed the window sash and bent to help Penny to her feet. That was when I heard the crash of glass, and the screams.

You know how it ended, I suppose. Poor Mrs. Westenra's heart gave out. Miss Lucy's own letter says a dog came through her window, though I never saw it; we found her lying pale and gray on the bed with her mother dead beside her. Penny, Kate, Alice, and I did the best we cold—covered the broken window, wrapped Mrs. Westenra in blankets, and took Miss Lucy downstairs away from the horror.

"Mother," she kept crying, and wanted to go back. But there wasn't no use in it, and besides she was too weak. I took everyone into the withdrawing room and found the liquor cabinet standing open. The brandy was empty—George, no doubt, which would explain the wrecked carriage—but the sherry was still full. I poured everyone a stiff measure, and we sat close to Miss Lucy while she wept. A sip or two of sherry was all she would take, though the rest of us drank up willingly enough; Penny even gulped down what Miss Lucy wouldn't.

"What'll we do, Mary Margaret?" Penny asked, her

eyes huge and terrified. She had a wound on her neck like Miss Lucy's, but she didn't seem the worse for it. Just tired.

"We'll stay here," I said. "Let morning come, and Dr. Van Helsing arrive, before we do anything more. Here, Miss Lucy. Are you warm enough?"

She was shivering, poor thing, though we'd wrapped her up. I felt warm enough. Over-warm, perhaps. Time passed, as time does even in the worst of circumstances; Miss Lucy wept, and we tried to comfort her.

It must have been near an hour later when I looked up and found Alice curled asleep in a red Moroccan chair. Kate had nodded off, too. As I watched, Penny dropped her glass and sank down on the fainting couch, her long dark hair spilling over the carpet.

My legs felt weak. When I tried to rise from where I sat, I found I couldn't. My arms had gone numb, and I could feel it stealing through me now like a cold wind.

Laudanum, to put us fast asleep.

"Miss Lucy?" I whispered. She didn't seem to hear me. The door of the withdrawing room opened without even a creak, and there in the dark stood Elizabeth Gwydion.

"Come," she said to Miss Lucy. And Miss Lucy, who hadn't but touched the sherry, wandered away, leaving the blankets on the floor. I couldn't follow, couldn't master my own legs enough to try.

Elizabeth came straight to me and looked me right in the eyes, grinning like a skull, and said, "My master's seeing to your Miss Lucy. But it's my privilege to see to *you,* you meddling cur."

I started to pray then, because I didn't think I could move. The world was going gray, the edges fraying, and she bent close to me, her lips cold on my neck, sucking like a baby at the breast, and I knew in the next instant she'd bite, and suck blood like red milk. I'd never feared anything so much, never felt such despair.

Something in my robe's pocket felt hot against me. Hot as the sun. *Holy Mary.*

Mrs. Westenra's paper knife! I grabbed it and stabbed for her, not able to feel my hand, nor the shock when it hit. I only knew I'd made the target when I saw her eyes go wide and strange, saw her stumble back from me and sit down clumsily on the floor with her legs splayed.

The hilt of the silver paper knife glittered on her black dress. I'd pinned it to her heart. She looked amazed.

"You—you English dog—"

"Irish," I snapped.

She was still trying to understand that when she died. Yes, I killed her—but here's the thing, Nora: as she died, she turned to ashes. *Ashes,* no different than you'd sweep up out of the grate in the morning. Ashes that stirred in the breeze of the door swinging open again.

Her master stood there, looking at the mess I'd made of Elizabeth Gwydion, and his lips drew back from his teeth. His face was ruddy now, his lips smeared with blood, and I thought of Miss Lucy with a terrible sick pang. I didn't have the knife anymore. I had nothing to protect me but my small crucifix and my fear.

"You've killed my servant," he said in some surprise.

"I'd kill her again if she'd get up," I said tartly. "Miss Lucy—"

"Is none of your concern." He walked around me, staring at me with red-flecked eyes. Like a lion that wasn't quite hungry enough to pounce. "I could kill you all tonight."

I couldn't think of any reason he wouldn't. Penny, Kate, Alice . . . all helpless. Me only a breath away from it. The laudanum was a thick black pool in me, and I was drowning in it.

"Go ahead," I said, as if I didn't even care. "If you'd stoop so low."

He smiled at me then, Dracula did. "For you, I might bend my principles, little one. Or make you my own."

"Go to Hell!" I shot back, amazed at my own bravery. I'd never cursed in my life, not like that, certainly not to a man. And still he smiled.

"Soon," he promised. "The dead travel fast."

I felt my knees buckle then, and I fell, face down in the ashes of Elizabeth Gwydion. I rolled over, spitting out the bitterness of her, and saw him looking down at me from such a far, far distance. His cold fingers caressed my face.

"No," he said. "I don't think I will do you the favor of killing you. Explain this tomorrow, to your betters. Explain your drunkenness and your dead mistress. Perhaps I'll come to kill you when you're starving on the streets."

His words struck fear in me, absolute fear, because he was right. I fought the dark as he walked away, but there was nothing I could do but fall. I dreamed, you know. This time no adders, no abbeys, no pale wasting ladies. This time I dreamed I was in a great cathedral, and I lit a candle to the smiling statue of Mary, and I prayed.

I prayed until the morning, when Dr. Seward arrived at the house and found Mrs. Westenra dead and Miss Lucy dying.

No, no, I'm all right. A fleck of coal dust in my eye, most likely. But it was a sad house, very sad. And no one to blame it on but four drunken servants, which Dr. Seward promptly did, though of course later he said he knew all along we'd been drugged.

It was Dr. Van Helsing who came to our rescue, finding positions for Kate and Alice. Dr. Van Helsing himself who gave me and Penny posts here in his house. Do you know what he said to me, Nora? He said, "There are monsters all around us, Mary Margaret. Some that people in my position will never see, but perhaps you will."

So here I am. Doing the same ironing, the same scrubbing, the same sweeping. Some things never change, as I said. And some do.

Yes, that one's good. Hand me the next. Now, you must put a good sharp point on them, Nora. Sharp enough to pierce skin like butter. It's got to go right to the monster's heart, you see? Dr. Van Helsing and the others are going after Dracula, but like I told you, this has nothing to do with Dracula. It's below stairs business.

Poor Penny's lying in her coffin in the parlor, waiting on the undertaker. And she were bitten by Dracula that night at Hillingham. If she wakes, we've got to do for her like the Doctor did for Miss Lucy. Test the knife. Sharp enough to cut bone?

Oh, wipe your tears, girl. And say your prayers. There's plenty below stairs who might need the same mercy, before this is all said and done.

We care for our own.

Dear Mr. Bernard Shaw

JUDITH PROCTOR

1st October 1893
22 Barkston Gardens
Earls Court, S.W.

Dear Mr. Bernard Shaw,

I write to you because I'm not quite sure who else to write to. You, I am sure, will tell me honestly and fully what you believe of these circumstances. I know you well enough to know that you will not gloss over anything in your reply and that if you feel I am being foolish, you will be blunt enough to tell me.

Be the critic for me once more and tell me if this speaks to you of something possible or simply an overactive imagination on my part. You're as firmly grounded in the real world as anyone I know— your play last year on slum landlords had all of London talking—usually to tear your name to shreds.

I'm wandering off the topic—I'm even being serious—perhaps that tells you how much this has distressed me!

We're playing *King Lear*. You know that anyway. . . . You see, I'm still dithering.

To begin—for I shall never get going if I don't—it started about two weeks ago. I think it was Wednesday, though it might have been Thursday.

Partway through the play, I became aware of someone in one of the boxes. Now that's nothing unusual. We've been playing to virtually full houses most nights and the boxes are popular. You wouldn't believe what people sometimes get up to in the boxes—the play must ·be quite a distraction to them. This man was watching the play though. He wasn't just watching it, he was virtually mesmerised. You'd think he'd never been to the theatre before. Henry was giving a bravura performance as Lear and I was doing pretty well myself. I'm really too old to play Cordelia now, but when the audience believes in it, I believe in it, too. It's a conspiracy between us and as long as they keep paying to see me, I'm happy to oblige.

The box made him hard to see in the darkness, but I knew he was there—I could feel him.

Last week, he was back haunting me again. That was definitely a Monday. It's easier to get tickets at short notice on Monday, because we're rarely full then. Same seat—he obviously preferred the boxes. There was something so intense about him—like a traveller in a desert who'd finally reached an oasis. He wasn't just thirsty—he was desperate. Something was different this time though; he wasn't watching Henry, he was watching me. Just me.

I've been watched before—you get all sorts in theatres. Some can get a little obsessed. This wasn't the normal admirer hanging over the balcony though. He kept back, and I could barely see him beyond the shadow of the box. I couldn't get a chance to look properly at him; I have to concentrate on the part when I'm performing. It's so easy to become distracted— sometimes the slightest thing can throw me and I lose my lines.

That's what was so strange—I knew he was watch-

ing me even when I couldn't see him. Have you ever
had that sensation? The feeling of eyes looking at the
back of your neck?

I'd swear his eyes were red, but it was probably just
a trick of the limelight.

I never did get a good look at his face. Even when
he stood to applaud at the end, he was still in the
darkness. All I could really tell was that he seemed to
be well-dressed; he looked like a man with money.

Actually, that's probably how he got along to Henry's post-show supper a few days later. Bram Stoker—
Henry's manager—has a real nose for possible investors. He does all Henry's correspondence and I honestly
don't know where Henry would be without him. He
corresponds with theatres for us, arranges tours, and
leaves Henry free to do what he does best—acting.

I knew the stranger was there the moment I entered
the room. He stood out in the crowd; there was a space
around him and you don't normally get much of that
at Henry's parties. I'll try and describe him for you,
though memory may make him more dramatic than he
actually was. He was tall, almost six foot in height.
He'd a real beak of a nose—you could have cast him
as Julius Caesar any day—a black moustache, a pointed
beard, and a hard cruel face. His teeth were pointed—
like a dog's canines. I didn't like the look of him at all.

He became aware of me immediately. Coming over
to me, he bowed. "May I introduce myself, Miss Terry?
Count Dracula."

He had a European accent, though I couldn't place
where from. It certainly wasn't French or German. I
really didn't fancy talking to him, but one has to make
the effort. One is expected to sparkle at such affairs,
so sparkle one does.

I made him feel welcome and asked him where he
was from. He wasn't too pleased at that.

"You can tell I am not English?"

"You do have rather a strong accent," though I

hastened to add, "but your command of our language is superb. You have obviously studied for many years."

That seemed to mollify him a little. "I wish to come among you as a gentleman, a man of learning. I have no desire to be taken for an inferior."

Well, I had his measure now. "That could never be," I assured him. "Your clothing, your manner, and your speech all declare you to be a nobleman by birth."

Now he was happy—positively preened himself. "The clothing is fashionable? I read your newspapers, but they are short of information on reliable tailors. I do not entirely trust tradesmen who advertise. I asked my legal representatives to recommend a firm to me."

I looked him up and down. You can't make a silk purse out of a sow's ear, but they'd certainly done their best. The cloth draped in the way that only really expensive fabrics do and the cut was excellent. "You must tell me the name of your firm," I said. "If their legal advice is as good as their choice in tailors, I might need them some day."

"I sent my measurements in advance; my wardrobe was waiting for me when I arrived."

I still didn't like him, but he was beginning to impress me. He certainly planned carefully enough—he'd *never* have made an actor. He'd also dodged my question, although I didn't think about that until later. Maybe he would have made an actor after all.

Loretta waved at me from the other side of the room and I tried to make my excuses to go and join her, but Dracula simply took no notice. He had that kind of natural arrogance that comes from having people leap to do your bidding all your life. At least he was polite about it—well, more or less.

"Miss Terry, I *must* speak to you about the play. Why is it different from what I have read?"

"Didn't the reviews do us justice?"

"You misunderstand me. The play was not performed as it was written. Why did you change the words of Shakespeare?" (You know, you'd have loved him. You're always criticising Henry's version of Shakespeare. You ought to be a theatre critic instead of shredding musicians.)

"A play is a complex thing. . . ." I began, when Bram came to my rescue. Or Henry's rescue if you look at it another way. I really believe that Henry has no more devoted fan than Bram Stoker.

"Henry Irving is a creative genius!" Bram declared. "The words written by a playwright are just the starting point. There is nothing sacrosanct about them. They are clay to be taken and moulded by an actor to suit his needs."

"I have re-read the play," the count declared. "Mr. Irving has changed the words. He has got them wrong."

Whoops . . . Beard not the lion in his lair. . . . (Do lions have beards?)

Bram exploded. When a six-foot-two, twelve-stone Irishman explodes, you tend to know it.

"Have you no soul!"

The count took an abrupt step back in the face of that fury.

"Don't you know genius when you see it? Henry Irving breathes life into cold words. He puts passion where there was only paper. There isn't his equal on the whole of the British stage."

Dracula's protest was washed away in the on-slaught. (I really do think you might have felt quite sorry for the poor man.)

"If you used that play as written, would it have the impact, the drama of what you saw tonight?"

"I—"

"Have you ever seen a better performance? *Have you?*"

I felt compelled to intervene. "Bram, dearest, he's only been in England a few weeks."

Didn't help of course. "So he thinks himself qualified to judge English theatre when he's hardly even watched any?"

Dracula finally got a word in edgeways. "Your theatre is excellent. I have greatly enjoyed the performances. But is it right to change what has been written? Would not the play be even more excellent if performed as written? Would you rewrite the novels of your great authors?"

Philosophy at that hour of the night? What is the world coming to? The argument was obviously good for ages yet. I took my chance, left them to one another's company, and slipped away to join Loretta. I spent the rest of my evening in dedicated pursuit of the trivial and I'm glad to report that I found it.

The next day, the 22nd, an hour before the show, I found Dracula waiting outside my dressing room. The stage doorman must have let him in. I wonder how much the count tipped him?

"My dear Miss Terry, I wish to apologise for last night. It was not my wish to embarrass you. May I apologise?" He held out a ring in the palm of his hand. The oddest thing—I hadn't noticed before—he had hair growing on his palm, black and wiry. It was rather unnerving; I've never seen anything like it before.

Let me tell you though, that ring was several carats worth of apology. (Tell me, why do men always give jewellery rather than money?) I accepted it with the best grace I could muster and thanked him.

"I find your city fascinating," he said slowly. "There are few people living in the high mountains of Transylvania and they are ignorant and superstitious. There are no men of learning there, no people who understand art or literature. It is possible for me to order books, to learn other languages, and to study the works of other great men. But with whom can I discuss these things? Who can make them come alive?

"Shakespeare is perhaps your greatest playwright. I

read his words on paper and thought that I understood them. I saw the play performed upon the stage and realised that I understood nothing at all. The rhythms and poetry of the words are invisible to me until they are spoken, and then they come alive. They speak of possibilities, of things that an old man had forgotten and the memory of laughter. It is a lifetime since I laughed, an eternity since I cried."

I get sickened by continual flattery, but he meant it. I'd swear he meant every word. What kind of a man did that make him?

"Is it really so empty where you live? Surely there must be towns? Theatres?"

"There are travelling entertainers who amuse the peasants with shadow puppets and old stories, but any attempt at a play is crude indeed. They play their parts with enthusiasm enough, but they do not *become* the part as you do. There is no emotion, no truth to it."

I felt then that he was drawn to the theatre because his own life had no emotion in it. All he could find to fill his need was the synthetic emotion that we supply to any who will come and watch. And yet there can be truth in a good play, of a kind anyway. I pondered that as I went into the dressing room and checked over my sticks of greasepaint. He stood, hesitant, in the doorway. I was reluctant to dismiss him, but I needed to get ready. I sat down and looked at my reflection—the empty doorway framed my head.

I heard his clothes rustle and spun round. He was still there!

I could not have turned back again to save my life. To turn around would not only have left him standing behind me, it might also have allowed me to confirm what the mirror had told me. There are some things that you don't *want* to be certain of.

My lips took over and started talking even while my mind was frozen in panic. "Count, I really must get ready for this evening's performance. Why not see me some time when I'm less busy? How about Sunday afternoon in St. James' park?"

He dipped his head in a gesture that was half nod and half bow. "Would three o'clock be suitable?"

"At the end of the lake nearest the palace."

"I will be there." He took my hand, and I'm proud to say that I didn't shake when he kissed it. Theatrical training has its uses now and then.

I was safe, at least until Sunday. A foolish invitation on my part, but I'd had to get rid of him fast and that was the fastest way I could think of. Anyway, I'd no intention of keeping the appointment.

What was he? A demon? An angel? Or do you think I imagined it about the mirror? I'm not sure myself now. Maybe I just had an attack of nerves because he was standing behind me? I don't know. I don't trust my own judgement any more.

I didn't tell anyone about it—I'd have felt such an idiot. They'd probably have decided my eyes were playing up again. It's not quite so hard writing to you, because I can put the words on paper and that's easier than saying them out loud. It's easy to imagine I'm talking to myself, just keeping a journal.

I actually did feel a little guilty about Sunday. Was it just his appearance that made me so uneasy? None of us get prettier as we get older. Men can't help the looks they are born with—Dracula had been nothing but courteous to me. I was almost relieved when I got a really bad headache that saved me the necessity of inventing an excuse. Besides, it was a terrible day, pouring with rain all afternoon.

Still, I should have known putting him off was just delaying the inevitable. He was waiting outside my dressing room after the show on Monday. I made a mental note to ask Henry to fire the doorman—I'd given strict instructions that *nobody* was to be allowed in.

"Miss Terry, I would not intrude upon you here and now, but I *must* speak with you sometime."

I tried to apologise for Sunday, saying that if I'd had his address, I'd have contacted him to say I was unable to make it. He brushed it aside—wasn't relevant. There were things he wanted to discuss—things that were important to him.

Why me? There's people enough in London. Why couldn't he talk to somebody else? No point in asking really—I recognised the symptoms all too well. People love me—not for what I am, but for what they imagine I am.

In the end, I'd no choice but to agree to another meeting. I probably wouldn't have kept that one either, except that George the doorman swore blind that he'd never let Dracula into the theatre that night. He'd never even seen him. I think the reason I believed him was that he voluntarily admitted to accepting a large bribe the first time. If Dracula was able to get into the back of the theatre without going through the stage door . . .

I met Dracula outside the actor's church on the Sabbath and trusted in the Lord to look after his own.

When I came out from the service, the day was bright and sunny. I could hear a blackbird singing somewhere, its song affirming everything that's good about life. Dracula stood waiting for me under the church portico. Daylight seemed to diminish him; he looked no different and yet—somehow—I feared him less when I saw him by the light of the day star.

He bowed and asked me what my pleasure was. I chose to walk. This Old Smokey was clear of fog for once and I wanted to enjoy it while I could. I had a need to be aware of everything around me, to have people passing and to see couples out strolling. I didn't offer him my arm and he didn't ask for it; instead, we walked side by side and just talked.

"Your friend Stoker told me that a hundred years ago, the ending of *King Lear* was changed to allow Cordelia to live. She marries Edgar and lives happily ever after. He said this version was popular, but now the proper ending has been restored. Why? What is the purpose of tragedy? Why is her death so important?"

"Tate changed the ending because people are fond of 'poetic justice.' They like good to triumph over evil. It reassures people, convinces them the world is a safe place."

"But Irving chose to use the original ending? Why? Cordelia is the heroine. She is young; she is beautiful; she is loyal. Why do you prefer her to die?"

"Because it means that you'll never forget the play. If Lear and his daughter both die needless deaths, you'll cry for them and you will think far harder as to the reasons why they died. Cordelia's love and duty carry more weight when she pays the fullest price."

He was silent for a while. I studied his profile as we walked, that beaked nose and the strong forehead. He reminded me of a bird of prey, something cruel that swoops down and seizes young birds in its talons. Eventually he spoke: "Is it more important to live or to be remembered?"

"It's more important to live—that's why tragedy exists. Tragedy gives us the illusion that other people will remember us when we are gone. We have no choice as regards death; remembrance is the closest we can come—we live on in the minds of other people."

I wonder if anyone will remember when I'm gone? Will they wander past my memorial and say "Ellen Terry? Who was she?" We all like to think our memories are immortal, but of course, they aren't. All things considered, they're probably more likely to stub their toes on my tombstone and curse.

I think Dracula understood people's desire for immortality. He asked me, quite seriously, if I would rather live for ever or be remembered for ever.

I laughed at that one (well, how can you answer a question like that seriously?), and said I'd look *awfully* decrepit if I lived for ever!

His answer was to ask if I would want to live for ever if I could stay as I am now.

"Well," I said, "if you're going to wave a magic wand, I'd rather be ten years younger." You realise, you'd probably be terribly disappointed in me if we met—I'll be a grandmother next year.

"Not you," he declared. "You should always be as you are now."

"You flatter me," I protested.

"You have more than beauty. You have intelligence, wit, and feeling. I have three sisters, and they are each worthless. They have no ideas in their heads that I do not put there. They do not read, they have no love of knowledge, they don't *think*. When I see you on stage, I see a woman different than the one I see here. That alone tells me the effort that goes into your work. Then I remember the emotion in the part you play and I know that must be a part of you, for it is impossible to truly simulate something that you cannot understand.

"My sisters tell me that I am incapable of love, but they lie. I recognise it when I see it and therefore I am capable of feeling it."

It struck me that this was a curious doubt for any man to have. Was love important to him because he had lived alone too long? Was there some dead love in his past? Almost on cue, he said—"You played *Othello* the year before last. Othello kills his love when he believes she has betrayed him, yet with her dying breath Desdemona seeks to protect him. How do you read that? Can a woman truly love the man who kills her?"

I love Desdemona for her perception, the way she loved Othello for what he was rather than how he looked. I couldn't help but wonder if Dracula had also raised the question for that reason. It would be hard indeed for a woman to love him for his face.

"It's a pity you weren't able to see it," I replied. "But yes, her love for Othello was always based on her understanding of him. Even when he is trying to kill her, she knows deep inside her that he still loves her. *That's* the tragedy of the play—he kills the person he most loves. If he hadn't loved her to such excess, he would not have been so enraged by her seeming betrayal."

"Do you think then that she forgave him?"

I pondered that one, because it's a tricky question. Love and a willingness to forgive don't always go hand in hand. "I think she wanted to protect him. I think she loved him. . . . Forgiveness? That's harder to say. He hadn't trusted her and that's always hard for a woman to accept."

"Suppose, for the sake of argument, she could have come back from the dead—would she have loved him then?"

He really did ask the oddest questions. Death seemed to be always at the forefront of his mind.

"I suppose she might. If a ghost is capable of love."

That seemed to really hit home. "It has to be possible!" he snarled. "There must be a woman capable of loving beyond the grave."

I touched him gently on the arm. "Who was she?"

"Everyone I have ever loved. Do you realise that it is possible for a man to live forever? To go on down through the centuries, never changing, never aging? But there is a price, and that price is to be for ever alone. Would you walk that path if you could take it?"

To never see my few grey hairs turning into thousands? To never feel the stiffness and blindness of old age? To be able to see my grandchildren grow to adulthood? How could anyone not want these things?

"It would be a gift beyond price, but you're wrong about being alone. No one need ever be alone."

There was a cat lying down ahead of us, sunning itself on the pavement in the way cats do. A butterfly carelessly darted within paw range and the cat had it at once. It teased it, and pounced every time the butterfly thought it had escaped. I shouted at the cat to go away and it ran, leaving the butterfly to struggle into the air once more. Such a pretty thing, all red and purple, the sunlight making the wings look as though they were dusted with gold.

"Do you know what my sisters would have done?" Dracula asked.

I shook my head.

"Pulled its wings off."

I pulled away in instinctive horror.

"The price," he said, "is to be unloved and always alone."

The butterfly flew higher and as I watched it, I heard the church clock strike noon. When I turned back to face Dracula, he was gone. Make of it what you will.—Yours sincerely,

Ellen Terry

Later—

I still haven't posted this. Maybe I never will. I'm still not sure what happened, or whether, indeed, *anything* happened. It's been a month now, and I've seen nothing of Dracula. Where did he go? *Why* did he go? Could he have been immortal as he claimed? I never liked him, but I'm surprised to realise that I'm concerned about him.

No, not concern—pity.

The Three Boxes

ELAINE BERGSTROM

London—August 19.

"The English is not difficult," the Count said, settling into a plush chair in his host's den, his reflection curiously absent in the polished mahogany top of the desk. His host did not notice, so intent was he on watching his visitor's face, his body.

"You might find it odd that I should sit like this. But I find the acts of sitting, standing, even breathing— or at least pretending to—so important now that I am surrounded by the life of this great city and must do my best to fit in."

His host did his best to listen to the tale. One that would end here in Mayfair, but began days earlier in a far less civilized corner of the country. He would say nothing in the hour that followed, for in truth there was nothing he could say as the Count continued. . . .

The Englishman himself is the puzzle. In my country, the poorest work the hardest, for they know it is only through work that they will survive. But here, after the ship ran aground and broke apart in the tide—that is good sailors' English for the matter, I think—with all the wealth the ship carried scattered across the beach, none of Whitby's poorest watching the ship break apart would provide me with any assistance in retrieving my sea-soaked boxes and getting them safely to shore.

So there was I, with not a soul to help me, dragging my boxes, heavy with soil and water, above the tide line. I had only the little money I had taken from the sailors. The bulk of my wealth was in jewels that I loathed to show to the lazy rabble lest they plot to rob me while I slept. Not such a fool, I worked alone, waiting for someone to come and offer service.

Someone did, but not at all the person I expected. To anyone less perceptive my helper appeared to be a boy, a youth of about sixteen. But I noted how the body moved, how weak the work it did, the slight scent of blood. No, not a man but a woman passing as one.

There were many reasons for such a disguise when I was alive—escaping slaves or willful women who did not like the husbands chosen for them. But I had come to understand from my solicitor visitors and from my readings of your land that a woman here would not need to hide. Not understanding, I did not let her know I had seen through her disguise.

I also did not have time to speak of it. Night was giving way to a dawn barely visible through the thick clouds. "How soon will the sun rise?" I asked my helper.

Face lifted to the sky, studying. "Noon," she finally said, and shrugged.

I understood, and she seemed so clear on it that I trusted her. With my life. But, you must understand, I had little choice.

As she predicted, the sun did not break through the mists for some hours. By the time it did, she had already been paid and taken leave of me, promising to meet me at the warehouse five nights later. And so I slept in the innermost box, thankful that two pounds and the promise of more covered the storage cost.

A happy meeting with a fine outcome. I was safe for the moment with time to get my bearings before I left for the city I would call home. For the next four nights, as I walked the cliffs near the city, watching men and women, absorbing language and manners, even while dining on a noblewoman of uncommon beauty, my thoughts returned frequently to the woman who had helped me.

I met her again as we'd arranged. Her clothes were the same as before, but were now ripped and muddy from the knee down as if she had been hiding in some swamp. Again, I did not ask for an explanation. It was not my affair.

"These boxes you need shipped, are they all yours?" she asked.

I nodded. "I have property near London. I need to take them there."

An interesting woman. She did not question the contents, instead asking, "You have money for this?"

"I have . . . means to obtain it," I replied, still wary—not of her honesty but of the possible slip of her woman's tongue.

She began a long explanation of currency exchanges until I stopped her with a wave of my hand, the gesture having some effect even on someone who did not know my temper. "I have the means . . . not in coin, but in goods. Do you know an honest person who would buy some . . . trinkets in gold?"

"Gold?" Her voice rose in curiosity, almost betraying her sex. "There are always those who would buy gold. As to honest, I can see what I can discover."

The person would, of course, be honest. I have ways of dealing with those who are not.

We spoke a bit longer then retreated to the first pub we found, where she and I sat in the larger room, one filled only with men and an occasional woman dressed in a way that convinced me that some professions are the same in any country.

I told her that I had already eaten, though in truth I was famished. I tried not to focus on my savior too closely, watching instead the men at the bar. Most were drunk or nearly so. When one stumbled out the door, I said I needed to step out back where the privies were built on the wharf. My partner shrugged and continued to devour her stew, gripping her spoon with her fist the way the men in the tavern did.

The building backed nearly up to the water, and there was no way to get to the front but through the pub or over the roof. Fortunately, the latter is not so difficult for one such as myself. Mist-like, I moved from back to front, finding my prey just as he was about to enter one of the foul-smelling hovels your poor call homes.

Too drunk to scream, he instead looked at me with wide eyes as I took form before him. Perhaps he even thought me some image of his sodden brain. No matter, he was mine in an instant. I moved his inert body into a narrow space between his building and the next and drained him. Even through his blood, I could feel the heat of the alcohol, so strong that I wondered if it would affect me. But I was not so foolish that I did not slit his throat before I left him.

His blood did give me a headache by the time I said goodbye to my evening's companion. But that was later, far after we left the public room.

Hunger gone, I could be more genial, enough that she eventually found the courage to say, "I am not what I seem."

I smiled, closed mouth, afraid that were I to open it I would laugh and she would notice my teeth and likely guess why. "I know," I said.

"So I thought. Thank you for being silent."

"And why such clothes?"

"I have reasons," she replied then looked at me, frowning, weighing my discretion. I must have passed, for she explained them.

I do not presume to understand her whispered lecture about women working in terrible conditions, living with brutes for husbands, denied land and a say in governing. But I did understand that last, the part that had her in so much trouble. "It is the same everywhere," I replied when she had finished. "Women have large families. They work too hard. They die young. At least here they have food to eat."

"And would have far more if they limited their children to two or three."

That was the number that would likely be left after plague and misfortunes and an occasional famished creature such as myself took their weaker offspring but I kept silent, believing that such a statement would not be well received by the woman. She went on, in a voice so close to silence that even I had to strain to hear her.

"I and my sisters came here to help as we have helped many in London with information on how to limit children. I have pamphlets that explain the basics to those who can read. To those who cannot, we hold lectures."

"And what do their men think of this?"

"Many approve. Others don't. But the government needs their soldiers and laborers and they do not approve. Nor does my husband. He forbade me to continue this work. I do not have his support in this endeavor."

"And why not?"

"He is a banker. They have reputations."

I killed a fair number of bankers when I ruled, and rarely pleasantly. "All bankers have reputations," I said, pleased when she understood the joke and laughed.

"So I waited until he left for business on the continent, then came here with my friends from London.

But they were arrested for public lewdness. Now I give the lectures, always ahead of the authorities looking for me."

"And so the clothes?"

"Exactly. But now I must return to Mayfair . . . that is, to London, by whatever means I can before my husband gets home on the 18th. Since my money was with my sisters I have no means. And I thought . . ."

She could not continue. Women, no matter how they play at independence, are not good at bargaining. "You thought one foreigner with a similar need might help?"

"A train ticket. Some money for food and I will help you get all your boxes safely to London," she said, leaning close to me as if we were partners in some crime. I needed the help. I agreed.

We were just leaving the establishment when some unfortunate woman found the remains of my night's meal. She screamed, drawing a crowd. My partner took a step toward the group, then moved back close to me. "It is good I have someone to walk with tonight," she said.

Ah, yes, this is not Romania. With luck it will stay so.

Such a charming woman, intense Sarah Justin. And she might not know how to bargain well but she got a fair enough price for the gold bracelet and ruby ring I gave her, and by the next evening all my boxes save three were being shipped to London through the efforts of the Billingtons, father and son.

Fifty boxes left my hands, but I am no fool. Fifty might be listed on Billington's records, but I kept the remaining three with me.

Those and my partner pulled out of Whitby a day later, on an afternoon train. I was safely resting in one of my boxes in a baggage car, not asleep but well aware of the train's motion; the faint, pleasant rocking as it headed west and south.

Would that I had been more aware of my companion. In truth I should have been wary. I have had a history of choosing the wrong sort of servant. Now that I have even more need for such loyalty, the matter has gotten worse. That lunatic Renfield, screaming out his fantasies in the charnel house you call an asylum, is the worst of any. But it matters little. Servants can always be replaced.

My thoughts wander and I only have the night to tell this story. You see, while I slept in the station warehouse, Sarah used the money I gave her for a first class ticket to pay the fines of her sisters in crime. They had means to leave and so all managed to catch the same train I was on, getting the lowest sort of tickets and sharing a section of one of the cars, plotting their next attack like the devil on All Hallows' Eve.

We pulled into Sheffield two hours before sunset. They were ready, leaflets in hand, departing the train for the meeting they had hurriedly arranged with one of those wire machines . . . telegraphs I believe Mr. Harker called them.

I can only conclude that the women thought they had right on their side and so were careless, because while Sarah in man's clothes had eluded them for days in Whitby, three women in skirts could not manage the same for even a few hours.

I was first alerted to the situation by loud-voiced men entering the baggage car. An employee of the railroad pointed out that the boxes—my boxes!—were not the property of the women they had arrested, but it made no difference to the local police. I heard one of them walk close to me, heard the workers argue with him one final time, then the pounding of an ax . . . thankfully on the box nearest the door.

Splintering wood. Creaking hinges. A man's voice, demanding, "What is the meaning of this?"

By which he meant, of course, what was the meaning of the earth inside. It was only then that I heard quick-minded Sarah reply, "Earth, sir. My traveling companion is . . . is a . . . a wealthy man. He has brought plantings from his native land and thinks that they will do better in their native soil."

Plantings! How well she put it.

I heard the policeman mumble something back, then the railroad official repeated his warnings. "And where can I find this man who pays good money to ship dirt, Mrs. Baxter?" he asked Sarah.

Clever woman! She never used her real name. "I believe he is in a private compartment."

"First class is at the front of the train, sirs," the railroad official added, no doubt trying to get them to leave the baggage car before they did more damage.

"Are we free to leave now?" one of the women, not Sarah, asked.

"Your fine was paid, and Mrs. Morgan's, but Mrs. Baxter's to be sent back to Whitby to see the magistrate with my blessing. Glad to get rid of the lot of you troublemakers."

Not acceptable, of course. I see to my servants.

The train would leave Sheffield at 10 o'clock, which gave me too little time to rescue Sarah. But I had to try. At sunset, I moved as mist outside the car then went to the front of the train, taking shape in the motor room, just behind the engineer. I disposed of him quickly, drinking nearly all of his blood. I was not particularly hungry but such an opportunity should not be wasted. At the end, to be careful, I broke his neck then stayed where I was, waiting for the rest of the . . . the crew I think they are called, to come and join him.

The second man reeked of sweat and soot, the third

much the same; these I killed quickly and in a violent human manner. Then, just to be certain the train would not leave with a different crew, I ripped through the wires of the engine. At the last, I dragged one of the bodies away from the front of the train, toward the passenger compartments farther back. We would stay where we were, at least until the passengers had been questioned. Plenty of time, I thought, as I made my way partly by instinct, partly by the help of strangers to the center of town and the police station.

As I had hoped, the bodies had been found and there was only one old man guarding Sarah and a male prisoner in a separate locked room. I had already decided to take the moderate approach to this problem— which is to say the human one—if only because a dead guard and an escaped prisoner would bring a great deal of trouble on Sarah Justin, and through her, onto me.

Besides, I wasn't hungry any more. In your land a vampire could grow fat.

The guard didn't even glance up at me as I walked into the room, though I made enough noise to alert him to my approach. He waited until I stood before his desk then looked up from the book he'd been reading. "Office is closed," he said.

"Closed?"

"You can't get legal work done, I mean."

"I think I can," I said and laid a gold ring in front of him.

"What's that?" he asked, making me wonder how he saw to read.

"Gold," I said. "Nearly pure. And if you pick up the piece you will notice four tiny diamonds along one side. Worth more than Mrs. Baxter's fine, I would think."

"We're not in the business of taking goods for fines, and she hasn't even seen a magistrate yet. It will have to wait until Whitby."

Not certain if I had found an honest man, or only a greedy one, I laid a second, larger ring beside the first. "I don't care if these pay the fine or not," I said. "I want her released."

"I can't do that, sir," he said, though he leaned forward to examine the pieces. As I took in breath to try one final, persuasive argument, I caught a scent that likely saved his life—alcohol, some cheap grain, recently consumed from the strength of it. If I had been more fixed on him than on my reason for being there, I would have noticed it sooner.

"I can't," he repeated, looking up from the rings and directly into my eyes.

"Give me the keys," I said after a moment.

He handed them over, but fought my suggestion that he sleep. A well-aimed blow to the side of his head placed him in a state close enough to sleep to seem so to the first returning policeman. Just to be on the safe side, I found the bottle in his pocket and spilled it across his desk. The rings were in plain sight. When the others returned, they would think he had been too drunk to hide his bribe.

In the back, I tried the key in the lock of the room where they had put her, but though it fit, it did not open the door. Apparently, the drunk was not trusted with an actual set of keys. I wonder if he knew it.

With no choice left me, I called to Sarah—awake now and wary. I told her to step back then flung myself at the door. It burst inward with such a crash that my first sight of her was with her face contorted with fear, eyes shut tight, hands covering her ears. "I thought you blew it up," she said.

"No need. It is not so thick," I replied, though my arms and shoulders ached with an almost human sharpness. "Now we need to catch the train."

"It would have left by now with your . . . boxes." She wanted to ask about the earth, but my only answer would be the one she gave the authorities.

"There's been trouble at the station. The train is still there. We must go."

She barely glanced at the unconscious guard as we passed him. Apparently my ruse fooled even her.

The station was filled with police. We waited in the shadows near the depot for the questioning to end. Two men passed close by, speaking of the murders. Sarah became pale as one of my brides, but I swore on the Bible and my mother's grave that I knew nothing of them. My soul is already damned, of course, and my mother, being a deceitful woman in life, would hardly be bothered by my lie.

We saw her friends. She started to call to them but I told her to be silent. "You must not be seen with them because they might be thought—" I hesitated, uncertain of the word.

"Accomplices," she supplied and nodded her agreement. So we sat, speaking little until the police went away and the train was fitted with a new engine. At the moment the wheels began to turn and the train pulled forward, blocking the view from the station, I pushed her toward an entrance. No coward she, she grabbed the handrail and pulled herself up. I followed with far less difficulty and soon we were sitting in the stateroom I had presumably rented for us . . . the first time we were together in it since the journey had begun. We had, I understood with some concern, less than two hours until sunrise and would arrive in London in midday rather than after dark. Like it or not, I was at her mercy. I had no choice but to explain matters as truthfully as I dared. To my surprise, I found that I did not wish to cause her anguish or take control of her mind, and not just because I needed her services.

She sat across from me in the little compartment, staring at the door every time someone went by as if the horror she would face lay outside our little compartment rather than on the seat across from her. Her hands clutched each other and the folds of her skirt, no doubt to keep me from seeing how they trembled. I reached for one. I had touched her before, but never for so long. I let my guard fall slowly, watching her face for some sign of understanding.

"Your hands are so cold," she finally said.

My usual means to approach the matter. "There is a reason for that," I said, and told her.

She listened to my story, more incredulous than horrified. A smile danced across her lips as if she wanted to laugh. "You are taking my mind off my troubles with this outrageous tale. You could make a fine living here as a penny dreadful writer," she said when I had finished.

I could have pressed her hand to my silent heart but that would have been too intimate, too . . . well, I would not. With only an hour remaining, I made her swear not to scream. And I changed.

I chose wolf form. A large and dangerous animal, it is true, but it has been my experience that women are far more afraid of bats.

Dear Sarah! When I lay across the seat opposite her in the form of noble beast, my muzzle resting on my paws so I would look as tame as possible, her hands shook but she reached out and brushed them across my fur, then buried her face in the back of my neck. "How wonderful!" she cried. "How completely wonderful!"

Such a woman, Sarah Justin! She watched with interest, not fear, as I shifted first to mist then to my own form. "And to think I have traveled with you all this time and never once suspected!" she said as much to herself as to me.

Now that she believed my story, I went on to explain that any exposure to sun would burn me as painfully as flames would her.

She understood and said she would see my last two boxes safely to Carfax. I told her she need not do this but she insisted. "I think of the men on the train with their axes and all you have done for me. Of course I will see you safely to your new home. The train stops in Purfleet. I will arrange for cart and driver then catch a later train to London. I'll have more than enough time to make it seem that I never left home at all."

Then she sat, hands in her lap again, watching me with a curious expression. Was it hope? She seemed to like the wolf and I enjoyed the feel of her hands on my pelt. But such a form is dangerous. I lose some human control and to have her touch me as she would not dare were I in human form . . . no, it was better to stay as I was and follow her conventions.

To pass time, I asked, "Tell me what you know of London."

She spoke of theaters and pubs and the banking district and the rest. I absorbed it all—particularly the places in your East End where one such as me can feed without arousing suspicion. Thanks to her, I feel almost at home in this marvelous city, and the hunting is excellent.

I left her just before sunrise, aware of her gaze following me. She had not given me her address. I had not asked for it. It would be better that way, for she belonged to another and I owed her too much.

When I rose again, I would see my new home. I was far too excited for sleep and so I was awake when my boxes were unloaded, feeling the sun even through the thick wood of my daytime refuge. I heard the rough voices of the loaders, the creak of a cart, the snort of a nervous horse, then Sarah's sweet voice asking them to please be careful.

"Done this longer than you've been on this earth, Miss. Now let us be," the man said.

I was being lifted, carried. I heard the train's whistle, the horse's nervous whinny, a crash, and last, Sarah's loud scream.

For a moment, I tensed, waiting for the burning of the sun.

Nothing. It was the other box that fell, cracked, my precious soil mixing with the dung in the road.

"Should we scoop it up, Miss?"

Just go, I thought, and heard her echo my words.

It was a long drive. The wood absorbed the heat and made rest impossible. When my box had been safely deposited in the cool confines of Carfax, I felt her hand brush the top of the box, a finger run the length of it. "Goodbye," she whispered, and was gone.

One night passed. Two. I found the old stone walls to my liking. I took the boxes of earth and scattered them through London, placing some in Belgravia and Bloomsbury and all the other places where foolish people walk the streets at night thinking there is nothing to fear. The rest, I hid on the Carfax grounds, a wild place with many hiding spots. And as I labored alone, I tried not to think of Sarah except to hope that her ruse had gone well and that she was happy.

On the third night, she returned to me, a little parcel of clothing in one hand. We met outside, the moonlight glittering on her tears.

"Are you hurt?" I asked, ready to kill the one who raised a hand to her.

"Yes. No . . . no. Really, I'm not."

"But you cry?"

"My husband learned of everything. I don't know how. He only said, 'Well, at least no one knew your name. Next time I'm gone, I'll lock you in your room and pay someone to watch you.' I cannot live that way. I will not. And then I thought of you, so kind and so helpful and so in need of a pair of daylight eyes."

"And you think I will take you in to help me?" I asked, carefully, praying her answer would be yes.

"Yes . . . and . . . no, to let me be with you, only

you. Let me stay here and work for you. Make me as you are."

Then she did something I could never forgive. She kissed me, betraying her vows and the loyalty and obedience she owed a husband.

I have been wronged by too many women, and they have all met the same fate. Would that Sarah had been stronger. But, out of respect for the help she had given me, one quick blow to the head and she was unconscious. I fed, and when she died I buried her beneath the crypt where I slept, using the box she had brought here as her coffin.

Tonight, I laid a jewel over the fresh-turned earth. And though I doubt God will listen, I said a quick prayer that, even though she broke her vows, he spare her soul. Then I went through her bag and found a letter addressed to you but never sent. It is a beautiful journey from Purfleet to Mayfair for one such as me. London. So beautiful. And so alive.

No, it will do you no good if you tip over the chair. There is no manservant to hear you, not any more. . . .

Dracula stood, moved close to his victim, inhaling the scent of hairwax and sweet tobacco and, just for a moment, of Sarah's perfume. "No, I do not understand you English," he said. "Such a woman, a prize among women, and you treated her as a servant. One bit of understanding and she would have loved you, passionately and forever. Instead you worried about little matters, and lost her.

"It is right to dispose of a woman who does not obey, to put her in the hands of God mercifully and quickly. But what of the man who pushed her away? What fate should await him?

"No mercy. Had you means to speak, you might even agree. No mercy. Fool! Perhaps she will be allowed to judge you in the next life."

And so the Count moved, silent as the mist to his bound prey. The last thing the man saw were long pale fingers coming toward his face, shifting swiftly into something more powerful, a beast to push his head back. No fangs here, nothing as soft and almost pleasant as fangs. No, it was the wolf who devoured him, feasting long after he had life to care. Licking the blood from furry paws.

With a quick, mournful howl, he was gone, padding away from the blood-soaked room, the silent Mayfair house. East he padded toward his retreat in Carfax. As he did, the almost-human part of him vowed that the next woman he took would be different—softer and sweeter, younger, and above all, obedient to her master.

When he reached Carfax, he found Renfield hiding just inside the gates. Seeing Dracula, he rushed out and gave a low bow, the solemnity marred by his laughter.

Better, his master thought, *far better than the other.*

Good Help

K. B. BOGEN

Not again! Dracula leaped from the sill and flew across the lawn toward the nearby trees. He landed amidst the small stand of English oaks at the same time the slender, cloaked figure entered the house at the Crescent. Shifting into human form, he turned to watch the window he had just vacated.

That irritating woman and her meddling! If she had continued her wanderings just a short while longer, I could have finished what I started. And if Renfield had not gotten himself incarcerated in that hospital, there would have been someone to waylay the nosy brunette. What a nuisance.

He really ought to do something about replacing the old lunatic.

At home, he had never required a full-time manservant to take care of everyday tasks. Anything that could not be done at night, the gypsies would do. For a modest fee, of course.

But here in England, it was different. So many people. So many annoyances. He really needed someone to prevent all the unnecessary interruptions. He simply detested having to eat and fly. It was bad for the digestion.

He shrugged and stared at the figure slumped on the windowsill until she stirred, moaning. After a few seconds, she rose and stumbled toward her bed. *Soon, my dear,* he thought to her, *soon it will be all over.* He ran his tongue over the points of his teeth, thinking how nice it would be when the time arrived.

A moment later, another woman appeared beside the first.

His eyes on the two women, he took a step forward—and fell the last ten feet. *Hellfire!* After all these years, he should have learned to land on the ground instead of the lower branches. He glanced around to see if anyone noticed. *No? Good.*

He wiped the dirt from his trousers and cloak, then spit out the dead leaves that had found their way into his mouth. After satisfying himself that nothing was torn or broken, he peered through the gloom at the two figures in the window.

The dark-haired woman, the one called Mina, put her arm around her sleeping-walking friend. The vampire listened intently, straining to pick out Mina's whispered words at that distance.

"Come, dear Lucy, we must get you back to bed. You'll catch your death in this damp, chill air!"

Dracula laughed to himself. *Somehow, I do not think the damp, chilly air will have anything to do with it.*

Mina gently helped her friend to her bed, still murmuring words of encouragement. As they left the window, Mina threw one furtive glance toward the trees, and Dracula quickly faded into the darkness.

He sighed. This Mina might prove an interesting diversion in the future. At the moment, her untimely return had proven—inconvenient. Miss Westenra would have to wait. There were other matters of importance to attend to.

*   *   *

His errand took him to the docks, past the row of darkened warehouses. The air smelled too much of salt and fish and waterlogged wood, but the gloom of the docks suited his mood as he stalked down the aisles between the crates. He was still seething about Mina's sudden return. Damned inconsiderate woman! He had been so close, and yet . . .

At last he found what he sought. Ethan Soarsby. His kind had been called many things over the centuries, but Dracula thought "wharf rat" suited him best. The little man might be just the distraction he needed. Dracula had been studying him for several days. He had potential.

Soarsby stood by one of the packing crates, pry bar in hand as he plied his trade. A moth-eaten wool jacket lay atop the crate, muffling the sound of splintering wood. A matching wool cap covered his head, leaving visible a fringe of mousy brown hair. On the ground beside him lay a pile of sacks.

A sudden crash at the end of a row of crates sent Dracula into the shadows to investigate. The last thing he needed was a witness. But the culprit turned out to be a cat hunting among the boxes, nothing more.

Satisfied his actions would go unnoticed, he returned to the now-open crate, but Soarsby had gone. Not far, though. Empty sacks still littered the ground and Dracula could feel the man's presence. The little thief was near. Very near.

What was the best way to catch a predator? The vampire knew that answer from years of experience. Pretend to be prey. He grinned and stood quietly, letting Soarsby step in behind him, a lion playing with a mouse.

The thief stepped silently into position. Silently to normal ears, at any rate. Dracula waited for him to make his move.

A hand snaked around his neck and a knife-edge

pressed against his flesh above the collarbone. The thief's skin was clammy and his breath reeked of onions and fish.

He noticed Soarsby had also had garlic for dinner and almost laughed out loud at the thought of that old wives' tale. How many times had he met with some would-be adversary who thought it was the *bulb* of the plant that would vanquish a vampire? So few people realized it was the *flowers* he found revolting. He really preferred roses. But, back to the business at hand. . . .

Centuries before, a knife at his throat might have caused Vlad Tsepes a moment's nervousness. But many battles and many lifetimes had passed since then. As it was, he found the situation— entertaining.

Seconds ticked by while he waited for the thief to make the first comment. Finally, Soarsby thought of something to say.

"Don't move a muskle, or ya won't be able ta move a'tol." Soarsby emphasized his threat by pressing the knife deeper into the flesh of Dracula's neck. Considering their height difference, the action was as much of a stretch as the threat itself.

"Really? How amusing." He deliberately kept his tone light. "I have a better plan."

The Count took the thief's wrist and gently forced it down as he turned to face the little man. Soarsby's features contorted from the effort as he tried to keep his knife raised. He failed.

Several emotions played across the thief's face. Surprise. Anger. Hatred. Fear. The fear won. His eyes widened as he began to understand the kind of force he was fighting.

Dracula continued amicably, "I have a proposition for you, my friend. . . ." He swept his cloak over Soarsby's shoulders and led him back toward the warehouses.

*   *   *

"I will be back by dawn. See that everything is in order."

"Yes . . . Master." Soarsby rolled the word around on his tongue, as if tasting it for the first time. In fact, he was. That vintage of it, at least.

Dracula left through the ironbound door, wincing as its rusted hinges screamed protest. It had been two days since his last visit to Lucy Westenra, and he looked forward to it. She was so—giving. He smiled at the thought.

He returned just before dawn, in much better spirits than on previous mornings. His visit with Lucy had gone well. Her friend Mina had not even noticed him. Having Lucy sit beside the window had proven to be a very good tactic. As long as she never left her bed chamber, her friend felt she was safe.

He landed just inside the wall surrounding the abbey. He was in such a wonderful mood, he felt like walking. A few wispy clouds trailed across the moon and a light fog had developed, lending Carfax an ethereal quality.

He took a deep breath, enjoying the salt/flower scent of the ancient apothecary roses that hugged the crumbling walls of the chapel. He was so engrossed in the smells, sounds, and flavors of the night that he completely missed the pile of rubbish some cretin had left by the corner.

Metal and wood scattered noisily as he stumbled through the pile of discarded building materials. A broken timber smashed into a pane of glass with a loud crash.

"What the—?" Considering the manner in which the things had been arranged, it almost looked intentional. But who would have done such a thing?

He limped toward the chapel, cursing in four different languages. Some of the words had not been heard in over three centuries.

As he approached the entrance, he paused, steeling

himself for the whine of the hinges. But there was no sound.

He opened and closed the door several times, experimenting. Neither a squeak nor squeal. Soarsby had located Renfield's underused oil can.

"Nicely done." Dracula entered the chapel quietly for the first time since his arrival at Carfax. He looked around, amazed.

Soarsby had dusted the spider webs from the corners, fixed the holes in the shutters and fastened them securely against the coming daylight. He had even removed the coffin lid and smoothed the soil within.

A fresh earth scent rose from the box, to mingle with the smells of old wood and wool in the ancient chapel. And there was something else. In the shadow where the lid overhung the edge of the coffin was a gift: Soarsby had left a bedtime snack in the form of a large rat in a wire cage. How thoughtful.

"Things are looking up," Dracula mused as he lay down for his nap. The picture on the inside of the coffin lid was a nice touch, too. He would have to remember to suggest to Soarsby that he replace the raw steak with one of those French postcards. Scented.

"Will ya be visitin' tha pretty miss this night, Master?"

"Not tonight. I have other business this evening. There is a stack of papers to go over and a libretto I, um, *borrowed* that I hoped to read. I shall be upstairs, if you require instructions. Miss Westenra will keep for a day or two." Besides, he was a little weary of trying to avoid Mina's notice.

The papers were, as expected, boring. Real estate contracts, accounting records, and reams of legalese he had not managed to escape for the last two hundred years. It constantly amazed him how many ways mankind had found to increase their load of paperwork. It got worse every century. Maybe he should start a campaign to save the trees and put an end to the document craze. Or invent something to take the place of paper. He dwelt on that thought an extra moment. It might be worth looking into.

Meanwhile, all that legal babble had given him a headache. Perhaps the play would prove more interesting. The title certainly looked promising: *The Pirates of Penzance*. Pirates were good.

An hour before dawn, a flustered Soarsby hesitantly entered the room Dracula had adopted as his office. He waited for his master to acknowledge him.

Dracula just chuckled and turned another page.

"M-master?" The laughter apparently confused the ex-thief. As if evil, bloodsucking monsters were not allowed to have fun once in a while.

Dracula looked up from his papers. "May I help you?" he prompted when Soarsby seemed reluctant to proceed.

"There be someone beatin' on the door, askin' fer ya. Tha *back* door."

Now who would . . . oh. Renfield. The Count reluctantly left his desk and that delicious libretto, and headed for the entrance to the chapel. Soarsby followed a few steps behind.

Renfield stood in the entry, fidgeting, clad in only his nightshirt. When Dracula started to widen the opening, Renfield protested.

"No, no! Leave it, Master! Leave it closed. They're after me."

Dracula pushed the door to and opened the small window set into it. He peered down at the old man pressed against the wood. "They are?"

"Yes, and they'll find me, soon enough. That they

will. But tell me, who—who was he, the man who first
answered my knock?"

Dracula paused, considering carefully his response.
"He is Mr. Soarsby, my—assistant."

"Assistant? A replacement? Oh, no, Master! I am
your faithful servant, still. You need not find others."

"Renfield . . ."

His cries became more fervent, even hysterical.
"You shall not have another! Not while I draw
breath."

"Renfield . . ."

"No, no! I shall—"

"Renfield!" If only the old man would let him
speak. . . .

Nearby, they heard a loud crash, followed by men
cursing loudly. The refuse Dracula had tripped on the
previous morning had been Soarsby's idea of a warning
device. It worked very well, as the Count knew from
personal experience. Now someone else knew, too.

Renfield listened to the sound for a moment, then
continued, his voice soft, but still tinged with hysteria.
"I am here to do Your bidding, Master. I am
Your slave. . . ."

*Oh, no! Not that "I deserve everything because I
have given everything" speech again. This could take
a while.*

Dracula leaned against a handy wall, arms crossed,
stifling a yawn. He thought of interrupting Renfield's
diatribe, but the ranting seemed to keep the old man
happy.

". . . await Your commands . . ."

He nodded off a couple of times, then shook himself awake. Dawn was fast approaching.

". . . in Your distribution of good things?" Renfield
finally wound down and his voice trailed off into a
whine.

More crashes and cursing brought Dracula out of

his doze. Renfield swung around to face the cause of
the noise as a group of men appeared around the corner. The Count recognized the leader as the doctor
from the asylum next door. Doctor Seward.

With a loud cry, Renfield rushed them. He fought
like a tiger, flailing wildly and without thought for the
consequences. The men with Doctor Seward had a
rough time bringing the old man down.

Renfield smacked one of the attendants with a piece
of wood. Another tripped and thudded to the ground
gasping, with Renfield's hands clutched around his
throat. Blood trickled down the old man's cheek from
a cut on his forehead. It was a circus, but it kept their
attention away from Dracula and the chapel.

The fight seemed to go on forever, but finally they
forced Renfield to the ground and wrapped him in a
straight waistcoat. As they carried him away, he risked
one last look in Dracula's direction while his lips
twitched into a knowing smile.

The Count watched them retreat toward the asylum. After a while, Soarsby broke the silence.

"Who were that, Master?"

"A mistake, Mr. Soarsby. One I should, perhaps,
rectify in the very near future."

"Rec-ti-fy?" He stumbled over the unfamiliar word.

"Fix."

"Oh, ya mean yer gonna kill 'im."

Dracula glared at Soarsby. Then he relaxed and
nodded. "Possibly, Mr. Soarsby, possibly."

The whole situation was quite unfortunate. Renfield
would have been a perfect assistant, if he could have
found two coherent moments to rub together. And he
did not seem very pleased at being made redundant. If
those fools at the asylum could not contain him, it
might become necessary for the Count to take care of
the problem himself.

*   *   *

He arose the next evening thinking about the events of that morning. He was still wondering how to solve the trouble with Renfield as he neared the Crescent. He also needed to decide what to do about Mina. It seemed a waste of Soarsby's talents to use him to prevent the woman from interfering with his visits with Lucy.

Dracula reached the edge of the wood near the house where the Westenras had rooms and stopped where he could see Lucy's window. He leaned against a large tree to watch for company.

The rough bark of the ancient oak dug into his back, as though to remind him that it deserved more respect at its age. *Hah!* Dracula himself had been alive almost two hundred years when the tree was a mere sapling. Still, it was good to know some things could last more than a few short decades.

Leaves rustled high in the branches, sending forth their earthy summer scent to mingle with the decay of their forebears already moldering on the ground. Shadows fluttered around him, caressing his face reverently, like sycophantic demons. He ignored them all. Life was fleeting illusion; shadows he was accustomed to; demons he would confront at another time.

He took a deep breath and leaped into the sky, changing shape as he did so. As he landed softly on the sill outside Lucy's room, he looked around. The window was open. Surprised, he cautiously stepped down from the ledge—and fell again.

Damn! I must be worried about something. That is the second time in less than a week I have done that. The windowsill was a little too tall for a bat. He transformed quickly and entered the room.

Lucy lay on her bed, the covers strewn wildly across its surface. She eyed him hungrily, her eyes burning. And she was alone.

"Please, come to me!" She beckoned to him as she reclined against the pillows, trailing one delicately manicured finger between her breasts. Her gown slid open, drawing Dracula's attention to her naked body beneath the silky material. The soft scent of lavender rose from her warm flesh.

This is different. He approached her slowly, a little suspicious.

She bit her lip in anticipation while an odd, almost predatory expression played across her face. "I am ready, my love." She leaned forward, head tilted, mouth open slightly.

Wrong move. Some latent, lingering shred of teenage rebellion asserted itself and he hastily revised his plans. He did *not* like being rushed. Especially by the victim.

He sat on the edge of her bed. Leaning forward, he caressed her cheek and whispered, "Not this time, I think." *Always leave them wanting more.* "Tell me, where is your friend Mina?"

"She received a message that her fiancé Jonathan Harker is in Buda-Pesth. He is in a monastery or some such, and very ill. She left to join him there." Her hands clutched at the edge of Dracula's cloak. He pulled away while he considered the implications of Lucy's news. Lucy pouted.

So—Jonathan Harker survived his final night in Castle Dracula. Bad news. He might serve as witness to the Count's true nature. He certainly must have some idea what the vampire planned for his new homeland.

And Mina had left to be with him. That was good. She would be out of the picture for some while.

On the other hand, they were certain to return to England as soon as Harker recovered from his illness. The two lovers would have to be taken care of when the time came.

To top it off, the girls were probably upset that their dinner ran away. If they ever managed to track Harker down, they would certainly find the Count as well. And he would be in almost as much trouble as his solicitor for failing to keep the young man properly contained.

Too preoccupied to dine, he left Lucy sleeping restlessly and headed back to Carfax.

When he landed outside the entry to the chapel, he found it cracked open and the sound of a struggle inside alerted him that Soarsby was not alone.

". . . not yours! I am to be the one. . . ." It was Renfield's voice.

Something thudded against the old oak, knocking it shut. There were several crashes. Splintering wood. A muffled cry of rage or pain.

Dracula burst through the door and found Renfield fighting with Soarsby. Soarsby seemed to have some idea of what he was doing and several times the thief got the upper hand. But Renfield fought like a demon. The older man was winning.

Dracula waded into the fracas and pulled the men apart. Twice. Finally, he shouted, "Stop this right now!"

They stopped.

He gave them both a shake before releasing them. "You should be ashamed of yourselves." He felt as though he were lecturing a pair of children. They stared at their toes, afraid to look Dracula in the eye.

"Who started this?"

"He did!" They replied in unison, each pointing to the other.

Maybe the comparison to children was not far wrong. It reminded him of all the times he and his brother Mircea fought for their father's attention. Dracula took a step backward, glaring at the two men. "You two have got to learn to get along. Now, shake hands and make up."

Soarsby started to say something negative as Renfield shouted.

"Never!" The old lunatic pulled a knife from his waistband and dashed toward Soarsby, slashing wildly.

"Renfield!" Definitely a strong resemblance to the relationship between himself and his brother. Including the mayhem and bloodshed.

He tried to get between the men, but Renfield was too fast. In a second, the old man had plunged his blade into Soarsby's chest.

"Heh heh! I am the one, the one who will be Yours forever! It is—" Soarsby's "alarm" went off again.

Renfield darted through the door, slamming it shut as he charged his pursuers. Dracula heard the sound of a vicious battle through the thick wood. Continuing to give ear to the fighting in the courtyard, he knelt beside the body of his erstwhile assistant. Soarsby lived. Barely.

He considered his alternatives. How disappointing! The thief had proven to be a very valuable aide, but Dracula had no intention of spending eternity with him.

What to do? He stared thoughtfully at the door, listening to the battle raging on the other side. "My dear Renfield, you certainly know how to make things difficult. I shall have to attend to you presently." He looked down at Soarsby's gasping form. "But for now, I think it is time for my morning repast."

He sank his fangs into Soarsby's neck, savoring the last few drops of life in the man's body. Leaning back, he eyed the pool of blood forming beneath the hilt of the knife.

Too bad Renfield had to go and waste Soarsby like that. He licked the last few drops of sweetly metallic liquid from his lips. *Good help is so hard to find.*

Everything to Order

JODY LYNN NYE

The bell rang precisely at the appointed hour of eleven. As the porter swung wide the door, Miss Violet Carr peered out at the three well-dressed women standing on the steps half-clad in darkness. At first she was cross with the porter for not lighting enough lamps, but she realized that the visitors were hanging back in the folds of the thick fog that wrapped around the London night. Miss Carr curtsied and dipped her beautifully coiffed head with the deferential half-bow she reserved for members of the titled class. They all wore heavy coats of velvet lined with the most expensive sables, with more furs wrapping them to the ears. Their hats were also black fur, from which depended thick black silk veils. The outfits must have been sweltering on an August night.

"Welcome to the House of Feldon, ladies," Miss Carr said, with deference and cordiality. Silently, the shrouded figures slipped one by one over the threshold. Once inside, they lifted their veils. Miss Carr scanned the faces and hesitated slightly, conscious of the possibility of making a dreadful faux pas and starting the evening out on the wrong foot. "I . . . I beg your pardon for asking—which of you is Countess Dracula?"

"We all are," the eldest said. She gave Miss Carr a smile as curiously undefinable as her accent. She didn't seem to be very much older than the youngest, who seemed as though she could boast the same number of years as Miss Carr herself, twenty-four.

Violet Carr was young for a vendeuse, but was grateful for the opportunity that the owner of the House of Feldon had bestowed upon her, to oversee showings of the house line to clients, to take orders, and to supervise fittings of the chosen garments. It was a position of trust, and she already had two—two!—titled clients who asked particularly for her when they came to the House of Feldon. She hoped to increase her status this very evening, if it meant she had to stay up until dawn.

"We must thank you for your indulgence in allowing us to come to you so very late," the eldest countess said. "We keep late hours. It is not an English custom. All of your shops are closed before sunset. How are we to make our purchases? Other houses of fashion of whom we made this little request were unable to accommodate us. It is most inconvenient."

"We endeavor to please," Miss Carr said, pleased for Mrs. Feldon-Jacobs's sake. It surely would be worthwhile having remained. These ladies were possessed of fabulous wealth. The necklace about the neck of the youngest countess was composed of real diamonds, each stone the size of Miss Carr's thumb tip. Such jewels had to be worth the value of a steamship. Those other couturiers would regret having refused, and Mrs. Feldon-Jacobs would have reason to be smug.

Her eagerness must have showed upon her face, because the eldest countess smiled. She had a most interesting face. It spoke to Miss Carr of high breeding and quality. The cheekbones were particularly beautiful, not too protuberant, yet with a piquant shadow

beneath. Her nose was high-bridged, narrow as a
hawk's beak, and she had large, deep brown eyes that
seemed to be a blend of black and red, and black-
brown hair swept up into sleek folds around her head.
She wore black velvet sewn with jet beads and fringe
that swayed gently as she moved. The second lady was
very much like her, the lineaments of her dark-
complected face spare as a sculpture, with large dark
eyes. Her dress, also of velvet, was blood red, trimmed
in jet and garnets. The third lady, clad in heavy blue
velvet, was equally striking, lovely in a more English
manner, with masses of blonde hair, fair skin, and
large, luminously blue eyes. At least their beauty would
be more pleasant if these ladies had the bloom of
health upon them. They were all so very pale. Perhaps
in Rumania ladies of quality were not permitted or
encouraged to take the air very often. It was on the
tip of Miss Carr's tongue to ask, but good manners
took over. It was not a question she would ever ask of
an Englishwoman. She must not allow her training to
desert her even though these were only foreigners.

Pages, yawning openly due to the late hour, assisted
the countesses in removing their coats and hats, and
vanished with the garments to the cloakroom. Miss
Carr took the lead, escorting her visitors into the salon.
She heard a murmur of approval from behind her as
she stepped aside to allow them to enter the chamber
ahead of her. The room, the most superior of the five
that Mrs. Feldon-Jacobs maintained, had walls covered
in Regency-striped oyster silk with dark wood trim and
doors. A vase of lilies stood on one occasional table,
and a vase of ostrich feathers adorned the other. She
was pleased to see that the porter had raised a good
fire in the marble-lined grate, and begged the visitors
to make themselves at home. The second-eldest countess took the most comfortable chair, a luxuriously padded, chestnut-coloured upholstered leather armchair
with mahogany legs that sat at one side of the fireplace,

and was chased from thence by a glance from her senior. Strangely, the eldest did not sit down in it herself, but left it for their fair-haired junior, who sank into it with the grace of a queen.

"How may our establishment assist you?" Miss Carr asked, standing before them a trifle nervously. In light of the byplay she had just witnessed, she did not quite know which one to address.

"We do not wish anything that has been worn before by anyone else," the eldest said, settling herself at one end of the bottle-green velvet couch at the other side of the hearth. "We are here for haute couture, nothing less. This house has produced handsome wares in the past. That is what we wish."

"Made-to-measure, then," Miss Carr said, inwardly jubilant. Bespoke gowns were worth to the establishment ten to twenty times the value of off-the-rack garments. She tried not to look excited as she opened her tiny notebook and raised her gold pencil. "Do you perhaps have a concept of what particular needs in your wardrobe you wish to fill?"

The youngest, enthroned in the great leather chair, waved her hand dismissively. "We have not had new wardrobes in ages, not ages! The whole ensemble, if you please. Evening dresses, walking dresses, night dresses! We wish to see it all."

Less explosively, the others agreed. "Yes, show us your current line, if it is not too much trouble."

"Not at all," Miss Carr said. "We are pleased to do anything that will suit your convenience."

The eldest countess smiled her enigmatic smile. "I am most delighted to hear you say that."

Miss Carr bowed herself out to go to the robing room where the mannequins were waiting to hear what garments they should don.

The girls sitting on couches and benches in their altogethers in the cloth-draped chamber looked up at her as she entered. They had been drinking tea and coffee to stay awake. A few of them had taken naps, but many of them were worn and a little pallid, looking older than their ages, which were from sixteen to twenty years. They had all expressed themselves willing to work late for the bonus wages Mrs. Feldon-Jacobs offered for this night. It was hardly a respectable time for young ladies to be out, but the owner constantly impressed upon her staff that the customer was always right, and three ladies who wished to be fitted for entire ensembles was not an opportunity to be missed.

"The whole line," she said. Excitement brought roses back into the girls' cheeks as they hurried to help one another dress. "The first walkthrough should begin in ten minutes," Miss Carr announced, pitching her voice slightly to carry over the hubbub. "Make your change in time for the second walkthrough and wait for my signal. Repeat your promenade in the same order until I inform you to stay or go back to your first costume." The girls didn't look up at her, busy as they were with corsets and petticoats, but she knew they heard her.

She returned to the salon, clasped her hands together nervously and beamed at her guests.

"We shall be ready to present our line to you shortly. In the meantime, may I offer you refreshment?"

"Thank you," said the second-oldest, raising her hooded eyes to Miss Carr. The glance was piercing and disquieting. Miss Carr suppressed a shudder. "But not just now."

"Of course," Miss Carr said, feeling her heart flutter. "I . . . Countesses, how shall I address you to distinguish among you? Are you perhaps sisters?" she asked, though she couldn't see how the third woman might have been related to the first two. "Or are your husbands brothers? Cousins?"

"We are all the wives of the great Count Dracula," said the second woman, with great pride.

"Our ways are not your ways, I know," the eldest

countess said. She smiled, showing her teeth. All three had red, lush lips framing perfectly white teeth.

"I hope you will not think that I am questioning your ways!" Miss Carr exclaimed, shocked.

"No. Of course you are not," the eldest Countess Dracula said, with a smile.

"Indeed, it is a fascinating concept of those of us in England," Miss Carr went on, "that a man should have three wives, rather like a Turkish sultan." The ladies, to her great surprise at women of such elegance, all spat on the white silk carpet.

"The Turks," said the eldest, disdainfully. "The Turks are barbarians."

"I apologize," she said hastily. "I did not mean to offend."

"It is not you," said the second-eldest countess. "It is the Turks who offend by their existence."

Miss Carr was relieved having just experienced an inner vision of the countesses sweeping out of the salon and into the night, outraged; and herself, standing on the very same stoop the next morning, unemployed, having wasted resources of the House of Feldon, then driven away the customers. She supposed that her grandmother might have made a similar gesture regarding the French, so perhaps the ladies' reaction was not so outrageously exotic as it at first seemed. What an odd thing it must be to be a co-wife, she thought, like those people who lived in the American states. What were they called, Mormons? Miss Carr had thought that the religion was new, but it might have originated in the Balkans, for all the proponent was a man called Joseph Smith. Perhaps there was a Rumanian equivalent of the name.

Mannequins swirled into the room like a bouquet of flowers. Each turned this way and that before promenading slowly around the room clockwise, then counterclockwise. In all, each spent nearly ten minutes displaying the dress she was wearing. The girls may have come from the poorer classes, but each one was attractive, perfectly groomed, and bore herself with the carriage of a queen, full tribute to Mrs. Feldon-Jacobs's rigorous training.

"You must tell me, Countesses, if there is any dress that appeals to you that you would wish to try on yourselves. We would be more than happy to assist you during the second showing."

The visitors chatted excitedly among themselves in their own tongue, leaving Miss Carr to watch the mannequins. One young woman was particularly good. Miss Carr recalled that her name was Claire Stimson, and that she was new to the House of Feldon. The dress she wore was Miss Carr's favorite of the season's line. The cream-silk evening dress daringly displayed a good deal of long, slender neck and the upper curve of the bosom before falling into becoming puffs of satin around the bust and shoulders, fitting tightly at the waist, and bustled with Alençon lace at the rear of the smooth skirts. Though the décolletage was much lower than a modest lady might find comfortable to wear, Miss Stimson still managed to assert dignity. Miss Carr watched her with approval. The three countesses sat up and showed great interest in Miss Stimson's ensemble, eyeing the model hungrily.

"Ah!" one of them exclaimed, in English. "Yes, this is precisely what we have come for."

They seemed particularly taken by the demeanor of the mannequin herself. Miss Carr thought that she would recommend the girl for promotion when the new line was brought out in the spring. The lovely gown concealed beneath it, Miss Carr happened to know, an entirely new kind of corset that Mrs. Feldon-Jacobs had designed for not only bestowing the wasp-waist so vital to the year's fashions, but subtly lifting the bosom. The undergarment was not yet complete, and had to be pinned together. It was surely very uncomfortable, yet Miss Stimson carried herself with aplomb.

"Ye-es," said the eldest, slowly, avidly, staring as Miss Stimson turned and pirouetted. "Exactly, exactly so." The mannequin looked to her employer. Miss Carr nodded, indicating she was to remain in the room. How could Miss Carr possibly send her away, with all three Countesses Dracula staring at the model gown with such interest that their mouths were slightly open. Miss Carr was faintly troubled by their very red lips. Such vivid paint was not the fashion for respectable women in England, but foreign customs were different.

And yet women talked the same the world over. The middle sister-wife had been keeping careful track of the various fashions that had been displayed.

"I want the evening dress in crimson. I believe it was the sixth dress," she said. Miss Carr went down her list to verify that it was so. "I shall also have the walking costume in midnight blue with white fur, the ninth selection. I shall look very elegant in it, should I not? The morning costume, number two in black and cream striped silk, is very handsome. I think highly of the fourth gown, the tea dress, although the dusty pink will not suit me. Does it come in other shades?"

"Of course, Countess. I have squares of the colors available for you to examine," Miss Carr said, adding up the value of each costume in her notepad and coming up with a most attractive sum, and the other two had not chosen yet!

Disconcertingly, the countesses appeared to divine her thoughts.

"You must not think we are extravagant, my dear Miss Carr," said the eldest, raising an eyebrow dark as a raven's feather on her pale forehead. "It is only our due from our lord and master. For the trouble he has caused us, he owes us much, to the very last coin in his treasury! Plucking us up from our native soil, and making us endure this arduous and dull journey into a foreign land . . . you must forgive me," she said, charmingly apologetic. "I mean no disrespect to your homeland, and you have been the most welcoming of hostesses."

"Not at all," Miss Carr murmured, embarrassed to overhear such private arguments between husband and wives. "It is difficult to travel such distances, although the summer is the best time in which to do it. How was your journey to England?"

"Abominable," said the middle one. "On the terrible little boat upon which we embarked from our beloved Rumania we sailed through a horrendous storm. All of our trunks were washed overboard. We barely came ashore with the vitals for existence still in our grasp."

"Your lives?" Miss Carr asked, gasping with excitement. There was an indefinable pause before the eldest broke the silence that had fallen.

"So to speak. And Magda retained our jewel box," she said, with an approving nod to the second-eldest wife. "She is always one to hold on to opportunity. Luckily our bankers had already received our letter of credit. If our lord had only followed our advice we might have saved the vessel—but he never does listen."

"We smelled the storm, but he enjoys such things," said Countess Magda. "Never mind that we have lost our whole wardrobes and everything we held dear."

He wrecked the ship on purpose? Miss Carr wanted to ask, but didn't dare.

"But, he will pay," said the eldest avidly, licking her red, red lips. "He will pay dearly. This is only the beginning of the price."

"Oh," Miss Carr said, uncomfortably, wishing to change the subject away from such personal issues. "Well. Did you land at Southampton?"

"No," said the youngest, sulkily. "Whitby."

"My goodness," said Miss Carr, with great excitement, "then you must have heard of the shipwreck there! It was in all the newspapers. A ship called the *Demeter* ran aground, steered by a dead man's hand."

Miss Carr thought the event sounded like a romantic and strange play that sent a frisson up her back when she'd heard. It was not gossip, but news, so it was a fair subject to broach, by Mrs. Feldon-Jacobs's rules. But it failed to intrigue her guests.

"How very . . . interesting," said the eldest countess, after another pause. "No. We had not heard of such a shipwreck."

The last mannequin curtsied lightly as she did her final turn, and slipped from the room.

"Well, Countesses," Miss Carr said, nervously. This was the moment when they would either make an order or find an excuse to leave. "Have we shown you anything that would suit you?"

"Oh, yes," the eldest countess said, with a lift of her dark brows. "We have seen many things that we wish to have. As you may guess, price is no object."

"Then, if you permit," Miss Carr said, "allow us to take measurements at this time, so that when you give your order, we may start at once tomorrow upon your choices."

The senior countess looked at the other two. "Yes, this would be acceptable to us."

With the assistance of three of the seamstresses, Miss Carr helped the countesses out of their gowns. Their velvet dresses, oddly heavy for the climate and the season, had a musty air about them, as though they had been hanging in a closet or folded into a chest for a very long time. Their undergarments were also curious, being extremely old-fashioned, albeit of the best fabrics and lace. One of the seamstresses prepared to wrap a tape measure around the bosom of the Countess Magda, when she jumped back in surprise.

"Oh!" she cried. Miss Carr hurried over to see what was the matter.

Spinning down along its own thread from a web just under the lady's décolletage was a large black spider, very much alive. Miss Carr looked at the countess in puzzlement. The creature was so large she could not possibly have missed knowing it was there. Perhaps she had no fear of them. Perhaps she liked them. Perhaps having a spider about one's person was a foreign custom, like the English tradition of letting a money spider walk across one's palm.

"Oh," the countess said, glancing down at the object of their curiosity. She seized a feather from the display in the vase on the side table, and whisked it to the floor. The spider promptly ran underneath a chair. Miss Carr made a mental note to send one of the page boys in to hunt it down and kill it as soon as the visitors were gone. When the ladies' measurements were complete, the seamstresses offered them dressing gowns and assisted them to sit down.

"And now we will show the line again," Miss Carr said. "You may stop any of the mannequins if you wish to try on her costume. Please let me know which you wish to order, or to add to the list for later consideration."

In the end the Countesses Dracula amassed an enormous order. Hardly a mannequin came and went without one of the three insisting that she must have the costume, with all the appropriate accessories and underthings.

"And when may we expect to have the first fitting?" the eldest countess asked, as the eighth model put in her appearance. Miss Carr glanced up from her notebook.

"I believe that Mrs. Feldon-Jacobs will say that it can be a week hence, er, also at night if you require."

"We do. You can do all this in a week?"

"Indeed, yes, madam," Miss Carr said with pride. "We have the best staffed and most efficient workrooms in London. I trust you will be satisfied not only with our workmanship, but with our promptness."

"That is most satisfactory. Ah! Here she is again."

Miss Stimson had returned for her second appearance in the perfect, pearl-white satin dress.

"Enchanting," said the youngest countess, her blue eyes wide. "We must have one of those."

"Two," said Countess Magda.

"Would you care to try it on?" Miss Carr offered politely, jotting the style number into each of the two younger ladies' measurement charts.

"Perhaps not now," said the eldest wife. "There is so much else to see."

"But, she must stay," the youngest wife insisted. Miss Stimson received her silent instructions from Miss Carr, and took up a languid-seeming stance against the wall near the vase of feathers, with one arm resting lightly on the tabletop. It was actually a restful posture, designed to ease the back when one of the mannequins must remain standing for a long time. Another girl swirled into the room in a walking costume of leaf green with sage trim. The countesses chattered to one another with delight, though their eyes kept returning to Miss Stimson.

Miss Carr was quite dizzy with delight by the time she finished writing up the order. Mrs. Feldon-Jacobs would have to put the workrooms on full alert, but it would be worthwhile. This order would be the talk of the industry. The last model was displayed and retired. The eldest countess clapped her hands.

"Brava," she said. "This is all very good. And now, we are feeling rather famished. Perhaps you may furnish us with that little refreshment?"

Their red mouths looked almost predatory, their white teeth sharp as an animal's. At once Miss Carr was horrified at herself for even thinking of such a comparison. "Of course!" she said. "Forgive me for not offering again." She nodded to one of the seamstresses, who left the room and sent in the page boy. Miss Carr gave the order for tea, sandwiches, and cakes. She risked a discreet look at her watch. The hour was long after midnight. She hoped the day's bread would still answer. Knowing that they would have night visitors who might require sustenance, they had wrapped a fresh loaf as well as they could.

The final group of mannequins began to withdraw. Miss Stimson, seeing release at hand, crossed the room to join her companions.

"Oh, no, don't go," the youngest countess said, catching Miss Stimson by the arm. "You must join us for our meal."

She drew the girl beside her and held her quite close. Miss Stimson looked unhappy, but she was afraid to refuse. She knew what it meant to them all if she should displease the customers. She smiled tremulously, looking to Miss Carr for rescue. Miss Carr was uncertain what to do, and wished the owner was there. She knew no respectable Englishwoman would touch another person so familiarly, but these were foreigners. She fancied that she saw their mouths open as if they would eat the girl right there.

What to do? The gown was lovely, and the girl did look lovely in it. Perhaps the countesses just wanted to have it there under their eyes while they discussed the final details of their order. Since the financial arrangements had not yet been concluded, Miss Carr was as paralyzed as Miss Stimson. She watched in horrified fascination as the youngest countess reeled in the girl like a fish until they were virtually eye-to-eye. Suddenly, the blond woman let out a horrified cry and threw the girl away from her. The girl landed in a heap of white silk on the floor. The countess pointed a trembling, accusatory finger at the mannequin's neck.

"What is that?" she cried.

Miss Carr went to help Miss Stimson up and investigate the problem. About the girl's neck was a tiny chain. Miss Carr hadn't thought a thing about it except that it accessorized the neckline of her gown and drew attention tastefully to the bare shoulders. Hanging from the fine chain was a minute gold cross, a small personal item that belonged to Miss Stimson herself. The mannequins were permitted to wear such jewelry as long as they were handsome and in good taste. The

tiny cross was real gold, classic in shape and irreproach-
ably modest. Miss Carr hadn't thought that the countesses might not be Christians and would find the
symbol offensive. They didn't look Jewish. Perhaps
there was another faith they followed in the Balkans
that went along with polygamy.

"I am so sorry," Miss Carr said, lamely, searching
for words to repair the damage.

"I can see that we are not welcome here," the
blonde said, rising to her feet with flashing eyes.

"Don't be silly," Countess Magda exclaimed, tug-
ging on her sister-wife's sleeve. "*Clothes,* sister! This
will be our only opportunity. He never shows remorse.
You know that. We must take advantage of this indulgence as we can."

"Ladies, please," Miss Carr appealed to them,
seeing hundreds of pounds fly out the window on night-
borne wings. "If the bauble offends you, I shall remove it."

"Please do," said the eldest countess, swiftly. "That
will suffice." There was a muffled outburst from her
co-wife, but it was quickly quelled by a fierce glance.

"I am so sorry, Miss Carr," Miss Stimson whispered, her fair cheeks crimson. "I thought it would be
all right. Please don't sack me."

"It is not your fault," Miss Carr said, unfastening
the tiny clasp and gathering the chain in her palm. "I
will put this in the dressing room on the table. In future
let us choose a different jewel for you to wear."

The girl's gratitude shone in her eyes. "Thank you,
madam." She gave an uneasy glance over Miss Carr's
shoulder at the visitors. "I . . . I do wish you would
not leave me alone with them."

"Nonsense," Miss Carr said briskly. "They will do
you no harm. They merely wish to look more closely
at the dress. Allow them to examine it as they wish."

"Yes, madam," the girl whispered.

"Refreshments, Countesses!" Miss Carr announced,

as the page boy entered, pushing the laden tea cart.
She was grateful for the distraction. It also gave the
mannequin time to recover herself and resume her station near the wall. The visitors waited as the page
poured tea and offered sandwiches all around.

"That is very nice," the eldest countess said, accepting a cup with a slice of lemon floating on the
amber tea in one of Mrs. Feldon-Jacobs's heirloom
cups. "Very nice. All is most satisfactory."

"Now, if you will excuse me for a moment, I will
go and prepare the papers for your approval," Miss
Carr said.

"Yes, yes," said the Countess Magda. "Everyone go
away. We wish to talk among ourselves. Not you, my
dear," she said, taking the girl's hand as Miss Stimson
attempted to follow. "We wish you to stay with us."

The last thing Miss Carr saw as she closed the door
on the salon was the girl's frightened eyes.

The invoice took little time to prepare. Miss Carr had
but to transfer to it the name and price of the gowns
ordered, note the name of the buyers and their
impressive-sounding address. Carfax Abbey, Sussex.
The owner would be pleased with everything from this
night's work.

She returned to the salon in time to see the mannequin staggering back to lean against the wall, pale as a
ghost, with a few drops of blood on her neck. She was
wrapped in a dressing gown, and the silk ball gown was
on hooks against the wall. No doubt one of the countesses had wanted to try it on, but the blood was a puzzle.
Perhaps Miss Stimson had been injured by the pins holding the incomplete stays together, which had to come off
over the head. Miss Carr checked the gown for spots.
The girl seemed to have had the presence of mind not
to bleed on the dress. Miss Stimson stood looking at her
employer with the dazed expression of a sheep.

"Are you all right?" Miss Carr asked.

"Yes, madam," the girl said, rather stupidly. She blinked at the lamp, her pupils shrunk to pinpoint size. Miss Carr saw how pallid she was, red rings around her eyes very much in relief to the parchment color of her skin, and put it off to the lateness of the hour. No wonder she had scratched her neck. "It's a trifle bright in here, madam."

"Perhaps," Miss Carr said. "You have done well, Miss Stimson. I will tell Mrs. Feldon-Jacobs so. You may retire and take tomorrow off. But I expect to see you here bright and early Thursday morning."

"Yes, madam." The girl tripped clumsily out of the room. Miss Carr was tired, too, but she didn't dare to give in to the sensation. Thankfully, the visitors read over the invoice with little interest. The eldest countess signed her name at the bottom beside the sum total, a colossal number that made Miss Carr want to dance, if only she wasn't so tired.

"Our bankers are Coutts & Co. The count has a substantial letter of credit with them. This should take a substantial bite out of it." As if it was part of an old joke, the senior countess showed her teeth, and the other two laughed. "We thank you very much for your hospitality, Miss Carr, but we must now be going."

Miss Carr dropped her half-bow, half-curtsy gratefully. It was after one in the morning. She'd be lucky if her bespoke cab would still be outside.

"Very well, Countesses. May I say, on behalf of the House of Feldon, that it has been a great pleasure to serve you? Is there anything else at all with which I may assist you?"

"No, thank you," said the youngest, rising from her grand chair and licking her lips. Miss Carr noticed again how very, very red they were. Was that a drop of rouge on her chin? "We have got everything that we came for."

Long-Term Investment

CHELSEA QUINN YARBRO

The coffins bothered him, no doubt about it. Ever since the foreign gentleman had hired him to supervise his warehouse, the coffins had bothered him—that, and working late, although he was not completely alone at any hour, for even at night the London docks bustled; ships tugged restlessly at their moorings out in the Thames and those secured to the vast wooden piers strained at the lines holding them. Lamps gave off a fuzzy glow, tingeing the docks with gold and lighting the busy efforts of all who labored here. Activity was everywhere: longshoremen worked steadily, loading or removing cargo from the waiting holds; sailors from a hundred foreign ports polished brightwork, swabbed decks, inspected rigging, bucked cargo, hauled lines, all as if it were midday. Many of the office windows in the warehouses were lit, testimony to the industry of the owners of the vessels as well as the men they hired. The brackish smell of bilgewater and the odor of tar hung on the air, stronger than the clean scent off the distant sea, although there was a tang of salt in the fog.

Edward Hitchin sat in the dusty office above the

warehouse floor and tried to keep himself busy. The foreign gentleman—calling himself Carfax—was paying him well: ten shillings for a day's work, and twelve when he had to remain past nine at night, handsome wages for a young man from Stepney who was little more than a watchman. He was determined to keep the job as long as possible, for he liked the jingle of coins in his pocket and the respectful nod from the patrolling constables.

A ship was due in from Varna, and Mister Carfax had told Edward to expect another load of coffins. "Not that we haven't a fair supply on hand already," he had added before leaving Edward alone. "Still, it is good business, is it not, to have an ample supply. Coffins are a long-term investment, are they not?" He had chuckled, which Edward found disquieting, but there were so many things about Mister Carfax that gave him pause that this chuckle seemed a minor intrusion.

"Too true," Edward said to himself as he looked out the window and down onto the warehouse floor where several dozen elaborately carved coffins were stacked. He had been thinking about Carfax's remark all evening—that coffins were a long-term investment; he had decided that in its way, the observation was witty. Coffins always got used, eventually. Another load of them and the warehouse would be more than half-filled, and that load would arrive in a matter of hours.

Edward was considering lighting up his pipe when a sharp rap on the entry door claimed his attention. Surely the ship had not yet off-loaded the cargo for Mister Carfax. When the knock was repeated, he bolted from the office, running noisily down the stairs as he called out, "In half a tick!" Opening the door, he found himself facing a man he had never seen before, but knew at once, though the man wore a suit instead of a uniform, that he was a member of the police. Edward blanched but held the door steadily. "Good evening."

"Good evening. Am I addressing Mister Carfax?"

"No," Edward answered, wondering what the police wanted with the tall, foreign gentleman. "He's away just now. I'm his . . . assistant. Edward Hitchin." He could not make himself ask what the police were doing here, so he waited while the policeman stepped inside.

"Do you have a little time to spare, Mister Hitchin? I am Inspector Ames of Scotland Yard."

This polite inquiry, along with being called "Mister" caught Edward off-balance. "Sure enough," he said after he thought about it.

"You've been here all evening?" The policeman took a notebook from his inner breast pocket, and a pencil from his outer breast pocket, and prepared to write.

"Is this official, you taking down my answers and all?" Edward asked, trying to conceal his anxiety.

"Should it not be?" Inspector Ames asked so mildly that Edward had to resist the urge to spring from the room. "Now, have you been here all evening?"

"Since eleven in the morning. I came in late because I have to be here late to receive a new shipment of . . . stock." He indicated the dimly lit warehouse.

"The sign over the door says *D. Carfax, importer and purveyor of fine coffins and caskets*," said the policeman. "Is this the stock on hand?"

"Yes," said Edward. "The bills of lading are in the office. What you see here comes from Varna, most of it. Very elaborate carving they do in that part of the world—very elaborate." He pointed to the nearest stack of coffins. "These are the simple ones. There are fancier toward the back. We even have some with bells to be secured above in case someone should be buried alive, and need to be dug up again." He had been told to mention this desirable feature even though he thought it ghoulish.

"Do you open them, or—" the inspector began.

"Oh, no," said Edward hastily. "It's not . . . seemly."

"Um. Very prudent," said the policeman indifferently, and handed a card to Edward. "Will you be good enough to tell Mister Carfax that Inspector Uriah Ames is desirous of speaking with him at his earliest convenience?"

Edward took the card, holding it gingerly. "May I tell him what this is about?" he asked, curiosity and dread warring within him.

Inspector Ames coughed diplomatically. "A body was found washed up on the Isle of Dogs. It has no identification, no clothing. It is likely the deceased was the victim of foul play. The dead woman has not been claimed or anyone of her description reported missing." He watched Edward closely. "We are asking all businesses along the docks, for it is likely that she was thrown into the water somewhere in this area, and we are hoping that someone noticed something." He paused, his pencil poised over his well-thumbed notebook. "Have you noticed any suspicious activities in this area in the last week or so?"

Edward shook his head. "I have been in the office, or on the floor, making an inventory for Mister Carfax. I take my tea inside." He shrugged apologetically. "I wish I could tell you something more."

"Provide me with your direction, and I suppose that will do for now," said Inspector Ames.

"Edward Hitchin, Beeks House, White Horse Road, Stepney," he said promptly, knowing that the address was far from impressive.

"Lived there long, have you?" Inspector Ames asked as he wrote.

"M'Mum and I have been there for ten years and more." He did his best not to sound defensive.

"Your Mum still there, is she?" Inspector Ames asked.

"Yes; she's not in good health." It was a convenient mendacity, for the melancholy which held her in its grip seemed as crippling as any misfortune or disease.

"Sorry to hear that," said Inspector Ames with the habitual sympathy of one used to bad news. "Stays in, does she?"

"Most of the time. I tend to her needs," Edward informed Inspector Ames, at once proud and wary.

"And you work here for long hours," said Inspector Ames.

"I am well-paid for my time," Edward insisted. "Mister Carfax is a generous employer."

"Worked for him long, have you?" Inspector Ames seemed disinterested in the answer, but Edward knew enough about the police not to be deceived by this ploy.

"Not long, no. Mister Carfax is a foreigner but recently arrived in London. He keeps a house somewhere in the country, but he has a place in London, probably in the toffy part of town—Mayfair, or Berkeley Square or some such. He's rich enough, and he has the manner." He felt that volunteering this information would show his willingness to cooperate with the police inquiries. "He comes here three or four times a week to tend to business and to instruct me in my duties."

"Then you expect to see him shortly," said Inspector Ames.

"Tomorrow, about four or five," said Edward promptly.

"Then you will give him my card and pass along my message, and I shall expect a call from Mister Carfax before the end of the week." This affable request, Edward knew, was an order. He nodded.

"I'll attend to it, first thing he arrives," Edward said, and tried to contain his fidgets.

"That's good of you," said Inspector Ames as he

put his pencil and notebook away, and with an uneasy glance at the stacked coffins and caskets said, "I'll let myself out."

By the time Carfax arrived the next afternoon, Edward had become distressed about what the Inspector had told him; dead women, murdered women, brought back memories of the Ripper, and with it, other, more personal recollections, as well as the uncomfortable awareness that the Ripper had never been brought to justice. So Edward was nervous when he passed on Inspector Ames's card and request. "The police are nothing to fash with, Mister Carfax," he added when he finished explaining the situation. "When there are dead bodies involved, the police are . . . are persistent."

"Ah, yes. English police. We hear many things about them in my native land," said Mister Carfax, examining the inspector's card. "What does he want of me, this Inspector Ames? You say there is a body— what has that to do with me?"

"There's an investigation into the woman's death. The police are gathering information about the circumstances," said Edward, wondering how Mister Carfax would doubt that: foreigners were unaccountable.

"What has that to do with me?" Mister Carfax repeated with supreme indifference. "I know nothing of this woman. Why should the police need to know that?"

"They want you to go along to the station and tell them what you can. You may know nothing, but they will want to hear of it from you." Edward tried not to sound too apprehensive, but he suspected he failed.

"But I have nothing to tell them. Dead women do not interest me." His accent grew stronger, as if his emotions had loosened his control over the English tongue. "It is most unseemly, to have to answer to the police, a man of my position."

Although Edward was not sure what that position might be, he said, "They just need to have you tell them you were not on the docks when the woman was killed—that's all."

Carfax looked indignant as he pulled himself up to his full, and considerable, height. "It is for the police to wait upon me. Send this Ames word that I will receive him the day after tomorrow in the early evening." He looked toward the newest arrivals. "How many in this load?"

"Twenty-three of the fancy, eleven of the plain," said Edward, grateful to have this opportunity to show his efficiency. "The ones with brass fittings are in the row at the center."

"Just so," Carfax approved. "Did you open any of them?"

Edward shook his head. "You said I should not."

"So I did," Carfax mused, then went on more briskly, "You have done well, Hitchin. I will pay you a bonus for your work." He strode toward the stairs. "Oh. I suppose you should know I will take nine of them, for delivery. Tomorrow a drayer will come to fetch them."

"You have a customer, then?" Edward said, relieved to hear it.

Carfax smiled. "In a manner of speaking." He paused. "I will tell you which are to be taken, so you will not load the wrong ones."

"Very good, sir," said Edward, secretly glad to know some of the stock would be leaving the warehouse.

As he climbed up the stairs, Carfax said, "This is going very well. By winter I should be established."

"There's always a market for coffins," said Edward, deliberately echoing Carfax's sentiments as he followed him up the stairs.

*   *   *

"When did Carfax say he would arrive?" Inspector Ames asked, glancing at his pocketwatch for the third time. It was twenty minutes past the hour Carfax had said he would be at his warehouse for their meeting. The afternoon was closing toward evening already; fall was beginning.

"He said four, but he was coming in from the country, and he may have been delayed on the road." Edward felt acute embarrassment at this predicament. "You may have to be patient. He was determined to meet with you, or so he said when he left day before yesterday."

"Well, I will wait a while longer," Inspector Ames said with a ponderous sigh. "He's the last one I have to interview from this area."

"Any progress?" Edward did not want to know, but he was determined to keep the inspector entertained during his wait for Mister Carfax.

"Not much," Inspector Ames admitted. "The woman is still unidentified, which hampers our work. We are doing our best."

Edward thought that did not sound promising, but he said, "No doubt you'll find the murderer, eh, Inspector?"

"Are you mocking me?" Inspector Ames asked suspiciously.

Shocked, Edward shook his head. "No, sir. Nothing of the sort. I only meant what I said, that you will catch the criminal."

Inspector Ames looked slightly mollified, but he glowered at Edward. "You . . . you poor people have no respect for the police."

"I am not one such. My father worked for the police, in the stationhouse. It got him killed," said Edward stiffly.

"Oh, yes?" said Inspector Ames, regarding Edward with slightly more interest. "How did it happen?"

Edward guessed that the inspector wanted to know so he could check out the story more than he had any genuine interest. "It was during the Ripper days. A man was brought into the stationhouse for Stepney, where my father clerked. He was under suspicion for savaging a . . . street woman, and some thought he might be the Ripper—the man in custody, not my father. The thing was, the fellow had a knife on him that no one knew about, and when he was being written up, he grabbed my father and used him for a shield to escape. Cut his throat on the stationhouse steps." He swallowed hard. "My father said that police are the best hope we have to make life safe. No, Inspector, I would not mock you, for his sake if no other."

"Just so," said Inspector Ames, making it serve as an apology.

"I won't say as police don't make me nervous," Edward went on, thinking he was saying too much, but unable to stop himself. "You said right when you said poor people—" He broke off. "Well, thanks to Carfax, I am not poor any longer."

Inspector Ames nodded and was about to speak when Carfax himself came striding in out of the foggy, fading day. "Mister Carfax," he said with energy. "I had about given you up."

"I apologize for my tardiness," said Carfax. "I have been at the zoological gardens. Most unusual. I must go again when I am at leisure to appreciate its occupants. I am afraid I forgot the time." He glanced at Edward. "I trust Hitchin has been looking after you in a satisfactory manner?"

"He has, sir," said Inspector Ames, not quite deferential, but less accusing than he had been with Edward. "I am sorry I must intrude, but there has been a—"

"—killing of a young woman," Carfax finished for

him. "Yes. So Hitchin told me." He indicated the steps to the office. "Perhaps you would be more comfortable if I offered you a chair?" Without waiting for an answer he went up the stairs.

"I am coming, sir," said Inspector Ames, tagging after Carfax.

Edward watched them go, feeling at loose ends. He had only the coffins for company, and he began to wander the aisles between the stacks of coffins. They no longer bothered him as they had done at first, although he was a long way from comfortable with them. He consulted his pocketwatch several times before he saw Inspector Ames emerge on the landing.

"Very good, Mister Carfax. I am grateful for your time." He bowed slightly and started down the stairs.

"If I think of anything that has bearing on your investigation, I will be sure to inform you," came Carfax's voice after the policeman.

"Much obliged," said Inspector Ames as he made his way down the stairs, pausing as Edward approached him to see him off the premises. He looked at Edward, his expression revealing nothing. "Odd sort of chap, your Mister Carfax."

"Well, he's foreign, isn't he?" said Edward as he opened the door.

"That he is," Inspector Ames agreed as he left the building.

The next body was found six days later: an amah coming from India with a military family was supposed to accompany the luggage from the docks to the family's house. She never arrived, although the luggage did. Now the waterfront began to hum with rumors, and the police sent more constables to patrol the narrow, noisome streets where warehouses sat chock-a-block with ancient inns and houses of dubious reputation.

Edward admitted Inspector Ames a day after the ghastly discovery was made. He noticed the dark circles around the policeman's eyes, and the downward turn of his mouth. "A terrible thing, Inspector."

"That it is," Inspector Ames agreed. "You know why I've come."

Nodding, Edward said, "You think it is the same killer, then."

"Yes. We have good reason to." He said nothing more specific as he glanced around the warehouse. "Carfax has moved out more coffins."

"That he has," said Edward, taking indirect satisfaction in this turn of events. He permitted himself to boast a bit. "He has sent more than a dozen out of the city. He tells me that more are to go before the week is out."

"He must be pleased," said Inspector Ames, and exhausted his capacity for small talk. "Hitchin, what have you seen? What have you heard?"

"Nothing that you haven't heard, or seen, sir," said Edward as a cold fist closed on his guts. "Why should I? I am indoors all the day long, and into the night."

"Do not tell me you while away the hours alone in that office upstairs?" The inspector's incredulity was insulting enough to sting.

"I will not tell you, if you are not prepared to believe me. But it is what I do." He could feel the heat in his face, and hear it in his voice. He struggled to cool his temper. "Why do you doubt me?"

"Well, you know, I checked up on your father, and on you. Your report of his death was reasonably accurate, but I must tell you that the scrapes you have been in since his death are very troublesome to me, very troublesome." He studied Edward a short while in silence. "You have been caught stealing, have you not?"

"Food. Only food. For my Mum," muttered Edward. "The pension doesn't go very far, and sometimes she's gone hungry."

"Very commendable, I'm sure." Inspector Ames's sarcasm was as bad as his disbelief. "You spent a month in gaol, my lad."

"That I did. Two years since." He could not conceal his bitterness. "My Mum nearly starved to death. No one cared for her."

"An unfortunate circumstance," said Inspector Ames smoothly. "You must be very grateful to Mister Carfax. Not many would employ the likes of you, not once you've been in gaol."

"Probably not," Edward said, keenly aware that the inspector was right. "But Mister Carfax, being foreign, is not so worried about these things as you are. He hired me—and I did tell him about what I had done." He did his best to look unconcerned, though the memory of that interview still rankled. "Mister Carfax is willing to give a man a chance."

"No doubt," said Inspector Ames. "And you are loyal to him for this."

"Certainly," said Edward staunchly.

"Good," said the inspector. "It would be unfortunate to see the man served a perfidious turn by one who should have only gratitude."

"I understand you, Inspector Ames," Edward told him. "I will not abuse Mister Carfax's faith in me."

Inspector Ames frowned at him. "I shall hope you do not. For I shall make it my task to be watching you."

By the time the fourth body was discovered, only five days after the third, fear was all but palpable in the air. Activity on the docks became hasty, furtive. More constables patrolled, and fewer businesses kept their offices open past seven in the evening except when it was absolutely necessary. Everyone looked upon strangers as dangerous, and occasional fights broke out as a result of quickened tempers and unlucky mistakes.

After sustaining a third visit from the police in as many days, Edward found himself wandering restlessly around the main floor of the warehouse, looking at the stacked coffins and trying to steady his chaotic thoughts. He knew Inspector Uriah Ames was suspicious of him; his experience of the police told him that once they had settled on a man, they were tenacious in their purpose, no matter how much in error they might be; the implications worried him. Why did Inspector Ames think he was guilty of some criminal act? How could any policeman believe that he was a murderer? He paused beside the largest stack of caskets, noticing that one or two of them were slightly out of alignment. Sighing with a sense of ill-use, but secretly glad to have something to take his mind off his problems, Edward did his best to shove the coffins back into position.

The uppermost coffin teetered, rocked, and fell, crashing onto the rough planking with an ominous crack as the lid split open at the lock, spilling out a load of dark-red earth on the warehouse floor.

Edward stood in silence, staring at the fallen casket and its unaccountable contents. He could not bring himself to move. *What was earth doing* inside *a coffin?* he asked himself, and found no answer. Very slowly he let his breath out, unaware until that instant that he had been holding it. He noticed that this coffin was one of the ones that had been tagged to be picked up by the drayage firm the next day, and that made him more puzzled than ever. Who wanted the earth, and what would he do with it? He had no answer, so he approached the matter from a different angle: why should any undertaker buy a coffin filled with earth? To whom was Carfax selling these coffins, and why?

The sound of a carriage in the street brought him back to himself. He swore obscenely and comprehensively under his breath as he resisted the panic that threatened to overcome him. He was aware that he had to clean up the dirt and make some attempt to repair the coffin before Mister Carfax could see what a mess had been made. This galvanized him into action: in a flurry of activity, he removed his jacket and turned up his sleeves in preparation for all he had to do, searched for the wide broom he used every night before he left to make a pile of the dirt, and he improvised a dustpan to collect it and stuff it back in the carved wooden box. The lock was a trickier problem, and it so engrossed him as he glued the various bits back together that he did not notice when the door opened and Carfax himself slipped into the warehouse, taking refuge in the shadows where Edward could not see him.

When he was satisfied that he had repaired the worst of the damage, Edward hurried off to the washroom to clean his hands and neaten himself up. He combed his hair with his fingers and patted cold water on his face to diminish the flush of exercise, then straightened his collar and tie before going to fetch his jacket. He stopped still when he saw Carfax standing in the doorway. "Good afternoon, sir," he said nervously. "I did not hear you arrive."

"I daresay," said Carfax, strolling into the center of the warehouse, his voluminous European-style cloak swinging around him. "Is all well?"

"The police still haven't caught the murderer, but your business is thriving," said Edward uneasily. He hoped that Carfax would not notice that the caskets were not stacked as they had been.

"Five bodies, is it?" Carfax asked.

"Four, actually," said Edward.

"Oh, yes. Four." He paused beside the first stack of coffins. "How sad." Then he turned abruptly. "If you will fetch the accounting books down from the office? I want to assure myself that our records are accurate. There have been enough orders for these coffins for a review of our stock."

Glad to be doing something useful, Edward bolted for the stairs; he did not see Carfax open the nearest coffin, take rumpled, stained clothing from under his cloak, and thrust the clothing inside; he closed the lid carefully, making almost no sound. Smiling slightly, he waited for Edward to come down with the account book.

"Here it is," said Edward, holding out the ledger. "You'll see I've ticked off all the coffins and caskets you have already shipped, and entered the date they were shipped here—" He pointed out the place in the columned paper.

"Ah, yes," said Carfax. "A good arrangement." He pointed to the inventory numbers of the next lot that would be shipped. "These are the ones that will be transported tomorrow?"

"Yes, sir," said Edward, unable to keep from glancing at the earth-filled casket.

"Very good," said Carfax, and turned his attention to other matters, which quieted Edward's dismay.

"I'll see the coffins get off all right and tight," Edward promised Mister Carfax shortly before that worthy left him that evening. "It will be good to have them gone," he said with genuine emotion.

"He denies everything. He claims to know nothing about the clothing or the earth. If you had not told us where to search, he might have got away with it," said Inspector Ames as his men struggled to return some order to the chaos they had created. "We expect that of such criminals. This one was no different, claiming someone had planted what we found, to fix the blame on him. I am sorry that we had to do this." He nodded as an indication of why he was apologizing: coffins and caskets were strewn about, most of them opened, as if a terrible desecration had taken place in an unlikely graveyard. The constables were doing their best to restack the coffins and caskets now that Hitchin had been taken into custody.   .

Carfax heard this out with every sign of distress. "But what did you find?"

"Enough to give the hangman employment," said Inspector Ames heavily. "In his drawer in the office there were some things he had hidden—of course, he denies any knowledge of them. They will be enough for the Queen's Counsel to make an unbreakable case."

"Are you so certain he is the man?" Carfax shook his head.

"Well," said Inspector Ames knowingly, "it's often the cooperative ones who prove the most dangerous in the end. No doubt he holds the police to blame for his father's death and his mother's decline." He held out his hand to Carfax. "And speaking of cooperation, I thank you for all you have given us, sir. Without your help, this case might not have ended so quickly."

Carfax accepted the inspector's hand. "I must admit I did not think it would come to this when I first admitted you to my warehouse." He sighed. "I can hardly stand to look at the place now."

"Give it time, sir; give it time," Inspector Ames recommended with a touch of sympathy.

"No doubt that is excellent advice." Carfax nodded as he looked about in mild distraction. "At least my business will keep me away from here for a while, so I may accustom myself to what has happened here." He stared up at the office above them. "I shall have to find someone else to manage this place for me, someone who can assume more of my duties in my absence."

"I can recommend an agency, sir," said Inspector Ames. "I feel a bit to blame for all the disruption you have endured."

"You have only done as you must. It is the murderer who has brought all this." He gestured to the disarray of coffins and caskets.

"Right you are, sir," Inspector Ames agreed. "But we're the ones as did the search, and we're the ones to put it right again." He did not add that this was a courtesy rarely extended to men in the visitor's position: had the search been unsuccessful, or had the owner of D. Carfax been less imposing, the police would have left the disorder for him to deal with.

"For which I am most appreciative," said Mister Carfax. "I could not look upon dealing with this without being appalled. I fear I should have had to hire others to do it."

"Understandable, sir," said Inspector Ames.

An uncomfortable silence fell between them.

"Inspector," said Carfax suddenly, "do you need me for anything more? If you do not, I will give you a key and ask you to lock up when you and your men are done."

"Of course, sir," said Inspector Ames, thinking that these foreigners were odd coves, going queasy over the damnedest things. "I'll return your key as soon as you ask for it."

"Thank you, Inspector." He turned his back on all the activity, then reached into his waistcoat pocket and drew out his key on a long chain. "I will go into the country for a few days, I think. To recruit myself. This has left me quite shaken."

"More's the pity, sir," said Inspector Ames, taking the key-and-chain from the visitor. "Just you rest up a bit. Don't let this unpleasantness spoil your taste for England." He wanted to ease Carfax's mind, so he added, "Hire an experienced manager and let him handle the business for a while. Take your time."

"Time," Carfax echoed. "You give excellent advice, Inspector. I have other matters to attend to just now. I would be imprudent to neglect them." He pressed his lips together, musing. "Your point is well-taken. With a competent manager, this place should prosper, whether I am here to run it or not."

Inspector Ames smiled. "Sounds the very thing." Very probably, he thought, there was nothing more pressing than the desire to get away from this place, but he could not blame Carfax for that, after such a grisly discovery. He would have patted the foreigner on the arm, but that would have been much too familiar a gesture. "What did Hitchin say you call this place—a long-term investment?"

Carfax paused in the act of leaving. "That's right, Inspector," he said with an expression that was not a smile, "so I did."

"Places for Act Two!"

BRADLEY H. SINOR

"Blimy, mate! You're out of your bloody mind!"

Liam Gideon stared down the length of his sword at the pale face that moments before had been a blustering, menacing figure.

"Crazy or sane, it doesn't matter," he said. "Because *I* am the one who has a sword at *your* throat. So I wouldn't be advising that you move too quickly or count on any help from either of your friends."

The pale-faced man's eyes darted to the far side of the alley where another man, dressed as shabbily as he, lay. This one was still breathing, but with two teeth dangling over the edge of his lip it was obvious he was coming to no one's aid. A second fellow lay on the ground, conscious, but not moving. A heavy black boot was planted across his chest. The boot belonged to a tall dark man, dressed in elegantly cut clothes, who the three had been attempting to rob.

"Now, sir," Liam said to the stranger. "I think it only right and proper that you make the decision about what to do with our friend, here. Should I run him through, perhaps cut him just a bit, say, remove certain portions of his anatomy; or should we just hold him and the others for the arrival of the police?"

"My first inclination would be to give them a long, very slow, very painful death. A public impalement might be a beneficial lesson to others." The man's dark eyes glittered with a strange redness to them. He spoke with the slightest hint of an accent, each word clearly, crisply, and evenly pronounced.

It occurred to Liam that perhaps English was not his native language.

"It would be an interesting sight, but consume far more time than I am willing to give to it." With those words the man lifted his boot from the thief's chest and half turned away from him. Liam had the impression of someone who had done with a matter, though he did notice that the stranger never fully took his eyes off the three thieves.

Liam drew his sword away from the first man's neck. The other one scrambled to his feet, watching Liam and the stranger with the look of a trapped animal. A moment or two passed as both men stood frozen, rain washing across their terror-striped faces. Then they grabbed their unconscious companion, dragging him down the alley.

"I imagine they will have quite a tale to tell once they hit the pub," said Liam.

"It is always wise to spread news of your prowess among an enemy. The story will grow with each retelling," said the stranger. "You never know how it might help you in the future."

"Hopefully, neither of us will have to deal with them again," said Liam.

"True, but with that sort of ilk it never hurts to have a reputation."

The stranger turned toward Liam. This was the first time he had had a chance to get a good look at him. His dark, somewhat disheveled hair, combed across the tops of his ears, gave him an almost feral look. There was something intense and controlling in his manner.

"Now, if I may inquire, who is it who stood to battle at my side?"

"Gideon. Liam Gideon, late of Dublin, Edinburgh, and parts beyond."

"Liam Gideon. I thank you for your assistance. It came at a most propitious time."

Liam had been minding his own business, hurrying to get back to the Strand Theatre on the west side of London. Passing an alley, hearing the sounds of a fight, he turned and saw three men attack a lone figure. He had hardly thought about it before he was plunging into the middle of the melee.

"You were holding your own pretty well against these fellows. I suspect that you didn't need that much assistance from me."

"None the less, you chose to ally yourself with me in battle. That is something that among my people means much. So do not doubt that you have the gratitude of Vlad Tsepes, Count Dracula."

"Thank you, Count. It wasn't that much of a decision for me. It was simply something that seemed needed doing. Something that I didn't think about, just did, my duty, and I am but a slave to duty," he said with a smile.

"A slave to duty?" Dracula looked at Liam oddly.

"Your pardon, Count. I was quoting a line from a play that I am in. It seemed fitting, somehow," said Liam.

"A play? You are an actor, then?"

"At times," he said.

"And what is this play?"

"*The Pirates of Penzance* by Gilbert & Sullivan."

"Gilbert & Sullivan? I am new to London, recently arrived from my native Transylvania, so I'm afraid that I am unfamiliar with either of these gentlemen. I must admit that they sound more like a law firm than playwrights."

"A law firm? That's novel," laughed Liam. "They are the creators of the most popular operettas in the last dozen years."

"Indeed? I may have to seek them out," he said. "That may, perhaps, explain your sword. Seeing a young man carrying one is a common thing in my homeland. But here in England, except for military ceremonies, I have seen none."

Liam held up the sword for his friend's inspection. Its surface was shiny as a teapot, the grip emblazoned with a dozen brightly colored stones amid Celtic knotwork.

"At first glance, it does appear to be a formidable weapon," said Dracula.

Liam could see that the Count had discerned the blade's true nature.

Liam cupped his left hand and sharply slid the edge of the blade along it. Then he turned his palm where Dracula could see it. Both men were smiling and not surprised that the flesh was uncut. "I'm afraid I couldn't have done much real damage to those three. It's a prop intended for the character of the Pirate King."

"The thing is, our enemies didn't know that. Their own imaginations were very potent weapons against them."

"Thank you, Count. Our company manager asked me to pick up a replacement for one of our principals, who broke his this morning. Since it was only a slight detour from where I was going, I was glad to do it." Liam pulled out his watch and flipped the cover open.

"Damn! I was due at the theater a full ten minutes ago. I'm sure that Mr. Bunberry will be snarling like a banshee!"

"Fear not, friend Liam. I am in your debt. You have stood to combat at my side. So I shall not abandon you. I will accompany you and explain about the delay to this Mr. Bunberry," he told Liam.

"Thank you, Count, but that isn't necessary."

"I feel it is," observed Dracula. "Besides, along the way you can tell me more about this Gilbert & Sullivan."

By the time Liam and his companion reached the theater, what had begun as a light rain had turned into a torrential downpour. As they rushed up to the stage entrance, Liam noticed that the new advertising poster had been put in place.

GILBERT & SULLIVAN'S
THE PIRATES OF PENZANCE
A SPECIAL LIMITED RETURN ENGAGEMENT

A theater in the midst of rehearsal a few days from opening night could resemble chaos personified. That evening the Strand was no exception. Yet to Liam's experienced eye there was an almost musical order to the whole scene, though he imagined Count Dracula found it quite confusing.

An entirely new operetta, *Utopia (Limited),* the first by Gilbert & Sullivan in some years, was scheduled to open in October. Yet at the last minute the decision had been made to reprise *Pirates,* using the group of actors who had been touring with it for well over a year and only recently returned to London.

"It is a matter of publicity, Liam," Alexander Bunberry, the company manager, had said. "We will still open with *Utopia* in October, but a brief reprise of *Pirates* can only help to generate interest."

"Liam! Liam Gideon! Where the hell have you been! I expected you back by half past four!"

The voice belonged to a tall skinny man, with muttonchop sideburns that seemed to cover half or more of his face. He came charging toward Liam from behind a huge Greek column that was part of the *Pirates* set. He seemed to be on the edge of pure fright. Hands were constantly in motion, pointing this way and that or flipping through the pages of a libretto that had seen better days.

"I'm sorry I was delayed, Mr. Bunberry. It couldn't be helped," said Liam.

"Couldn't be helped! You know that Everett is screaming that he can't rehearse unless he has his new sword," said Bunberry.

"I well know all his complaints, sir," said Liam.

"Then why were you dawdling about! I'm still expecting him to fall in the pit deliberately, just to spite me!"

"I doubt that."

"Sir, Mr. Gideon was not as you say it, dawdling about," said Dracula.

"And who would you be?"

"I am . . . Count Dracula." Dracula's eyes fastened on Bunberry's. Neither man blinked. "Had it not been for the timely intervention of Mr. Gideon when three thieves were attacking me, I would have found myself in a grave situation. He did the only thing that a man of honor and duty could do."

Bunberry stood there for a moment, his eyes glassed over, a thin sheen of sweat on his forehead.

"Well, if it was something like that I can understand the delay," he said. "Just get that sword to Everett. The old hen will be fretting his life away, sure that his performance will be ruined and his career over, until he gets it. Then run down to the costume shop. They need to measure you for your new Frederic costume."

At that, Bunberry whirled on his heels and headed off in the direction of the pirate ship set that filled much of stage left. Just before he got there, a large fat man that Liam didn't recognize, dressed in a tailored waistcoat with a top hat and cane in hand, stopped him. The two men began to speak in whispers.

"I expected him to be quite a bit more vehement about the whole thing," muttered Liam.

"Perhaps it was something I said," mused Dracula.

"Look, you blinking Irishman. If you don't stand still, Effie is going to skewer that pretty little bum of yours with a very long needle!"

With those words ringing in his ears, Liam made a conscious effort not to move. If Effie Ferguson made a threat, she meant it. Looking somewhere between thirty and sixty, she was the absolute mistress of the Strand Theatre costume shop. She had the reputation of being able to make a gunny sack, four buttons, a flower, a skein of thread, and some glass beads into the fanciest ball gown.

Facing the mirror, Liam could see the woman's hands moving swiftly, marking with a long piece of chalk on his pants leg. Then she produced a rather formidable-looking shaving razor and slid it along the cloth from the back of his knee to his ankle. He could feel the cloth parting, but never once felt the touch of the metal.

"You just tell me what I need to do, Effie, and I will do it."

"Now, that's a good lad," she told him. "We want you looking only your best, now, to go on for Their Highnesses."

"Highnesses? What are you talking about?"

Effie chuckled but did not look up. "Now tell me, Mr. Liam Gideon, are you trying to say that you don't know about our 'guests' for opening night?"

Liam drew a breath and forced a smile. He had played this little game with Effie before. "No, Effie, I don't. So would you please share that information with me?"

"Well," she said. "I suppose if they had wanted you to know someone would have mentioned it to you."

"Perhaps. Or perhaps everyone thought that everyone else had told me. So why don't you tell me?"

"Maybe I should. After all, it isn't often that poor little common actors get the chance to perform for the high and mighty likes of 'themselves,' now do they?"

"Yes?"

"It seems that opening night we will have some people in the audience that will bring all of the 'right' sort of society as well as the commoners in."

"Who in hell are you talking about, woman? Is St. Patrick himself coming to see the show?"

A sharp pain drove its way into Liam's calf. He could barely keep from moving, knowing that Effie would do much worse if he did.

"No, you Irish gobashit, it isn't St. Patrick, nor is it Grace O'Malley or even Finn MacCool! Trust an uncivilized Irishman to think of those insignificants in a case like this," she said.

"Insignificants! Strike me, woman, there are moments I wonder about your sense of who is or isn't important," Liam said. "So, now, who would it be, if it isn't *those* noteworthies?"

"Simple; it is himself, Albert Edward, Prince of Wales and heir to the throne of England, who will be gracing these premises on opening night. Seems that he and his wife think that seeing a performance of *Pirates* would make a grand way to spend her birthday," Effie said.

"I suppose they're renting out the entire theater? Just an intimate little gathering of 1,500 of their closest friends," said Liam.

"No, they aren't renting out the entire theater, you Irish idiot. You don't think Bertie has that many friends?"

Another pain shot through Liam's calf to punctuate

Effie's words. There was a muted chuckle from the costume mistress.

"Woman, you enjoyed that!"

"Me? Of course I did. Now, stand still!"

"I wanted to stop in and wish you good luck, Liam," said Dracula.

"I appreciate the sentiment, Count. But I really wish you hadn't said it."

"What?"

Liam smiled. Explaining theatrical traditions to non-theater people was something that every actor had to do now and then. He led Dracula into the Strand Green Room. The Green Room, which was painted a mottled brown, was a large lounge in the back of the theater where actors and stagehands could take a few minutes and relax. Why it was called the Green Room Liam didn't know. As a matter of fact he had never been in one that was green; it was just another theatrical tradition.

"It's an old theatrical custom. If you wish a performer good luck before they go on, you don't say those words; they'll bring him bad luck. Instead, actors say 'break a leg.' Every actor knows what you really mean."

Dracula raised an eyebrow at this. "I suppose each profession has its own customs. Very well, let me bid you to 'break a leg.' Figuratively, of course, not in reality."

"Thank you," said Liam.

"Are you nervous?" asked the Count.

"A bit. A very wise actor once told me that if I weren't at least a little bit nervous before each performance, then that was the time to worry."

"Your friend had the right attitude."

Just then the door to the Green Room flew open,

as if a storm was behind it. Bunberry came barreling in, followed by Effie and several stagehands.

"Liam, there you are. I've been looking all over the theater for you!" said Bunberry.

"Is there a problem? Everett has his sword and knows the new choreography backwards and forwards."

"I don't know what he does or doesn't know, and it doesn't matter. Everett is incapacitated and won't be going on tonight," said Bunberry.

"Incapacitated? Is that a fancy way of saying he's drunk again?" said one of the other actors.

Effie answered them with a *humph,* and a look of disgust. There were tales that Everett had, over his twenty-five-year career, given some of his best performances drunk.

"He's passed out and no one can rouse him. He's breathing, so I assume he is alive. I spoke to the gobashit earlier, not an hour ago," said Effie. "He seemed fine then. I certainly didn't smell any alcohol on him then."

"Could he be sick?" suggested Liam.

"There's a doctor in the audience. I had him come back and look Everett over. He says nothing appears to be wrong with him; he is just asleep and no one can wake him up."

"The thing is, we are going to need a Pirate King and neither of the usual understudies is available," said Bunberry.

"Are you saying what I think you're saying?"

"We can use Gene Yearson as Frederic, but not for the Pirate King. I want you to take the role," he said.

The words hung in the air. Liam felt the bottom fall out from his stomach. He glanced toward the big clock that hung near the door. It said 7 o'clock.

"And curtain is at half eight," he muttered. "The thing is, I don't know half the songs or the dialogue. I'll try, but I'm afraid that I will end up making a fool out of myself and disgracing us in front of the Prince of Wales."

"That's a chance that we are just going to have to take. Effie, can you alter his costumes and fit him out as the Pirate King in time to go on?"

"A moment, Mr. Bunberry," said the Count. "Liam will do what he has to do; that is all any man can do. Understand that I do not doubt Liam's abilities, but I may have an alternate possibility that you should consider."

"Count, right now I can see no other answers, besides Liam, short of sending a man on with script in hand," said Bunberry. "But, I'm willing to entertain any ideas. Just make it quick."

"Very well, then I suggest you leave Liam in the role for which he is prepared and put me in the role of the Pirate King."

There was utter silence in the Green Room. Every one of the actors had heard Dracula's words; none was more surprised than Liam.

"You, Count?" asked Liam.

"Yes."

"You're an actor?" said Bunberry, a tone of disbelief in his voice. "In university, I suppose."

"There and in other places. I was in fact considered very good," said Dracula.

"You never mentioned that you were an actor," said Liam.

"It was a long time ago. Besides, Liam, you never asked." His eyes locked with Bunberry's, as they had the previous night. The company manager didn't appear to breathe for several minutes.

"You know the libretto? The songs, the dialogue?" said Liam.

"Every word."

"Only two days ago you hadn't even heard of Gilbert & Sullivan, let alone the *Pirates of Penzance*," said Liam.

"Meeting you and seeing this company made me curious. Shall we say I borrowed a copy of the libretto someone had left on a chair, read it over, and was amused by it. I even slipped in last night and watched the rehearsal."

"That would help with you knowing the blocking. But you say you read the libretto just once?" asked Liam.

"That's right. Anything I read I remember, every word of it."

"Your voice, sir?"

Liam, Bunberry, and the others looked toward the door. A man, dressed in evening clothes with a neatly waxed mustache, stood there.

"Mr. Gilbert!" said Effie.

"Your voice, sir? What do you sing?" demanded William Schwenck Gilbert. The fifty-seven-year-old lyricist spoke with the manner of a sergeant-major demanding something from one of his troops.

"Baritone."

"And you say you know my words?"

"Indeed." Dracula began to sing. *"Oh, better to live and die, under the brave black flag I fly. Than play a sanctimonious part, with a pirate head and a pirate heart."*

Gilbert stood silent, his face unmoving and emotionless.

"Effie!" said Gilbert. "Can you alter Everett's costume quick enough to fit the Count? I can have them hold the curtain an extra ten minutes, but not a second longer."

"I'll have him looking like those clothes were made for him."

"Do it."

"Still nervous, Liam?" asked Dracula.
The two men stood in the wings, looking out at the back of the great gold curtain that covered the

front of the stage. Effie was standing just behind them, tying off several threads in the Count's costume.

"A bit. But I should be asking you if you're nervous. After all, you came to see the play, now you're a part of it."

"I am a bit nervous," said Dracula.

"Then break a leg, Count."

"Thank you, Liam."

No one heard a shot. With the orchestra well into the act's final number it would have been impossible to hear anything short of a cannon going off. Liam would have never known that anything happened if he had not been looking straight toward the Royal Box.

Something struck the plaster wall edging just above the Prince and Princess of Wales, sending a shower of powder down across the duo. Their Royal Highnesses looked around, as puzzled as everyone else. A moment later they began laughing as the elaborate dance on stage ended and the curtain rolled down.

As Dracula exited behind the waterfall curtain, Liam grabbed him and explained what he had seen.

"It was not your imagination, Liam, nor was it the manifestation of this ancient theater exhibiting its aches and pains. I saw it as well. I suspect a rifle shot," he said.

"A rifle? In the theater? Why, and who would be using it?"

"I'm not sure," said Dracula. "I suspect that it came from somewhere above us."

Liam's eyes traced the edge of the curtain up into the darkness high above the backstage area. It was a landscape of catwalks, curtains, and ropes, all helping to add to the illusion that was projected on stage. There were a few figures moving around on the catwalk, high up in the air, where they could raise and lower the curtains. But it was higher that Liam looked, nearly a hundred feet, near the top of the building itself. He saw nothing, but apparently Dracula did.

"Follow me," said the Count.

Liam was only a moment behind him. Attached to the back wall of the theater was a ladder that ran all the way to the roof. Dracula was thirty feet onto it when Liam began climbing, moving upwards into the darkness.

More than a dozen heavy black curtains, along with an equal number of smaller, lighter ones, hung from railings that were in turn suspended from beams embedded in the walls of the theater itself. Below and all around them Liam could hear the sounds of the stage crew busily changing the set to get it ready for act two.

Once they reached the highest level there was little light. The catwalks were nothing but long boards, a foot or so wide at best, that had been placed along the girders to provide a path for workmen. A single misstep could send someone hurtling down.

That fact did not bother Dracula. He moved quickly, with a confidence that seemed inhuman. Liam tried to keep pace, but it was not easy. When Liam finally caught up with the Count they had made their way back across the stage area and stood next to the top of the huge waterfall curtain.

"Observe," said Dracula. His long slim fingers pointed downwards. From this perch they had a clear view of the Royal Box. "I would say this is where the assassin shot from."

"Thank God he missed," said Liam. "But where is he now?"

"I think close by." The Count motioned for Liam to be silent, his eyes blazing red. Dracula was a hunter seeking his prey.

Liam heard the soft sound of a board creaking. He turned and found himself confronting a figure, dressed in the same pirate costume that the actors wore. In the semidarkness it seemed a fearful apparition that was trying to slip by the two men.

"Oh no, you don't," Liam said.

He moved to intercept the assassin but missed his footing and stumbled, ramming his head hard against a metal strut that supported the curtain. It was only the purest luck that he was able to keep from falling from the girder. Around him the world whirled for a moment, transforming the stage light below into a rainbow of colors.

That was when he noticed the fog. It came from nowhere; it was just there, flowing around the upper part of the theater. Liam tried to focus on Dracula, dressed as the Pirate King, who stood now facing the assassin in the crewman's costume.

The words that Dracula had sung earlier in the Green Room ran through Liam's mind, echoing in the Count's strong baritone. *"Oh, better to live and die, under the brave black flag I fly. Than play a sanctimonious part, with a pirate head and a pirate heart."*

Then Dracula was gone, replaced by a huge silver wolf, the fog blending into the beast's coat. The animal's growl was an otherworldly sound that seemed to Liam something out of a nightmare. The assassin screamed and tried to back away.

Liam's eyesight began to clear and he could see Dracula again. The fog was gone and so was the wolf. The Count was grappling with the assassin. In a single motion he managed to hurl him against the curtain. The impact made a dull thud that sent the figure collapsing into an unconscious heap.

Liam got to his feet and made his way over to their prisoner. There was enough light coming through the top of the curtain that he could see the figure's face.

"Effie?!"

*   *   *

With the help of a couple of stagehands, Effie had been taken down from the theater aerie. She now lay stretched out, unconscious, on a pallet of curtains and sacks, a thin trail of drying blood running from a cut on her scalp.

A crowd of actors and stagehands surrounded them. Gilbert, Bunberry, and the large fat man that Liam had seen earlier had appeared out of nowhere.

"It looks as if we have what we were hoping for," said the fat man.

"Is there a doctor in the house?" said Gilbert. That it was one of the oldest theatrical clichés ever didn't seem to matter when William Gilbert said it.

"I think having a doctor look over both Effie and Liam would be a good idea," said Dracula.

"Arguably," said the fat man. "Send one of the stagehands to box A17. There is a doctor named Watson with the A.J. Raffles party."

"Are we going to be able to finish this show?" asked Gilbert.

"Oh, yes," said the fat man, "if Mr. Gideon and the Count are able to carry on, and I think there should be no doubt of that. By the way, Count, I thoroughly enjoyed your performance. You have a wonderful voice and a real talent for comedy."

"Look here, Holmes." said Bunberry.

"Holmes?" said Liam. He knew that name, as any regular reader of *The Strand* magazine did. "Are you?"

"That was my late brother. But it doesn't matter who I am, young man, because you never heard that name mentioned in this theater, and I was never here," said the fat man. "Consider that an order from Her Majesty's Government."

"Yes, sir," said Liam. He had other questions he wanted to ask, but discretion seemed the better part of valor right now.

"Perhaps you could explain things to me, sir," said Dracula. "Would I be correct in assuming that this whole matter of the reprise of *Pirates* was part of an elaborate plan? Who is Effie?"

The fat man, who wasn't there, removed a cigar case from his inside jacket, opened it, and offered one to Dracula. The Count declined.

"As to your first question, you may be right or you may be wrong, that is all I can say. Effie, my dear Count, besides being the costume mistress for this theater, is an expert with a one-shot air rifle. I know of only one better, a former Indian army colonel. Those skills earned her a position as an assassin for hire, working this evening for a Scottish anarchist group," he said.

"And you want her to tell you all about her employers," suggested Dracula.

"It would be very nice to hear news of her current and past employers. She can choose to cooperate with us, or face a hangman's noose. Her Majesty's Government had long suspected her, but we never had any proof. Tonight, we have the proof we needed. Thanks to the cooperation of Mr. Gilbert and Mr. Sullivan, Their Highnesses, and a pair of very good actors who portrayed them this evening. Had she not missed, and even the best miss occasionally, it would have been a most inconvenient matter to explain things to the public. Now, I have matters that require my attention. May I wish you, Count, and the rest of the cast the best of lu—"

"The proper phrase is 'break a leg,' I believe," said Dracula.

"Ah, yes, quite right. Very well then, break a leg."

Others came crowding around Effie, Gilbert, and the fat man, so Liam and Dracula withdrew to the far corner of the stage.

"Count, I have to ask you something," said Liam.

"What is that?"

"Up there, when you were fighting Effie, did I see what I thought I saw?"

"And what was that?"

"I would swear that I saw one of Finn MacCool's wolves. But then it was gone."

"Are you sure of what you saw? Any more sure than Everett is that he did not have a visitor earlier this evening? One that told him to take a long nap?"

"Perhaps not. But why, Count? Why did you do it?"

"Partially curiosity. When you are as old as I am you embrace the unknown. By the time we encountered Effie, I had no choice. I was a 'slave to duty,' " he said with a remarkably toothy grin.

Before Liam could speak, the assistant stage manager came up behind the men.

"Places for act two, gentlemen," he announced.

Beast

AMY L. GRUSS AND
CATT KINGSGRAVE-ERNSTEIN

"I told you." Jerry gloated from behind Al's shoulder. "I told you Poltwhistle'd come asking for those books. I told you you shouldn't just go making free with valuable and delicate antiques, but did you listen? Oh no! What's old Jerry Cartley got to say that the great and powerful Al—"

"Look!" The taller youth whirled on his heel and glared, stopping his coworker dead in his boots. It was a good one, that glare; it had often served him well when the school bullies looked for a thin, asthmatic boy to torment. Al did not scrimp on it now. "I heard what Poltwhistle said, same as you did. 'Keep them safe,' he said." Al shoved his hands into his pockets and looked over his shoulder at the sunset. "They wasn't safe up there with the mice in the attic." He sniffed and strode off down the street again.

"Roof leaked up there," he muttered, more as comfort to himself than by way of explanation. Jerry was useless in Al's estimation, more interested in the pastry shop next door than in the volumes of treasure at Poltwhistle's Papers and Antique Oddities. Tonight of all nights, when speed and secrecy was what Al needed, the dolt found the single streak of determination that beat in his flabby heart.

"Wettest summer since I came down from Scotland," Al grumbled, once more finding his stride on the sooty cobbles. A fast stride, in hopes of outdistancing Cartley's endurance, if not his curiosity. "Rained all August, practically. I did Poltwhistle a favour, getting those books to a dry place, and he knows it! I kept them safe! Now there's a buyer that wants them, I'll just bring the trunk back to the shop, is all."

Jerry laughed, a phlegmy, unpleasant sound.

"What's funny then?" Al demanded through clenched teeth.

"You. All noble; which is why you kited off with the Sefer Yetzer-moth, and the Sumerian wotsit, and that grim-thingummy, and left the Voltaire and Dumas up there for mouse food."

"Give me strength!" Al pleaded of the smudged sky, just visible between the last of London's outlying warehouses. "Any idiot can come by a Voltaire, and there are so many first-edition Dumas in London you could wipe your arse with them!" He turned and backed Jerry into the blood-slimed steps of a fishmonger's alleyway. "But the Yetzeroth—in English? Unheard of! The Egyptian Book of the Dead—and the handwritten grimoire of the last witch hanged in England? That box held a dozen treasures, and I . . ." He let the sentence trail off, aware, suddenly, of the street behind him. Not crowded, but hardly bereft of curious onlookers.

Cartley's eyes bulged in alarm. The smell of his sweat, strong in the evening's chill, overcame the alley's fishy ambience. Al coughed, moderated his tone, and put on a smile. "I put them in a safe place. I'll have them at the shop first thing in the morning, just like Poltwhistle said." He patted Jerry's woolen coat, flicked a bit of dust, and backed away. "Now if you don't mind, I'll walk the rest of the way on my own. Get on home to your supper now, eh?"

Jerry's eyes narrowed. "You just don't want me to see if you got anything else from the shop hidden away that hasn't been missed yet," he accused. "It's stealing, Al. They may call it whatever they like in Scotland, but in London it's stealing, and it's wrong. You go to Hell for stealing."

Al smiled grimly. Just like a Londoner to take a jab at his nationality when he couldn't win an argument any other way. "You go to Hell for buggery too, Jerry, but that doesn't stop you and that newsboy, does it?" He relished Jerry's ragged gasp as he realized that Al knew his most dreaded secret. "It's getting late; what say you run home now, else I walk along with you," he called. The fat fool backed away, mouth still agape with horror.

"Sorry, Limey," Al muttered as Cartley turned and ran into the gathering fog creeping with the evening from the river Thames. "Can't have you tagging on after me. Not tonight." The thin youth shoved his hands into his pockets and turned back toward his treasure trove's hiding place. What a perfect hiding place it was, too. He scowled in annoyance. Hardly anyone from London ever went out by way of Carfax House and the locals were all scared to. He'd heard the tales told in Purfleet inns when his studies had kept him late into the night; a clutch of witches, burned in their sleep by Elizabeth the Great's witchfinders, haunting and wailing and searching for their lost souls—or failing that, the soul of anybody who came near.

He only told the story once, to a flirtatious pub wench who knew no more of the old place than he, and whose eyes grew round at the fear of it. Total fiction—he'd only been thinking of a tumble then, but within the month Al had heard the whole, embellished tale on three separate occasions. He seized the opportunity to add further grisly detail to the history in order

to secure absolutely that solitude which his study of
the lost arts required. With the caged lunatics baying
in the sanitarium next door and Al's own little addi-
tions to the place—hollow pipes to moan when the
wind blew, branches in the chapel's ruined belfry that
clattered like bones, the occasional well-placed lantern,
mirror, and pane of glass—the ghost story had spread
like wildfire. It was perfect.

Perfect until a month ago when a horde of carters
tramped through his haven, setting huge boxes on the
ground without regard for any of his carefully drawn
glyphs. Bad enough that all his experiments had been
smudged into oblivion, but the idiots had put the big-
gest one—a trunk seven feet long, five wide, and four
deep—just at the entrance to his hiding place, making
it impossible for him to get to his precious books.

Then the real haunting had started, more profound
and horrifying than anything he could orchestrate;
grisly murders in the city, sightings of fierce rats and
dogs with demonic, red eyes, the dead ship appearing
in Whitby harbour after a freakish storm. Inspecting
the damage after the carters had left that first night,
Al had noticed that every one of the boxes that littered
Carfax were marked with the doomed vessel's name:
Demeter. He hadn't dared go back there.

Still wouldn't go, given his preference, but he
daren't lose yet another job or his father would, as he
had promised, call him back home. Al would rather
face down the devil himself than wind up trapped back
in that Scottish bog of a village.

"You!" A voice shrilled from above his head, scar-
ing the wits out of him. "You boy!"

Al swallowed his heart. The Lunatic—again. Every
time he worked up the nerve to come near the house
that mad bastard was at the window, baying like a
watchdog. But Al couldn't afford caution this time,
couldn't hide from the threat of guards or the shadowy,
half-glimpsed figure that lurked in the ruin. Al hunched

deeper into his collar and tried to ignore the wild-eyed man's yelling.

"I know why you come here! It won't work! The Master has promised it to me and you shan't have it! You with your pitiful scratchings in the dust—you don't know how to serve him!" Somewhere nearby, a dog began to bark.

"Look, you daft bastard," he hissed, glaring up at the madman, "I don't give a haggis about your master—it's my master's going to have the Peelers down on me if I don't get my books back! So do us a favour and shut your gob!" Al peered at the crumbling wall, hoping his dismissal was obvious enough. From the sanitarium's well-tended garden, he could see Carfax House, the chapel with its cracked steeple bulking darkly athwart the night sky. From the outside, it looked impenetrable, however. . . . *Yes,* he thought. *There's still the crack in the wall, overgrown with vine and weeds.* With a sigh of relief, he started forward.

"Oh little boy," the Lunatic called, sweet-voiced. "Would you like a treat?" He thrust one hand through the bars of his window, fingers pinching at something that wriggled.

"Sod off." Al seethed as the barking grew more frantic. "Shut it, or that dog'll wake the whole of Essex!" He glared as the madman started to giggle.

"Think that's a dog?" Another giggle, and the man howled suddenly, full-voiced and lusty. "It's a wolf! The Master's servant, just like me! Like me! And not like you!" The arm thrust through again, bony finger pointing, shaking with rage or palsy. "You wheezing ninny! You've not enough lives in you to serve him! You're pathetic, you hear? Don't you walk away from me! You forgot your treat! Come back! Don't leave me alone!"

He burst into tears, and was still wailing when Al scrambled over the wall and out of earshot.

"Quite a piece of work, that one. Bloody barking

Limey. Harumph." Inside the chapel, Al leaned on the huge box and sulked. The answer to his worry was just there, blocked in by a crate he just couldn't budge. "Ought to cull out Cartley's tongue." He grumbled, " 'Tongue of fat, buggerin' bastard' ought to be an ingredient in some spell or other. First time in his life he'd be useful!" He snickered briefly, wiped grime and sweat from his face, then sighed. "Ballocks."

Suddenly, Al remembered his Aristotle. He searched the chapel in a sudden fit of motivation. "Leverage!" A fallen roof-timber poked out from under a tattered curtain of cobwebs. Al seized it. "Perfect!" Wedging the board between the wall and trunk, he heaved.

The huge box creaked, shifted. Al held his breath, put a boot against the wall, and shoved harder. Just when he thought his lungs would burst, the crate slid back with a lurch and a shriek of nails on stone. Al scrambled to try the door. "Ahh, not quite—bloody hell!"

Losing the last of his patience, he clambered over the box and slithered into his hiding place, too annoyed to care when he tore his only coat. He found the lamp by touch and examined the door's lintel. As he'd feared, the chalk was an unintelligible smudge where the trunk slid down the wall. "Dammit, they ruined everything! I knew I should have scratched that glyph into the stone. Blast and damn!"

He turned back to the worktable with a fierce scowl and began digging through the piled volumes thereon. "Now which book did I find that in?"

Drakul fed vigorously that night on grubby street Arabs and opium-dazed Chinese from the far reaches of the English Queen's empire, like spice and savour to his jaded palate. Even the tame English were a welcome relish after five hundred years of bland Rumanian peasants. Delicate, these English were, and decadent as the soft, green land that spawned them. He thought of Lucy, pink and sweet as the roses in Hillingham's sprawling gardens, and barked a laugh. A sweetmeat too cloying for every day, that one—better to sip a bit at a time than spoil her worth with greed. Especially with the luxury of variety to be had at no more expense than a brief journey to London.

Besides, he played a delicate game at Hillingham estate—one he had no intention of quitting untimely. Drakul had chosen his first bride, and the chase was exhilarating for all the little obstacles that her caretakers threw in his way. His animal servant had not shirked at their garlic or guards or crosses on the window, and at Drakul's bidding had opened the way for him into the lush expanse of his bride's private chamber. He laughed, the memory of Bersicker's feral joy sparking fire in the back of his brain. This night would not soon be forgotten in the Westenra family, such as remained of it.

The wolf had known his business; to open the way and to terrify. Not like that idiot Renfield, who ranted and babbled and was very nearly more aggravation than he was worth. As he thought of the man, Drakul felt the contact between them flicker to life, though he had intended no such communication. A moment later, the man began shouting his usual promises of loyalty and adoration, flailing his arms through the bars and in general making a canker of himself. With a mental reminder not to drink the blood of opiated Chinese again, the Lord of the Un-Dead wheeled around to approach his sacred earth from the east, with the distant threat of dawn to his tail, and the shrieking lunatic out of earshot.

He came to earth among the weather-tumbled stones of the chapel's burial yard, long desanctified by blood and fire. Like the chapel in his own castle in the Carpathian Mountains, no prayers had been sung here for hundreds of years, and the only sacred work being done within the crumbling walls was that of the beetle and the fly.

"The perfect place for me," he said aloud, rolling the English words around his tongue as he had done with the life-blood of the Chinese girl with the flat, glassy eyes and sweet-burning pipe. "From this place of murder and sacrilege, I, Vlad Drakul ride out to meet my destiny as master of this green and pleasant land." He laughed. "Let any come against me who dare!"

The wind answered with a rush, made the trees in the sanitarium's manicured park creak and thrash, and left behind a breath of something at once new and familiar. A boy, on the verge of manhood: his scent had haunted the chapel where the vampire's precious Wallachian earth lay hidden. The nuances were clearer now: the boy was frightened, he did not eat well, and was not at all strong. The scent of his fear was tangible—sharp, but sweetened with an undercurrent of hunger, almost greed. He was also very, very close. Intrigued, Drakul listened, heard the rasp of fingers on paper echoing in a bare stone room, heard a slight wheeze in the boy's breathing, the hiss of a burning lamp. *The Crypt,* he thought with a smile as he entered the chapel.

One of his boxes had been moved, and behind it, a door revealed. From under this door came both a delicate life-scent and a thin streak of light. Drakul looked in. A lamp's glow warmed a tiny room, outlining a gangly youth. He sat with his back to the door, hunched awkwardly in a chair too small for him. A table and crate—the only other furniture the cell afforded—were buried under precarious stacks of books, papers, bags, leaves . . . doctor's things, but the youth was no doctor. Drakul smiled, sharpened his sight to pick out details that uncertain light might have hidden from any other hunter.

The youth had ruddy hair, coarse and apparently resistant to attempts at England's respectable grooming. No beard. He wore the threadbare garments of a clerk—junior clerk more likely—or he could have been a shop boy in his Sunday best. But he wore the boots of a peasant instead of the shoes that London's gentry and all who aped them wore. Drakul liked boots. You knew what to expect from them, and the people who wore them. The vampire absently shifted his earth box out of the way and stepped around the door. The interloper did not so much as twitch. Drakul smiled. Imagine not knowing when one's destruction stood at one's shoulder! He cleared his throat.

The boy didn't move. His breath did not even quicken. The smell of his mortal fear still pervaded the cell, but without the spike of panic that Drakul expected. He took a step nearer and coughed again. Still no stir, still no alarm. Drakul scowled. He was the Hammer of the Turks, terror of his country, the lord of the night, and this intruder ignored him in favour of . . . what?

He took another step, brought his shoes down on the stone with a clack. Still the youth did not notice, but now Drakul could see why; he was reading. The Count thought about killing him there, in the old way he might have done to a Turk on the battlefield; a quick twist of the head, and a jerk backward so he might be the dying man's last sight. Then he caught a glimpse of the book and it gave him pause; a familiar pattern, arcane and ancient lay under the boy's fingers. Scholomancy! Here in this place, this land and time of reason. In the hands of a shop boy. Unacceptable!

"What are you reading?" Drakul growled into the youth's ear. At last the boy started, ancient book dropping to the flagstones with a flutter and thud. A ragged gasp escaped him as he tried to whirl in his seat, entangling his legs and upending the whole, himself, coat, chair, odds and ends from the table, and half a dozen more books into an undignified sprawl. Drakul did not laugh at the sight, though he wanted to.

The boy opened his mouth to speak, made a noise like a rat, then swallowed and tried again. His voice was tenor and loud with panic. "What's it to you?"

Impudence! Drakul bent to pick up the book, which purred with force in his un-dead fingers. "It?" He gave the youth a broad smile, for effect. " 'It' is of no consequence to me. You, however, have invaded my home, taken refuge in my holy sanctuary, and you annoy me." The smell of the youth's alarm mingled with the lingering opiate in Drakul's blood and rushed to his head like a tide. Pleasant, but inopportune.

The youth pressed his lips together, all colour draining from them. His nostrils flared with quick, shallow breaths as he gathered himself into a less precarious seat on the floor.

Drakul waited only so long for a response. "Make no mistake, boy, you are no match for me. I demand answers and will have them. What are you reading?"

"Words." He smiled, actually smiled, and an unwelcome scent wafted past Drakul's nostrils. *Satisfaction? Inconceivable!*

"Clever. So clever, but you must not believe that will win your life from me." He stood, turned the book over in his hands. "I have seen times when clever men like you were burned, hanged, broken, and," a smile to remembrance here, "impaled simply for possessing such a volume." He looked down. "Knowledge of the Devil, the men of God called it, as they did the Devil's work against science."

"I don't believe in God." The boy jutted his chin in defiant dignity. Drakul raised an eyebrow at the claim, and he elaborated, "I believe in what I see. I've never seen God or the Devil." He swallowed, the apple of his throat bobbing. "They don't exist."

"You have seen the Devil now!" Drakul reached out his shadow to the cheap lamp, smothered the flame effortlessly. In the sudden and shocking darkness, his eyes were as blind as those of his prey, but the youth's gasp and scramble betrayed his movements. The vampire laughed, reached with a clawed hand toward the radiant terror. "I expect that you will call out to God before we part!"

Suddenly the boy scrambled forward, threw his arms around the Count's person, and slapped something against his sternum. "By Gevurah I invoke you!" Those words were half-familiar, but the power quickened the air, this Drakul knew.

"By Chockmah and Netzach I invoke you!" The incantation rose to a breathless shrill as Drakul seized the boy's narrow throat. "By Kefer and Malkuth I summon you! Come Uriel, Archangel of the Dead to my aid!"

Ghost light, chill and blue, swirled around the vampire, searing, freezing his long-dead skin. A million tiny motes coalesced into a ball of fire, then shocked like lightning, like a battering ram into Drakul's breast. The force flung him into the crumbling wall as his prey scrambled out of reach, then bolted for freedom.

Half a mile down the road, Al risked a backward glance. "He's—he's not coming after me. It worked. It worked!" He slowed, but his thoughts did not. "Ye gods, it worked. It's for real!"

Al's disbelief found its way into sporadic mirth. He vaulted a stile and took off across a pasture, hardly minding his wheezing lungs. "Fancy, I did that. Me! I could have—out of the way, bleedin' sheep!—but I didn't—bastard!—and now—" He shouted gloating laughter to the sky. Across the river, London's great clock tower chimed four.

He reached a village and slowed to a trot, sensing safety in the surrounding cottages, though he still rambled aloud in wonder at his discovery. "The power in

those books! I could rule the world! The books—oh
ballocks!" Cold reality jolted him out of his smugness:
in his panicked flight from Carfax's ancient crypt, he'd
left the books behind—all but the one he clutched.

The breath caught suddenly in Al's chest. Pain
squeezed it tight. He stumbled to a halt, sobbing for
air as he tried to examine the lone book he'd managed
to win. It was too dark, and the moon had long since
set. Al turned the rough leather over in his hands,
peered close, held it up to his face, and squinted some
more. All in vain. He swore heartily. Then, through
the tangled hedgerow, a gleam of light caught his eye.
A church! Dozens of candles in the window, and a
bench out of the wind in which to read. St. Catherine's,
the carving over the door read. Al took only that much
notice of it as he strode up to the church's window,
looked at the book, and swore.

"Holy sodding ballocks of Christ! It's the buggering
German one!" Suddenly he felt like crying. Al trudged
back to the church's front steps and sank down to
brood. "You have to go back, you know," he told himself, sniffing. "Nothing for it. You have to get those
books. Poltwhistle will serve you up to the Peelers if
you don't." His foot began to cramp. Al absently
yanked his boot off, getting sheep dip on his hands in
the process. Dammit! He wiped the filth on the
church's steps, then massaged his foot, mind racing.

"He's dead. You killed him, you know. You saw
him." He paused, for he hadn't actually seen. "But you
felt it happen." Al stood up, hopping on one foot to
pull his boot back on. "There now. Going back. For the
books. Off you go—" The back of his neck prickled; a
pair of glowing garnet eyes blazed out of the darkness
at the end of the lane.

"Shite!" Al lurched toward the door, boot half on,
and pulled at the latch with all his might. "Ballocks!"
Tripping across the threshold, he hit the stone floor
and rolled. His boot flew free. He snatched his foot to

safety, watched in horror as the creature appeared out of the darkness. Skin white, bloodless, and waxen but for a single slash of red across the forehead, lips pulled back in a rictus of fury. Pointed, long teeth like a feral wolf in those red lips. His hands were talons. Al felt his heart skip as the eyes, crimson and filled with hate, bored into his for a moment. Then the spell of horror broke and Al realized that the monster was coming toward him. Fast.

"NO!" he screamed, scrambling back. "Get away!" The creature reeled from the church's threshold with a furious snarl. After several breathless moments, Al worked up the nerve to shut the door.

No sooner did the latch click than the monster spoke from the other side in a voice as cold as the grave and rumbling with anger. "Open the door. Now."

Al backed away, hysteria tightening his laugh to a giggle. *I sound like the Lunatic!* He swallowed hard. "Not bloody likely, sunbeam!"

Something hit the door, made the ancient timbers creak and shiver like matchwood. Al jumped, backed farther. A reek of scorched hair filled his nose as the steely voice commanded him again. "Let me inside!" The tone, icy, murderous, shook Al's bravado to the core.

"Oh no!" Al whispered, shaking his head. "I will not open that door! You can just stay outside and rot! By Gevurah I inv—"

"DESIST!"

With a sudden horror, Al found that the Qabbalic names of power fled his mind like water. He couldn't remember them. Any of them!

A paving stone hurtled through the window, scattering the candles across the floor. Al scrambled to stamp out the flames, his breath coming in sobs as he realized the trap in which he'd snared himself. *Much good all that study does you now,* he thought, sinking to the floor beside the church's font.

He screamed as another stone smashed in through the window, splintering the rear pew. *Couldn't grab Agnes Nutter's grimoire, could you? Couldn't grab the Yetzeroth. Oh no! You had to go and get a bloody useless book in bloody useless German!*

"Come out and your death will be quick!" the monster bellowed. "I'll spit you on a sharp stake. I'm merciful." That won a giggle from Al. "Laugh, do you? My servants will hunt you down and destroy you! You cannot imagine my reach!" His rant grew desperate, more a child's tantrum than a devil's promise. "Animals, elements obey my will! I have mastered the arts in which you merely dabble! Your lifetime is the blink of an eye to me, your insignificance so slight it is—insignificant! Damn you—open the door!"

Al whirled to shout at the door and the horror it held at bay. "SOD OFF!" He sobbed, "Shut up, shut up, shut u—" His breath and his litany of despair caught short as he realized that there was only one thing to do.

The door opened. Framed in the threshold slumped his lanky tormentor, head down, defeated. Drakul blinked, then laughed, scenting victory in the boy's terror. "Come forward, slave. Come and meet the death I promised you." He crept from the shelter of his holy sanctuary like a dog on its belly. Drakul licked his lips, tasting already the rush of triumph. This one he would kill utterly. No un-death for this boot-wearing, too-clever peasant.

Drakul seized his prey as he came within reach, shook him to see the fear in his eyes. "Now who is the clever one?"

In answer the youth spit, spraying a mouthful of burning holiness into the vampire's face. It blinded him, sending him reeling to his knees.

"That would be me," came the boy's voice, choking a little with laughter or holy water as he backed away.

Drakul clawed the air, snarling, howling as the lingering fire deepened his agony. "Your name!" He thundered the battlefield cry of old. "Give me your name, little beast, that I may remember you properly!"

Retreating footsteps were the only reply.

A l was well and truly wrecked by the time he got back to Fleet Street. Grinning, he wound his way through the crowds of London's working class, the hard-won book in one hand, his lone boot in the other. Al didn't notice the tall man in the traveling cloak waiting on the bookstore's front step until he'd nearly run into him.

The man turned to scowl, bushy eyebrows lowering as he took in Al's dishevelled state. He looked down himself, suddenly self-conscious. Begrimed and smelling of sheep, bare feet muddy, trousers filthy to the knees. God knew what his hair and face looked like. Al's temper flared and he flushed to the ears.

"What're you staring at, you old shite?" he demanded. The old man's eyebrows shot up, but he looked more amused than insulted. Al ground his teeth and brandished his boot. "Laugh at me, you southern pansy, and I'll feed ye this!"

"CROWLEY!" Al jumped like a scalded cat at his employer's thundering voice. Poltwhistle loomed in the doorway, fists on his hips, towering in apoplectic fury. "How dare you speak so to my client!" Al yelped as the old man grabbed his ear and hauled him into the shop. "What have you to say for yourself?"

Al straightened up, and met the old bastard's eye with a grim smile. "Here. I brought you your book."

He didn't even try to duck as his employer dealt him a staggering cuff to the ear. The German book went flying, fetched up against the customer's shoe.

"Dr. Van Helsing," Poltwhistle said as Al picked himself up, "My apologies. This little thief stole the volumes you ordered but never fear. A brief stay in gaol will remind him of their location."

"Do not to trouble yourself, good sir." The old man stooped, reverently retrieving the volume. "This is the book I require most urgently. Note the title—*Wampyre*." Poltwhistle began to object, but the doctor ignored him. "This book will stand between mankind and a beast most unspeakable. Good!"

He stood, snapped the little book shut, but stopped as his eye fell over Al, wiping the corner of his mouth. The doctor extended a hand to him.

"You should not fire such a steadfast boy—curiosity is no crime."

"Beastly Aleister Crowley? Steadfast?" Poltwhistle asked, incredulous as the two shook hands.

The doctor grinned, stepping out into the bright golden dawn. "So. And even a beast can learn, if properly taught."

A Most Electrifying
Evening

JULIE BARRETT

London—fortunately for me—is a city of many diversions. From the high-society theatre crowd to the lowlife in Limehouse, I have had plenty of opportunity to experience it all. One might say I have taken a taste of all this city has to offer. I daresay that my presence in this great city may have had some small bearing on the recent fashion trend of high-necked blouses.

And now, having experienced all that is London to the point of un-deadly boredom, I find myself spending more time in my Piccadilly rooms, reading.

Amazingly, I find myself fascinated with some of the recent scientific advances of the day. Of course, the changes in weaponry over the centuries have not escaped my eye. The lance eventually gave way to the cannon as the sword to the gun, and as a watchful lord of my property I took note of the trend (slow though it was to reach my secluded property) and trained my servants accordingly. After all, it does not suit my purposes to have a poorly defended castle.

The latest trends in inventions met my eye with mixed emotions. Perhaps the most intriguing of them is the electrification of the cities. London has been electrified in places. Indeed, my sitting room has been outfitted with an electric lightbulb. I find the light harsh, and much prefer the softer glow of candlelight or gas. Yet it is not the lightbulb, but another application of electricity which has taken my interest.

A young scientist in America by the name of Nikola Tesla is said to have patented several electric motors in the last year. News of his astonishing experiments with electricity would no doubt have reached my backwater lands within the year, for his experiments hold great promise. His tinkerings with motors are most fascinating to me. Based upon my reading, I surmise that it would be quite possible to create a sanctum within my castle with doors operated by these electric motors. This would make it possible to move solid stone doors with great ease. I also surmise that it would be feasible to create electric locks. Such devices might make it quite impossible for prisoners to escape.

I must say that it was with a certain amount of glee that I read the news that Tesla himself would be lecturing in London. While this lecture was by invitation only to the greatest of scientific minds, gaining admittance would be an exercise in trifles. After all, it would be very easy to convince a member or two of the scientific society that I am an eminent scholar in my own land. The task was embarrassingly easy, for the milquetoast young man in charge of the invitations became "convinced" with minimal energy on my part and only a slight headache on his part. He will think twice about taking a second glass of sherry again.

A lecture hall at St. Bartholomew's had been chosen for the occasion. I slipped into a seat at the rear of the hall, leaving the front spaces for those with less-keen senses. Precisely at 7:30 a hush fell upon the hall. A tall, well-dressed man whom I took to be Tesla himself approached the podium. After arranging the pencils on the lectern in a precise pattern, he began to assay the decanter of water. I'm sure very few beyond the front row heard him mutter the phrase "64.7 fluid ounces" before pouring himself a glass with a white-gloved hand. I, of course, heard the expression clearly. He took a sip of the liquid, cleared his throat, and proceeded to talk.

"My fellow scientists, thank you for allowing me to speak with you this evening." Tesla's voice boomed through the hall. Even the elderly amongst them could hear him clearly. While he had lived in America for the past nine years, his Hungarian accent and method of speech had not altogether faded.

"I come to lecture to you tonight on new advances in the field of electricity. Even as I speak the first alternating current electric plant in the United States of America is being constructed at Niagara Falls, in New York. The falls will provide enough energy to light the entire city of Buffalo, with electricity to spare. Electricity will be cheap and plentiful. It will replace steam in the factories and gaslight on the streets. Soon our homes will be heated by electric energy."

The scientist then asked for the gaslights to be turned low so he might show a series of lantern slides depicting the great plant. When the gas was turned up, an outlandish apparatus stood in the middle of the room. Chairs squeaked and voices hummed as the assembled gathering of scientists positioned themselves for a better view.

"Gentlemen, I give you the induction coil." A large, ring-shaped piece of metal stood atop what appeared to be a tube around which wire had been tightly wound. Several feet away stood a lightning rod. He gestured to two of the more elderly of the crowd who had moved their chairs forward to further examine the device. "Please move your seats back, sirs. Otherwise I am unable to guarantee your safety."

I cannot comprehend most of what I saw at that point, but when he worked the apparatus an enormous bolt of lightning sprang from its crown to the lightning rod. I felt a tingle run through my body. Mr. Tesla explained the sensation as stray electricity in the air. Whatever it was, I must say I was quite amazed.

"So much for the parlor tricks," he exclaimed as two men threw a cloth over the apparatus. "I will also speak tonight about the new methods to which electricity may be put to use. In America, I have just patented a means by which telegraph signals may be sent through the ether. The signals can be conducted by the electricity in the upper atmosphere." The scientist paused to allow a murmur to pass through the room. "Not only will man be able to pass telegraph signals through the ether, but one day he may transmit his voice, and perhaps even pictures."

Tesla spent the next hour expounding upon one astonishing theory after another. I do not consider myself to be of small intellect, but I had a difficult time grasping much of what he had to say. Indeed, it seemed as though some of the eminent minds in attendance could not fully comprehend parts of the lecture.

I shook my head in disbelief as I filed out with the group of scientists. Transmitting signals through the air was without a doubt the most fanciful idea I had ever heard, and believe me, I've been around long enough to hear much. Still, something about this man intrigued me, so I allowed myself to follow him and a small party of scientists to Simpson's. During the part of our trek when I was in human form I detected another following behind. Any mortal nostrils could have performed this feat, for the scent of cologne that reached my nostrils when the wind shifted was quite overpowering. Another discreet admirer, perhaps, yet I sensed a different type of excitement than what was felt by the party I trailed.

Dining in such an establishment is one of the few pleasures that elude me in my present state. Still, I persuaded the captain to seat me along the wall near a large potted tree. Normally it would not have been considered a good table at this fashionable restaurant, but it suited my purposes well. Not only could I hear Tesla clearly, but the plant afforded a ready receptacle for the glass of wine and bowl of soup that I ordered. As I attempted to secret a small amount of soup away, a stranger approached my table. It was his cologne that had assaulted my senses moments earlier.

"I see you're fascinated by the great scientist." He was an American, judging by his accent and clothing. "May I sit down?" As much as I would prefer to listen to the conversation at the nearby table, I allowed him to join me in hopes that I would be able to rid myself of him quickly, one way or another.

"My name is Jack Danielson, and I represent the Buffalo Power Company." He slid into the seat opposite me, blocking my view of the great scientist. "You look like an intelligent man."

I nodded.

"I am prepared to offer you an investment opportunity in the greatest electric power plant in the world."

Another familiar scent came to my nostrils. Rat. It went strangely well with his overly pungent cologne. This man had targeted me, and I planned to make him sorry for his intrusion. "I was under the impression that this project was funded by the government and Westinghouse Electric."

The man swallowed almost imperceptibly. I could hear it. "Sir, we are a subsidiary of Westinghouse. Allow me to show you some materials." As he began to open up a small leather portfolio, a woman stopped before the table.

"Mr. Danielson," she exclaimed. Her demeanor was quite calm, if not regal, but I could sense her heart beating quickly out of anxiety. "Has my money been invested?"

"Of course. May I speak with you about dividends for a moment?" He excused himself to take the woman to the rear of the room, near the kitchen door. I focused my ears on their conversation, and was able to hear a few snippets amongst the bustle of the wait staff.

"—of course, this investment cannot pay off until the plant is operational—"

"—my son the duke will be requiring his dividend—"

"—soon—"

"—reclaim my necklace."

I let the conversation go and studied the woman's profile. Of course. I had seen her picture in the newspapers. She was a dowager duchess whose family had fallen on hard times after the death of her husband. Her son had just come into the title, and rumor was she was trying to marry him off, no doubt in expectation of offspring to carry on the title, preferably to some American heiress. Poor woman. Her son had rooms below mine, and the walls are thin for one of my powers. It seems he does not prefer the ladies at all.

A picture formed itself quickly in my mind. This Danielson was the worst sort of predator. Van Helsing and his coterie portray me as a vicious stealer of blood, but I can assure you that those who join my circle do so because deep within their hearts it is their desire. Danielson, however, was a destroyer of souls. I'm sure he mistook my old country dress and ways as a sign of gullibility and planned to take advantage of it.

The leech and his victim rejoined me. Her agitation was noticeable to even most mortals. Normally I wouldn't feel much in the way of pity for this woman. The titled rich manage and mismanage their funds over the course of generations. Most of these families find a way to keep up appearances until the next windfall arrives. Yet she was the victim of this predator who had single-handedly ruined my quiet, educational evening. I bade the duchess to rejoin her party while I took Mr. Danielson off to a quiet corner of the smoking room and convinced him that he had made a grave mistake and would be refunding the money to the investors.

It took a little more persuasion to pry the location of the necklace from him. Once I did, I couldn't get him to be quiet. He proudly told me how he had taken the necklace, promising its return to the duchess as part of a dividend payment. Instead, he would be using it to pay off a rather substantial gambling debt. His creditor had said something about using the proceeds from its sale to construct an air gun which could be disguised as a walking stick. Ingenious, but I let his rambling stop at that point. I instructed the under-handed Mr. Danielson to return to my table and finish my glass of wine. Slowly. That should hold him while I performed my errand.

I took the form of a bat and made my way to his East End lodgings. The necklace was where he said, under a floorboard. It contained a single brilliant ruby. The setting was simple, allowing the gem to shine in all its brilliance. Such a jewel would sparkle upon any woman's bosom, and it crossed my mind to simply re-treat to my rooms and keep it for myself. It would look stunning on Lucy. But I had already started other events in action, so I hung the jewel around my neck and reverted to the form of a bat, keeping to the shad-ows so the light would not flash upon the ruby.

Upon my return I found Mr. Danielson seated at my table, dutifully obeying the suggestions I had left with him. I handed him the necklace and bade him to return it to the duchess. Return it he did, but I was unprepared for the noblewoman's quite earthy reaction. She began to beat the man about the head and shoulders with her handbag with such fury that two waiters were required to separate the pair. Presently a policeman arrived and the duchess proffered her charges.

The great scientist Tesla, seemingly engrossed in calculating the volume of his coffee pot, looked up at the commotion and approached the duchess after the leech had been taken into custody. Although the inci-dent was not directly of his doing, he offered his most sincere apologies for any distress caused to her person. As he spoke, his eye was drawn to the ruby necklace dangling from her hand.

"Madam, would you allow me to examine your ruby?"

She understandably demurred.

"You may hold onto the necklace. Please, hold only the gem up to the light." He gestured in the direction of a gas lamp. He studied the stone for a long moment, inspecting the way in which the light refracted through its facets. He thanked the mystified duchess for her kindness then returned to his table, his thoughts still clearly with the ruby. Next he took a long, slow sip of coffee then proceeded to arrange the spoons at his place in precise alignment with the salt cellar. The waiter delivered a brandy snifter, the volume of which Tesla absentmindedly calculated. He took a sip, then recalculated the remaining amount of liquid. After a moment a smile began to play upon his lips, and his eyes shone with the brilliance of scientific thought.

"Gentlemen," he addressed the somewhat startled assemblage at his table, "what do you suppose would happen if you were to shine a very intense light through a ruby which has been cut so as to precisely focus that light?"

"A very focused red beam of light?" ventured one fellow.

"That could be quite useful during your magic lantern slide presentations," concluded another.

"The world is not ready." Tesla sighed as the waiter refreshed his snifter, then addressed the man. "Did you know that you have precisely forty-two ounces of brandy left in your decanter? I'll double your gratuity if you can divide that equally between the glasses at this table." There was a hearty laugh all around as I retreated to my own place to settle up my bill. My heart sank as I noticed the waiter had refilled my wine glass and brought a fresh, steaming bowl of soup.

Ah, well. I would simply leave a generous tip and explain that a recent sea journey had left my stomach unsettled. I had learned that there are as many excuses as there are long, lonely nights in London.

An Essay on Containment

GENE DeWEESE

(From the Secret Journal of Radoslav Coulson)

London
August 7, 1893.

I greatly fear there will soon be trouble for us all. The so-called Count has made landfall, I know not where.

For days I have sensed his approach, so powerful is his aura. But it is not his power that is the source of our peril, it is his damnable ego, his utter lack of discipline.

We have known of his existence for more than a century, so perhaps the current dilemma is as much of our own making as it is of his. We should have acted decisively decades ago and not continued to place naive confidence in his obvious intellect and the instinct for survival that we all share. It is apparent that our quiet counsel, even our more pointed warnings, have gone unheeded. Had he paid the slightest attention to our words, he would at least have contacted one of us to help prepare the way for his journey, not one of them, with whom he must always be on guard, ready with justifications for behaviors that to them are bizarre but to us are only what our nature demands.

But perhaps I am being unduly alarmist. Perhaps those very contacts will cause him to apprehend the danger more clearly, to begin at last to act with the discretion that is essential in dealing with the ever-increasing perils of the modern world. Such, at least, is my hope.

Nonetheless, we shall begin our preparations immediately. I only hope that our skills have not atrophied in the decades since we were last called upon to make extensive use of them.

August 9, 1893.

Once it was determined by consensus which of our unwitting accomplices to employ in this matter, it required only a single night to verify that our choice was viable. The extensive conditioning he was given nearly half a century ago in his youth still holds sway. He has become precisely the person we intended, precisely the person we knew we would someday need. Now preparations for our little drama can begin in earnest.

August 12, 1893.

As I had hoped and expected, the initial phase went remarkably well.

Indeed, it is at times like this that I can understand what drives the Count to engage in his reckless behavior. There is undeniably an incomparable satisfaction to be taken in exercising one's mental powers, causing memories to shift and alter by mere whispered suggestions in the night. As I observe the intricate patterns of change we weave within the minds of our oblivious subjects, I can imagine that the feeling we experience is not unlike that which their master musicians achieve when giving a virtuoso performance for an appreciative audience.

My only regret is that for our virtuoso performances

there can be no audience save ourselves unless it becomes necessary for the subjects to act out the scenario dictated by those deceitful memories. Contrariwise, my dearest hope is that, for the sake of us all, such actions are never required and that the memories themselves, untended, will gradually retrogress, unnoticed, until the minds that housed them are left only with dull reality.

We shall see.

August 17, 1893.

Carfax!

The fool has actually moved into Carfax, bringing with him not one but *fifty* boxes of his precious native soil, a needless luxury at best! If he persists in such recklessness, he might as well shout his nature from the rooftops!

I should not have delayed even these few days. I should not have allowed myself to entertain for even a moment those same false hopes that had already kept us from acting for nearly a century. I should have paid stricter heed not only to the power and the undisciplined nature of his aura but also to his shameful record of almost mindless self-indulgence. I should have seen that, like anyone, he is shaped by his past experience, and that *his* past experience consists of centuries of indulging his every whim without concern for the effects. For centuries he "lived" alone in a backward and isolated area where superstitions of all kinds were so deeply ingrained in the mortal populace that no one would even *think* of defying even the most ludicrously unlikely creatures who claimed, let alone openly demonstrated, supernatural powers. Drink a little of their blood while they slumber unaware, steal one of their daughters and bend her to your will, causing her to rise in the night in answer to your silent summons, and they cower in their hovels, scrupulously avoiding any show of defiance or even of discontent for fear that anything short of servile obedience would only worsen their situation.

The civilized world which he has invaded—*our* world—is far less deferential, as he is already discovering. If he alone were involved, we would not devote a moment of time to his plight. If he wished to draw attention to himself and himself alone, I would wish him well and quietly await his demise, which would surely soon be upon him. But his antics, his foolish attempts to "live" as he had "lived" in that welter of mindless superstition that is Transylvania, will call attention to us all. Here in the civilized world our strength—and our safety!—lies not in our modestly superhuman powers but in our anonymity, in the fact that our kind is rarely believed to be more than the fevered imaginings of superstitious fools and that when one of us *is* found to exist, he is easily destroyed if only you follow certain arcane and nonsensical rituals. If ever we lose that advantage, our already meager numbers will quickly dwindle to nothing.

Tonight it begins.

Sept. 1, 1893.

It is with considerable relief that I record the fact that our elaborate preparations have not been in vain. Dr. Seward, one of many who benefited from our recent ministrations, questioned none of his recently acquired memories when he was called in to examine the unfortunate young woman the Count has become enamored of. Nor did he hesitate to immediately contact our chosen accomplice, ostensibly his "old friend and master" from school days and, fortuitously, an expert in the very maladies of the blood from which the young woman is suffering.

Dr. Van Helsing arrives tomorrow, and I am confident that, with our clandestine assistance, he will meet with spectacular success in ridding the land of this creature that menaces us all.

Berserker

NANCY KILPATRICK

Here, it is so unlike your homeland. The land where your blood and that of your father and his father before him rusts the soil. Where you can rest untormented, and be at peace.

But this place! Even the brilliance of daylight cannot disguise an obscenity: the parody of life. Around you swells a perpetually flowing, ever-renewing river of unawareness from which you intend to slake your thirst at will. But rampant mindlessness offends you. Do they not deserve your scorn?

Such pathetic trees! Scrawny as the Cockney children racing by. Feeble roots cling to the island's soil. So bare, as if stripped of life's nourishment. These denizens of the modern have cleared and clipped the bushes as though natural, wild beauty is repugnant. What a society! What a mockery! Cutting vegetation into the shape of animals! These mortals have too much time on their hands! Time is their enemy, even as it has become your friend.

So this is what you have read of, what the British call "civilization." A "park." You came to this place for several reasons, not the least of which is that you seek refuge, a temporary respite, a few moments where you may recapture for refreshment's sake the comfort of nature's calming familiarity. But it is a sham! An illusion. You have been tricked. This is not the verdant growth of your homeland. The tight green carpet beneath your feet screams in distress. These short hairs resemble the preposterous muttonchops stuck to the cheeks of the mortal males surrounding you. They look ridiculous, foolish, and yet these beings have the nerve to call your countrymen barbarians! Madmen! Once you have supped on their blood, and they have tasted your wrath, truly they will come to know what the word "barbarian" means.

"Good day!"

"Good day," you reply to the just-so gentleman in the summer frock coat, accompanied by a timid, plain woman and two frightened children.

He and his family stop, wanting to continue this pointless exchange with a stranger. "The weather has turned for the better," he remarks.

"England possesses a most fortuitous clime," you comment.

"Yes," the wife responds nervously, glancing furtively at her husband as though seeking approval for her vocalization.

She is plainer, that is certain, yet she resembles Lucy—fair hair and eyes, arched brows, high cheekbones, long, slim throat. . . .

The man leans upon his ivory-tipped cane, content with his lot in life, the world his oyster, it seems. "I take it you are from Europe." His face smiles, yet you are keenly aware of the distrust beneath this facade. He has encountered a foreigner. One alien. He must assess you rapidly, fit you neatly to a slot in order to "know" you.

"Indeed," you say, "you are correct. I am Transylvanian."

The woman, eyes dulled by incomprehension, stifles a gasp. The girl child a yawn. The boy his urge to run with the pack of children from the lower class, their shirttails flying, short breeches dirty. Children his mother looks on with disapproval.

The man repeats, "Transylvania," scanning a mental map. You see that he has pegged you. "Eastern European," he now says confidently. "Northeastern Balkans, correct me if I am wrong."

"You are not wrong," you inform him, although the satisfied nod is annoying. He feels he now has you classified and can rest. He wears the mask of intelligence laced with safety and certainty. A veil of correctness that hides control. Control born of fear.

Perhaps you should inform him that this meaningless exchange will not assure that blood remains in his veins. That if you had a mind to bleed him dry like an enormous leech, you would do so, could do so. His destiny rests in your hands.

"James Holbrook," he says, extending a hand. "Barrister-at-law."

You shake his hand, the current custom here, adopted from North America apparently, and revel in the warmth of this mortal's flesh and the throbbing cauldron ablaze beneath that epidermis. These sensations cause you to tremble slightly with anticipation. "Count Dracula," you inform him.

His thin eyebrows lift. He is impressed with your station, as he should be, and yet more relieved. Here he is, in the presence of what he deems to be his own class, no, a class to which he aspires. "My wife Elizabeth," he says informally, adding, "my son John junior, and my daughter Caroline," and he pats the little girl on the top of her head of yellow curls. Caroline stares up at you with large eyes that provide no challenge, since she is already under the natural spell of childhood.

"It is a pleasure," the wife says, beginning a curtsy,

which she curtails because of indecision. She is not quite certain what to do with foreign royalty.

In the distance, a familiar howl, one you recognize. The sound sends a shiver through the woman. She is as one entrapped behind a glass prison, a prison whose panes you could easily crash through and shatter—

"I take it you are a visitor to our England," the man says crisply. "Am I correct?" He asks questions as if they are statements, as though he is in a court-room, before a judge, arguing a case rather than engaging in a dialogue.

"I am."

"We are very proud of our city of London. And the gardens here. I hope you've been enjoying your stay in our fair land, taking in the sites, the marvels of the modern, civilized world." His hand sweeps with a gesture of ownership, as though he not only possesses but has created all of which he speaks.

You have been on this unfamiliar soil but a short while and yet you far prefer the ruggedness that is your heritage to the cultivated "marvels" he so obviously idolizes. In Transylvania, the harsh beauty reminds you that survival is always a struggle. The environment it-self forces a warrior to be alert to danger, rather than lulling him into a torpor which leads to demise. This man is surrounded by a hundred dangers yet has con-vinced himself he is invincible. Your attitude, the one you were born with, the one you died with, the one you continue to rely on in this existence is in tune with nature—for are not the animals, even the insects, on guard always, alert to predators? That is nature's way. What is wrong with these Englishmen that you can walk among them, speak with them, touch them, and their every sense is dead to danger?

They laugh and talk and ignore you, other than the odd glance or remark focused on your foreignness, which always fosters comments to prove they are supe-rior. They delude themselves with silly thoughts that suggest supremacy. It is their weakness, and will be their downfall.

"Have you been to Piccadilly?" the wife ventures.

You stare into her faded eyes, a bold gesture, and watch as conflicting emotions dance within her— she is trapped by your gaze. Attraction and repulsion vie for position. Paralysis is the outcome.

The man instinctively feels this threat and takes her elbow, which causes her to look away. Her cheeks redden with embarrassment.

"Well then," the man says. "We shall be off. The children want to ride the carousel, you know. And we would hate to impinge."

You feel a twinge of respect for him now. At least he has the sense to recognize peril in one regard.

He tips his hat, and you return the gesture, glancing at him, bowing slightly to his wife, who seems afraid to look at you again, and that causes you to smile. The distracted children are like barely ripe plums, not ready yet for the brandy maker. But the woman . . .

The family turns by rote at the cue of the man and begins to wander toward the carousel. You watch them stop at the cotton candy vendor. The children receive a cone each of pink sugar fluff. The wife surreptitiously glances back in your direction.

"Yes, my lovely," you whisper. "I could easily shatter the walls of your prison and you would belong to me as you so long to."

A delicious look of lust and dread flickers through her eyes, and she turns away abruptly.

You laugh, drawing stares from the crowd.

So many warm-bloods! Their numbers spiral to infinity, like drops of water in the ocean, stars in the sky. They bask in the sunshine, light which has, over half a millennium, become increasingly abhorrent to you. It would not surprise you if soon you can no longer tolerate these fiery rays and prefer to sequester yourself entirely in the indirect light of the moon. You are so

unlike these mortals, who believe the light beneficent.
Who have recently created sunlight in small globes of
glass and this, like their other inventions, leads them
to believe they are conquering nature. All in an attempt to master death. But it is you who are the Master
of Death. And you have done this by adhering to your
true essence, something these peasants cannot imagine.

That they should envision themselves greater than
nature, that they believe they can control eventualities
with their industries, both amazes and amuses you, the
latter in a grim way. You survey the skyline of London,
blotted with inky smoke from their factories, fumes
that choke the air, and you wonder: are they insane?

They cannot breathe. They die of illnesses brought
about by their own wicked habits, and yet they place
such childish faith in science—even now, they believe
they can replace the blood in the veins that you have
drained, blood that calls to you as the lark calls to her
mate. Oh, these straight-backed fools! The strict and
serious men arrayed in silly top hats, the prim parasol-
carrying women who believe themselves better than
one another, their rosy-cheeked children skipping
across the lawns as if they will never age. As if their
blood will never cease flowing through their veins . . .
and into yours.

You cannot even pity them. Are they not less worthy of compassion than these caged animals you approach? The mortals ignore their carnal instincts while
you indulge yours. They are to you as the beasts are
to them—inferior. It is your right by virtue of your
superiority to take them. They will become your eternal storehouse at which you will sate your hungers.

They call this park the London Zoological Gardens.
To either side are structures the living have built to
amuse themselves. Such romantic, pastel buildings,
with domed roofs and arched wrought iron gates.
There! Close up. The electrical carousel, the painted
ponies dipping and lifting to the music, in imitation of

the horses you once rode into battle. It amazes you that barely more than a decade ago, in your part of the world, a clever inventor generated electrical power for the first time and it is that which drives this frivolous machinery. This is yet one more indication of the inevitable downfall of this century.

At least there are the remnants of nature. The flora, though cultivated, inspires you. Color splashes the lawns, the flowers still as the dead, their brilliance enhanced to your eyes by the growing darkness as the sky following you becomes overcast.

Ahead, an abomination! You are assaulted by sounds and smells. Caged wildlife! A horrifying concept. You see one animal familiar to you. You reach back into your memory where this furry humped spitter emerges from a time long ago when your father offered you and your handsome brother to your mortal enemies, the Turkish Ottomans. He betrayed you to save himself, abandoning you in a foreign land with strange customs and intense cruelties. You learned a lesson well at a vulnerable age, one you have carried with you all of your long existence—none are trustworthy!

A pachyderm from India is chained to a spike. This enormous beast you have read of, have seen sketches of, yet have never before experienced. Dusty grey flesh, pig-like eyes, ears that could be wings, a snout functioning independent of the rest of its body. And the scent! Sharper than that of the camel. This beast emits a strong mix of the hay it consumes and the natural result of that consumption. It bays, but not like a horse, more like a horn. This giant of a creature even now recognizes you in the crowd, turns towards you, rearing back on legs like tree trunks, then kneels before you. . . .

You pass by quickly. There are other, stranger sights here, and you have a mission.

Birds of all sizes and colors flutter in the aviary. And the lion, ruler supreme of the jungles of the world, roars in your direction, shaking its mane, bowing, prepared to relinquish his reign to one supreme.

These wild beasts that once roamed free on the earth are now caged in spaces far too small for such majestic life. If you were capable of pity, you would pity them. Where *Homo sapiens* invade, the extinction of a species follows.

This is the natural extension of Darwin's theory. He is an Englishman, one of their own, and yet you know they have not paid heed to his work. But you have. The origin of the species is linked with natural selection. These feral creatures are doomed. Only the strongest survive, and you know in your heart that you prevail absolute over humanity, even as they rule the beasts.

The animals are fearful. They sense you. Sense the danger. Their muscles lock in terror, their eyes bulge. The felines pace with tension and the airborne take frantic flight. These reactions alone make them superior to the stunned men surrounding them.

Your acute hearing identifies a sound you heard but moments ago, so familiar. It is the reason you have ventured so far into the land of the living on this sun-drenched day. The low panting emanates from the far end of a row of hideous metal cages. He is confined, the area cramped for one of his proud nature. You have command over all animals, including this kindred spirit—he will do your bidding.

The wolf pauses, sensing your approach. He turns to face you. His nostrils flare. He recognizes a species akin to his own, but not of his pack. Indeed, he has no pack, no mate. Like you, he is far from home soil. He is alone.

"All the way from America, they brought him, they did." The keeper, a fat man with a suit official but too small, looks at you, hoping to impress you with his knowledge. "Fearsome beast, ain't he? Tore a man's heart right from his chest in a minute, he did."

"Is that so?" you say calmly.

"Oh, absolutely! That's the wolf for you. They've rid the continent of them a hundred years ago for that very reason. That's why they had to bring this one over the ocean."

The wolf glares at the keeper and growls low in his throat. Clearly he understands the meaning of the human's words. His feral odor becomes sharp to your nostrils, betraying his fury.

The gray wolf of the timberlands stares at you, savvy to your understanding. The glint in his eye tells you that his wild nature has not been tainted by years in captivity.

"Name's Berserker." The keeper interrupts your thoughts. "On account of his being so deranged and all."

"A fitting name," you say, "for clearly he is not predictable."

The wolf's ears prick in your direction, for he knows you speak of him and to him. He knows you know him deeply. The madness in his eyes is the spark of passion that aligns with your own.

Suddenly, the keeper reaches for a wooden pole. He jams it between the bars. Berserker growls low, and snaps at the wood, his large teeth gouging the birch.

"See what I mean?" the keeper says, jabbing at Berserker again with the pole. The wood slams hard into the animal's furry side, causing him to yelp. Fear and fury claw the airwaves as his savage scent turns sharp with this provocation.

Patience, I tell him. *Your revenge will be sweet.*

"In Transylvania," you say, distracting the keeper, "such beasts freely roam the forests still."

"That right? Well, this one shoulda been shot long ago. He's a menace, he is."

You survived Europe's encroaching civilization. Planned destruction forced these wondrous animals further back into the wilderness until their numbers became few. You know intimately of their habits, though, for you have spent centuries among them. They are not the werewolves of mythology, nor the killers of legend, but gentle, timid mammals, akin to the dog—indeed, you have kept them as pets on occasion. It is rare they kill anything as large as a man, and then only out of desperation. They nurture their young, travel together for protection, the strongest male with the strongest female, working in tandem to defend the pack and its territory.

The moronic keeper grabs up a slab of raw meat in his fist and slaps it through the bars. Berserker sniffs at the stale flesh, then licks it twice for the blood. He stops, raises his head, and stares at you, the insanity in him the result of incarceration. *Soon,* you assure him, *you will have fresher flesh, and dine with a lost hunger borne of exertion.*

Berserker nods. He bows his graceful head slightly, ears pressed back against his skull. His tail droops between his legs. Now, he haunches down on all fours, watching you, waiting.

"See the way it is?" the keeper says. "Let 'im know you ain't scared. Show 'im who's the master, ain't that right gov'ner?"

"As you say," you tell the stupid man, whose flabby throat you would tear out yourself were there not the crowds still littering the grounds.

Berserker is a noble brute. He is so much like you, frustrated by his fate. He longs to find purpose again. He longs for the hunt. He longs for revenge on the weak and the stupid, and to bring down the brazen. Given a fair altercation between the two, this keeper would not survive. All three of you know that to be true.

Berserker stares into your eyes, his yellow orbs speckled with hope and despair. You watch the pupils dilate then contract, and again. He bares his teeth, but just once, then you hear the whimper of submission as he bends his head even lower, muzzle resting on the floor of the cage, eyes still fixed on yours.

You laugh in delight, thrilled to find one unbroken here, amidst the tamed.

The keeper jerks his head around to stare at you, askance.

"A storm approaches," you say. "One that will devastate this city of London, and this country, leaving dead and near dead in its wake."

The keeper's small eyes turn fearful. He follows your gaze to the blackened sky. Lightning cuts through the darkness, diving toward the ground near his feet, startling him. Thunder rocks the earth you stand on.

The mortals scurry for cover. The keeper turns to run, crying after him, "Best to find safety!" and then he is gone.

Every animal in this evil zoological garden responds to the elements. The pungency of their scents clog the air as the storm rampages towards you. You hear them screech and roar in terror and hope. The finches in the aviary fly hysterically, like bats. The larger animals pace and stomp, trembling. Berserker twitches, on his feet now; you have captured his soul. He and the storm become aligned in agitation. You see the ruthlessness in him and it cheers you.

These animals have more sense than the men fleeing for cover. They know where danger lies, and where it does not. The mortals have much to learn from what they deem inferior life-forms. But they are prideful, willful. And alienated. These traits spell their doom.

"We will stake our claim to their thin blood!" you cry, and Berserker throws back his head and howls in tandem.

Your laughter equals the explosion of thunder. Oh, how the dark rage buries the blinding sunlight! Berserker paces, races back and forth in his prison, excited, eager for freedom. His wild eyes are alive, brilliant with awareness of your authority. The earth trembles as if in awe, sensing he will do your bidding.

In the century in which you were born, the French deemed what lay above as the macrocosm, the greater world or universe, reflected here on this tiny earth as the microcosm. You are in touch with this reality that equates the inner with the outer, the small and insignificant with the grand and incomprehensible. It is the source of your strength and to draw from it is your right.

You contemplate the earth itself, so abundant with the flicker of warm-blooded creatures. Their metallic scent seeps through their wet pores, wafting along humid air in a tantalizing manner—the scent of steaming blood! In the blackness that has descended, you see them here and there, glittering stars with the added dimension of being aromatic.

You have always acknowledged nature. Respected her. You know you are her equal. Nature is, perhaps, all you respect, for you believe only in the natural order. You are the culmination of Darwin's evolution. The one who has evolved over time to become the most advanced life-form on the planet. You are master of this terran universe. The English naturalist would have been thrilled to meet you.

These mortals would declare that such notions disease the mind, although you do not permit dis-ease to infiltrate your crystal awareness. Berserker is a worthy assistant because beyond all else, he is like you: adaptable and cunning, dominant traits imbedded in your genes as Herr Mendel discovered when he played with peas. Dominant traits which are the foundation of potency and preeminence!

The storm crashes around you, drawn to you, for you are the source of division. Berserker leaps at the bars that confine him, as if crying "Death or Freedom!"

Over 400 years of existence have developed your organic talents. You will adapt to England. But England will never adapt to you. You will infect these bleeders as the Frenchman Pasteur predicted. You will spread through the population like a germ, a plague darker than black, leaving them helpless, unable to resist. Imprisoning them in their own weakness.

Your laughter expands, drowning out the thunder, and Berserker begins to howl in earnest, bashing his body against the bars, drawing blood. The smell of it intoxicates you. The mortals for miles around tremble at the unfamiliar sound and scent of wildness that strikes a primal cord.

The wolf's victory cry delights your ears, riding sharp and crisp through the wind. You are a pair, in unison, like lovers, or father and son, master and slave. Two warriors, unstoppable.

You raise a hand to the sky and lightning follows where you point, splitting a birch down the middle. You are a warlord now, as you were *vivode* throughout your existence. One deemed so fierce—mad even—that your countrymen fear you still. They learned to respect and fear you in the past, when you drove the Ottomans back from your boundaries, back over the Carpathian Mountains, back to the land where they belonged. They respected and feared you for preserving the law, for enforcing Christian values. Did you not punish the dishonest, those who would steal and lie and cheat for personal gain? And even as much as those you ruled respected and feared you, they loved you. Then, and now. Your reputation survived, even as has your body in this supple, corporeal form you continue. You are a hero to your countrymen. The British who have colonized so much of the world are simply modern Ottomans. You defeated the turbaned ones, you will erode from within this society that wears the high hat symbolizing the pinnacle of civilization.

You are Ruler of Transylvania, King of Terrors,

Lord of the Undead. You are invincible. That truth causes your lips to split apart and a long hiss to escape your throat, swirling through the air like a current that will crush everything in its wake, mingling with Berserker's mad howls. The wind whips the soul of every soon-to-be corpse in this park. It slices through to the subconscious Freud postulates. But humanity's creative inventors and astute thinkers cannot save them!

You have read that Kierkegaard preached an acceptance of fate, which includes suffering. That philosophy is repugnant to you. It is Nietzsche who speaks your creed. You and you alone are of paramount importance. The prattle of Marx and Engels will dissolve in the vapors of time—there is little strength in a collective without a strong leader. Machiavelli, your contemporary, knew this. He spoke from your era, where politics sired all.

Berserker's instincts are aligned with your own. He understands all too well the rules of power and control as crucial for survival. He cannot cower at your just fury because he shares this reaction. You cannot bear to see him entrapped this way. It is not sentiment which inspires you but a sense of reestablishing order.

These mortals will pay for their insolence! Let them gloat for now. Their telegraphs and telephones and phonographs. Their printing presses and cameras. Their refinement of pistols and rifles and gunpowder. None of it will help them! All will incinerate in the blaze of a power greater than their own. All of their knowledge will crumble to dust.

Your knowledge has been gleaned over many lifetimes, knowledge that covers the spectrum of life, that totals the grains of sand on all of the beaches of the world! Mortal philosophy is correct in one thing—they will taste divine suffering through their servitude to you, their master. Your violent kiss will bequeath this destiny to them. They will languish in the knowledge that they will be like you but never be your equal.

With the strength of ten men, you direct the forces of nature. Your hand sprouts talons that claw the lock on the cage. Instantly, sparks shoot through you. In the deluge, the metal sizzles and melts. You grasp it in your hand, snap the lock, and pull open the door of the prison.

Berserker does not hesitate. In one leap, he is on the ground, before his master. "Go!" you tell him, mentally directing his instincts toward Whitby and Hillingham. Toward the glass that separates you from Lucy, as if such tangible reality can stand in your way!

Berserker swivels his head to stare in the direction of the keeper. "When you have served me and my work is done," you remind him, "then and only then will you will reap your reward!"

He hesitates but a moment. Then, swiftly, he sprints over the drowning grass and into the trees. Free. Alive. As lucid as can be.

Curtain Call

GARY A. BRAUNBECK

(From the unpublished papers of Charles Fort)

I have been, for most of my life, a collector of notes on subjects of great diversity—such as deviations from concentricity in the lunar crater Copernicus, to the great creature Melanicus and the super-bat upon whose wings it broods over the affairs of Man, as well as stationary meteor-radiants, the reported growth of hair on the bald head of a mummy, the appearance of purple Englishmen, instances of amphibians and blood raining down from the heavens, apparitions, phantoms, the damned, the excluded, wild talents, new lands, and "Did the girl swallow the octopus?"

But my liveliest interest is not so much in things as in the relations of things. I find now, in the twilight of my life, as I pour over the endless data that I have assembled throughout my days, that I think more and more about the alleged pseudo-relations we call "coincidences." What if these events, rather than being happenstance, are the final result of great, secret, dark machinations of the Universe interacting with the subconscious to produce an event or events which guide humanity down certain roads its members were destined to take?

I am writing now of a brief period I spent in London when I was thirty-six, in the early months of 1912 (nearly ten years before I decided to move there), and of a most singularly peculiar bookshop, its even more peculiar proprietor, and a bit of London Theatre history which none before me has ever recorded.

I was staying at a very comfortable rooming house in Bedford Place, just around the corner from the British Museum in Great Russell Street (since my visit to London was solely to search through the museum's vast archives of manuscripts, the location of my rooms could not have been more advantageous for my purposes). On this particular day—kept from my research at the museum by a cryptic note delivered to my room early that morning—I was exploring the narrower, less-often traveled streets of the vicinity, in search of an address which seemed more and more to me a flight of fancy in the mind of whomever had composed the note, when the heavens opened wide and within moments the rain was pounding down violently. I was in Little Russell Street, just behind the church that fronts on Bloomsbury Way, and there was no way for me to find immediate shelter from the storm. The address written on the note was obviously someone's idea of a joke, for I had been up and down this street no less than three times.

So why had I not noticed the little bookshop before?

It seemed that as soon as the sun was obscured by the rain clouds, the tiny edifice simply appeared out of the rain, set between a baker's and a haberdashery where before there had been only, I am certain, a cramped alleyway.

I shall state here that, despite the path of research my life has been dedicated to, I am not a man who is given to either hallucination or flights of fancy. I neither believe nor disbelieve anything. I have shut myself away from the rocks and wisdom of ages, as well as the so-called great teachers of all time; I close the front door to Christ and Einstein and at the back door hold out a welcoming hand to rains of frogs and lands hidden above the clouds and the paths of lost spirits. "Come this way, let's see if you can explain yourselves," I say unto these phenomena, always taking care to look upon them with a cold clinician's eye. I cannot accept that the products of minds are subject-matter for belief systems. I neither saw nor did not see a bookshop hidden away on this street. It simply *was,* at that moment, where the moment before it was not.

I crossed the street and entered the place, nearly soaked through.

The first thing that assaulted my senses was the so-very-right *smell* of the place. Perhaps you have to be a true lover of books to understand what I mean by that, but the comforting, intoxicating, friendly scent of bindings and old paper was nectar to my soul.

I called out, asking if anyone were there. When no response was forthcoming, I removed my coat, draped it on the rack near the door, and—after patting down my hair and shaking off the remnants of rain from my shoes and sleeves—proceeded to browse through the offerings.

The walls were lined from floor to ceiling with sagging shelves full of books, and I could see at a glance that, though the stock contained everything from academic texts to the usual classics, its primary focus was on matters philosophical and occult; everywhere I turned there were books such as Agrippa's *De Occulta Philosophia,* the ancient notes of Anaxagoras of Clazomenae detailing his conclusions that the Earth was spherical, *The Gospel of Sri Ramakrishna,* the Hindu *Rig Veda,* the poems of Ovid, the plays of Aeschylus, Lucan's *De Bello Civilia.* . . . My heart beat with tremendous anticipation. What treasures would I find here?

It was only as I was admiring an ancient copy of the *Popol Vuh* which sat under a glass case in the center of a great table that I became aware that I was no longer alone. How I knew this I could not then say, though what was soon to follow would make the reason clear.

I turned and saw the proprietor.

Though he appeared to be only a few inches taller than I, there was, nonetheless, a sense of power and great, massive presence about him. His fierce, dark eyes stared out at me from underneath thick eyebrows that met over his knife of a nose. His heavy white moustache drooped down past the corners of his mouth, drawing my attention at once to his red and seemingly swollen lips, which were flagrant and somehow femininely seductive against the glimmer of his face. Though he was obviously an older gentleman, he carried himself with the grace and power of a man fifteen years my junior.

"Mr. Fort," he said, in a heavily accented, full, rich *basso* voice the New York Opera would have swooned to have sing upon its stage, "I am so very pleased you were able to accept the invitation." He offered his hand. "It is a great honor to meet a gentleman such as yourself, who shares my interest in matters of data that Science has excluded."

I shook his hand. His grip was steel. I winced from the great pressure and the pain it sent shooting up my arm.

"I beg your pardon," he said, releasing my hand. "I sometimes forget that, in my enthusiasm, my handshake can be a bit . . ."

"Formidable?" I said, massaging my fingers.

His smile was slow in appearing but total in its chilling effectiveness. "What a kind way to put it." He turned and started toward a door near the back of the shop. "If you'll be kind enough to follow me, sir."

I did, though somewhat reluctantly. After all, what did I know of this fellow or his intent? True, in my studies I had come across many strange tales told by sometimes stranger individuals, but (at this point in my life, at least) I rarely had to meet any of these people face to face. Still, I must admit, my curiosity was stronger than either my anxiety or trepidation.

I need speak in a bit more detail of the cryptic note which was delivered to my room as I was readying myself for the day's research at the museum. It arrived in a heavy envelope which contained—aside from the letter itself—several newspaper clippings, which I will summarize momentarily. It read as follows: "My Dear Mr. Fort: I know that you will read the enclosed with great interest, but also with your Intellectual's eye. Come to the address written below before the noon hour and I will give you irrefutable proof that these incidents are, indeed, based on fact and not myth. I urge you to keep this appointment."

Below the body of the writing were these words: *Denn die Todten reiten schnell* ("For the dead travel fast," a line from Burger's "Lenore").

The letter was signed only: *A.S.*

Having read with great delight Mr. Jules Verne's famous novel, I found myself smiling at the thought that I might encounter the fictitious Arne Saknussemm at the end of my own "journey."

The clippings came from newspapers such as *Lloyd's Sunday News,* the *Brooklyn Eagle, Ottawa Free Press,* and the *Yorkshire Evening Argus.* All of them detailed stories of various bodies which were discovered to have died from massive blood loss—often the bodies were drained totally of their blood supply. All of the deaths had another fact in common: each victim, though at first thought to have been the target of a robbery-related assault, was found to have "tiny puncture marks" near or on a major artery. Sometimes there were more than one pair of these marks (a body found in Chicago had at least thirty such puncture marks on her legs) but, in each case, saliva was found within these punctures, leading, naturally, to the conclusion that each of these victims had been killed by "mentally disturbed" individuals who suffered "the delusion of vampirism."

My hope is by now you will understand why my curiosity overpowered any anxiety I might have been experiencing.

The proprietor opened the door and led me down a long stone stairway which emptied out into a surprisingly cavernous basement. Lighting a kerosene lantern, he proceeded to lead me down a slope in the floor to an area which I can only describe as being a sort-of hidden theatre; there were a few rows of seats (which smelled of old fire) and a raised stage, more than a few of whose boards still bore the black marks of a fire.

As I sat where the proprietor directed me, I noticed the insignia of the Lyceum Theatre on the back of the seat in front of me, and realized at once that these seats—as well as portions of the stage before me—had been scavenged from the great fire which destroyed the Lyceum in 1830. (That they might have been scavenged from the wreckage of the 1803 fire did not, at the time, seem a possibility to me.)

The proprietor wandered away into the darkness, the light from the lantern growing smaller and more dim as he made his way through a curtain off to the side. I heard him moving around backstage, then a few squeaking sounds, a cough, and then the curtain fronting the stage rose slowly to reveal a series of chairs and small podiums, each on different levels, arranged in a manner befitting a "dramatic reading"—what is often called "Reader's Theatre" in America.

There was, however, only one person on the stage as the lights came up, and he was neither standing nor seated behind one of the podiums.

He was in a wheelchair, downstage center, illuminated by a spotlight from above. His face was half in shadow, even after he raised his head to look out at his "audience."

Newspaper clippings of blood-drained victims.

The Lyceum Theatre.

A.S.

I knew even before he spoke in his watered-down but still musical Irish brogue that I was in the presence of none other than Abraham—better known as "Bram"—Stoker.

"Mr. Fort," he said, barely above a whisper. "Thank you for coming. Have you paper and pen?"

"I do," I called from the darkness of the theatre, then produced said items from my jacket pocket. (Fortunately the light from the stage bled forward enough that I could see to make notes.)

"Excellent," said Mr. Stoker, then wiped at his mouth with a dark-stained handkerchief he clutched in one shaking, palsied hand.

I knew—as did many of his admirers—that Stoker had been in seclusion for the last few years. Ill health was rumored—a rumor which I saw now to be sadly true (though whether or not he was suffering from the final stages of untreated syphilis I had not the medical knowledge to ascertain). I can tell you that the rumored feeblemindedness was true, for several times during his narrative did Mr. Stoker begin muttering gibberish for minutes on end, until he would fall into something like a brief trance from which he would emerge lucid and articulate.

"I am a great admirer of your writings," he said from his place on the stage. "You must assemble your articles into a book for publication one day."

"That is my intent," I replied, suddenly aware of the single bead of perspiration that was snaking down my spine.

"May I suggest, then," said Stoker, "that you call your work *The Book of the Damned*?"

"Why?"

He laughed. It was not a pleasant sound. "Because all so-called 'unnatural phenomena' comes from damned places, sir. Speak of damned places and you speak of places where powerful emotional forces have been penned up. Have you ever been within the walls of a prison, Mr. Fort? Where the massed feelings of hatred, deprivation, claustrophobia, and brutalization have seeped into the very stones? One can *feel* it. The emotions resonate. They seethe, trapped, waiting for release, waiting to be given *form*, Mr. Fort. What you might call an 'unconscious confluence' were you to label it in one of your articles.

"You now sit in the remnants of one such 'damned place,' sir: the charred remains of the Lyceum Theatre. These stage boards, the curtain above me, the very seats which surround you and the one in which you now sit, were discovered by myself in a basement storage area of the Lyceum during my time there as manager—along, of course, with Sir Henry Irving, my own personal vampire."

He spoke Irving's name with a level of disgust that was absolutely chilling to hear. Even though Stoker attempted to hide his true feelings about Irving in his biography of the famous actor, it was now well known that, during the twenty-seven years Stoker worked as stage manager at the Lyceum, Irving treated him little better than a slave, paying him so very little that, upon Irving's death, Stoker was forced to borrow money from friends and relatives in order to survive; when he was no longer able to borrow money, he was forced to write such drivel as his latest (and, I suspicioned, what would be his *last*) novel, *The Lair of the White Worm.*

I could not help but share the sorrow of this broken man on the stage before me; there had been a potential for true literary greatness there, once, but no more . . . and the late Sir Henry Irving was as much to blame for that as were Stoker's so-called "personal indulgences."

"Remember as you listen, Mr. Fort: emotions resonate. They seethe, trapped, waiting for release, waiting
to be given form."

I wrote down his words, though they seemed more
the ramblings of a mind surrendering to the body's
sicknesses.

Stoker coughed into his handkerchief once again.
Even from my place in the "audience," I could see that
he was coughing up blood. His handkerchief was useless to him now. I took my own, unused handkerchief
from my pocket and rose to approach the stage and
give it to him, but was stopped by the appearance of
a great, dark wolf by Stoker's side.

It wandered on from stage left and seated itself next
to his wheelchair. Even sitting on its haunches, it was
nearly as tall as he. I had never seen such a magnificent
and terrifying creature in all my life. It looked upon
me with pitiless eyes that, in the light of the stage,
glowed a deep, frightening crimson.

I returned the handkerchief to my pocket and took
my seat once again.

"You'll come to no harm, Mr. Fort," said Stoker,
reaching out to rub the fur at the nape of the great
wolf's neck. The beast growled contentedly. I thought
of a line from Stoker's most famous novel, about the
Children of the Night, and what sweet music they
made.

What follows is my transcription of Stoker's narrative. I have taken the liberty of removing the
sometimes-prolonged pauses he took between words,
as well as excising those instances where his crumbling
mind led him down rambling paths of incompre-
hensibility.

I ask only that you remember this was a man who
could have achieved true literary greatness, but who is
now only remembered as the author of "that dreadful
vampire book."

Even now, I still sorrow at the thought of What Might Have Been, had Fate been kinder to him.

The Narrative of Abraham (Bram) Stoker, as told to Charles Fort.
Little Russell Street, London, 1912.

I was born in Dublin in 1847, one of seven children. Though I was a very sickly child, I was nonetheless my mother's favorite. During those years I spent in my sickbed, my mother tended to me with great and loving care. Having fostered a lifelong fascination with stories of the macabre, she entertained me with countless Irish ghost stories—the worst kind there is, I should add. As a child I was lulled to sleep each night with tales of banshees, demons, ghouls, and horrific accounts of the cholera outbreak of 1832.

My mother was a remarkable woman—strong-minded, ambitious, proud, a writer—she hoped that I, too, might one day become a person of letters—a visitor to workhouses for wayward and indigent girls, and above all, she was a proponent of women's rights—much like her close friend, the mother of Oscar Wilde. I sincerely believe that, were it not for her kind ministrations on my behalf, I might have surrendered to the illnesses that plagued my early years. But she gave me strength and a sense of self-worth, and for that alone I shall always cherish her memory.

When I became of college age, I was accepted at Trinity on an athletic scholarship—you would not know it to look at this pathetic body now, but there was a time when I was a champion. I was a record breaker, in my day . . . and, I must admit, I gained a reputation among the members of my class for a somewhat exaggerated masculinity—some would even call it polemical. But I assure you that I was never less than chivalric toward the ladies with whom I kept company. I often wonder now if my way with the ladies back then is not the reason I am being punished in my final days with a wife so distant and frigid I might as well be wed to a corpse.

In 1871 I graduated with honours in science—Pure Mathematics, which enabled me to accept a civil service position at Dublin Castle. That same year I began to review theatrical positions in Dublin, and in 1876 I was privileged to review Sir Henry Irving's magnificent performance in *Hamlet*. Shortly thereafter, we became great friends—or so I thought.

The great actor is a strange beast, indeed, Mr. Fort, for his ego is such that it requires—nay, *demands*—constant feeding. Sir Henry was much like a child in that way. He took more of my friendship than he ever did return, but I was simply too awestruck by the man's genius to take notice of this.

I became his stage manager when he took over management of the Lyceum Theatre. That same year, I began to publish my writings—*The Duties of Clerks of Petty Sessions in Ireland*. It was released to unanimous indifference from critics and the public alike. Sir Henry urged me to explore more "universal" themes in my work, much as Shakespeare and Milton and Marlowe did in theirs. The man was simply hoping that his lapdog assistant would, perhaps, compose a play in which he might once again take center stage and be the focus of attention . . . but I digress.

I served Sir Henry well and loyally over the years. His opinion of my writing remained, as always, dismissive . . . until I wrote *Dracula*. On this, he at last expressed an opinion. "It is absolute, pandering rubbish," he said. Still, in "reward" for my many years of service and friendship to him, he agreed to allow me to stage a dramatic reading of the novel before its release from the publisher.

The novel was, as I'm sure you know, quite dense, and so several long, sleepless editing sessions were required in order to make the work an acceptable length for theatrical presentation. During this period in the latter part of 1896, I insisted on being able to rehearse with a cast so as to determine the success of my editing process. Sir Henry would not allow his personal company of actors to be "inconvenienced"—his word—with a "work in progress," and so left it up to me to assemble a cast of unknowns with whom to rehearse the piece. It took me several weeks, but at last I had my cast—with the exception of an acceptable actor to portray Abraham Van Helsing. But I shall come to that.

You need to understand that, during this period of intense concentration, the character of Count Dracula became even more alive to me than he was during the years of research it took to create him and write the novel. He was so alive to me, in fact, that I often found myself talking with him as I would stagger home nights after hours of emotionally draining rehearsal. "My dear Count," I would say, "have I lost all perspective where you are concerned?" I did this to relieve my anxiety: if the novel were not reduced to an acceptable three-hour theatrical entertainment, Sir Henry made it quite clear to me that he would not permit me to present the work to the public . . . not in his precious theatre. And so the Count became my constant companion, sir, my father-confessor, my only true friend.

I began to realize that the only way for the work to be made right was to necessarily make the cast believe in the Count as fiercely as did I. I spoke to them one night of my imaginary conversations with the Count, and though they were at first amused, they came to understand that my dedication to the project was unflappable. I have to say, they were far more accommodating to me than Sir Henry's personal players would ever be with him; being unknowns, there were no egos to soothe or feed. Until the last rehearsal, it was the purest, most enjoyable theatrical experience of my life.

Soon, all of the cast were holding conversations with the Count. I recall encountering the actress who portrayed Mina Murray one night during a break in the rehearsal: I found her off-stage left, sitting with her book, eyes closed, whispering, "Why does someone as remarkable as you, dear Count, have to be so very, very wicked?" It *moved* me, sir, to hear that—and not only from her, but from all of the cast members. Oh, the stories I could tell you of their conversations with the Count. They came to believe in his existence as much as I.

Remember: emotions resonate. They seethe, trapped, waiting for release, waiting to be given form.

The deadline for my final draft of the performance text was rapidly approaching, and still I had not found an actor who I felt would adequately convey the essence of Van Helsing. It may seem a somewhat selfish point, but the other actors had so refined their vocal interpretations of my characters, had given them such life, that to bring in an actor who would be less than their equal would have been an insult to them.

Then one evening, after having ended rehearsal early, I found myself in this area of Little Russell Street, and came upon this very bookshop. As I wandered among its many volumes, the proprietor took me aside and asked, "Are you Mr. Bram Stoker, author of *After Sunset?*"

"I am," I replied, seeing with some delight that he held a well-read copy of that very short story collection in his hands. "I am a great admirer of your stories," he said, offering the book to me, "and I would be honored if you would inscribe my copy."

I took the book from him with thanks, and proceeded to uncap the pen he offered, but somehow I managed to cut the tip of my thumb in the process. I bled a little upon the first page—not enough to ruin it, but enough that it could not be easily or neatly wiped away. "Please do not worry yourself," said the proprietor to me as I signed my name to the title. "It can be taken care of."

After I returned the volume to him, he took it behind the counter and knelt down behind a shelf of books. A few moments later he emerged and showed me—much to my surprise—that the blood had been successfully removed from the title paper. I noticed—but did not think much of—his licking his lips several times after rising from behind the counter. "I must say, Mr. Stoker, that I am greatly anticipating the release of your new novel."

"You may be one of the few persons in England who is," I replied, and we shared a jovial laugh at my remark.

Something about him seemed terribly familiar to me, and as I listened to his voice with its weary, sand-like quality, I came to realize that I was looking at my Van Helsing. I proceeded to tell the proprietor of my problem, and asked him if he would be willing to read the part of Van Helsing for my presentation to Sir Henry at the end of the week. He was deeply flattered, and of course accepted my offer.

When the time came for the rehearsal, I found him outside the theatre, nervously pacing by the performers' entrance. "My dear fellow, we are all waiting," I said. When he said nothing in reply, I opened the door wider and said, "Please, come in and join us." He did so, and the rehearsal began.

It was the most magnificent reading of the novel I have ever witnessed. He captured not only Van Helsing's weariness, but his near-mad drive to destroy Dracula, as well. His performance was a prism of compassion, fury, wariness, dedication, sadness, and strength. When it came time for his "This so sad hour" speech, he had all of us transfixed. He *was* Van Helsing.

Then, at the conclusion of the scene, he began to laugh.

It was the sound of an ancient crypt door being wrenched open.

The spell was immediately broken. "My dear fellow," I said to him. "May I inquire what you find so humorous about this very tragic scene?"

"That you see it as tragic at all is what amuses me," he replied, only this time his voice was not that of either Van Helsing or the sandy-voiced proprietor I had met at the bookshop the previous day: it was the voice of Count Dracula—not only as I had heard it in my imaginary conversations with him, but as the others in the cast had heard it, as well. I looked upon all their faces and knew that *this* was the voice of the Count as we had come to believe it would sound.

Speak of damned places, Mr. Fort, and you speak, on some level, of belief. Emotions resonate. Electrons dance. Equations collapse and are replaced by newer, equally possible equations. Call it the collective unconscious or the hive mind of the masses, but the emotional charge had built and surged down the cumulative lines of our psyche and found not only focus but *form*.

He changed before our shocked eyes; from man to bat to wolf to rodent to owl to insect, then back again, then a hybrid of all creatures, plus man—a sight so unspeakable I have never been able to bring myself to put its description onto paper for fear of being labeled mad.

Count Dracula rose up before us in all his dark, majestic, terrifying glory. "My thanks to all of you for our little talks at night," he said, smiling a lizard-grin and exposing his awful teeth. "I have searched for centuries for a proper form in which I could enter your world, and you have so thoughtfully provided one for me."

We began to run for the doors, but he became shadow and beast and speed itself: none of the cast made it any farther than the stage-left dressing room entrance before he fell upon them and opened their veins with his teeth. His strength was superhuman, his speed that of the wrath of God Himself—if indeed such a Being exists at all.

I huddled behind a stack of risers, listening to the terrified and soon-silenced screams of my cast as the Count fed on each and every one of them. After what seemed an eternity, he found my hiding place and lifted me up as easily as one would a newborn child.

Holding me by the throat, he glared at me with his glowing red eyes and said, "I wish to thank you personally, Mr. Stoker, for giving me life. But you have also made it necessary for the others who populated your novel to enter this world behind me, and so I must take my leave of you for now. Since I now know the ending of your story, I feel it is my duty to change it on this side . . . but you needn't worry about further revising your manuscript. I think it will be satisfactory to have the world believe that I am a fictitious creation who was summarily dispensed with at the conclusion of your little melodrama."

And with that, he released me, and disappeared into the night.

Shortly thereafter, the members of my cast rose to their feet, undead all, and made their way down into the basement of the theatre and, from there, into the sewers of the city. They are still there to this day.

And I sorrow for what I unleashed upon them and the world. Dear God, how I sorrow.

I sat in the darkness of the theatre in stunned silence for several minutes after Mr. Stoker finished telling his incredible tale. The man was obviously mad . . . but there still lingered in my mind a whispering doubt. And there was, after all, that unearthly wolf on the stage with him.

"How can I help your unbelief?" came a voice.

I had been staring at Mr. Stoker. His lips had not moved. I looked, then, at the wolf by his side.

It spoke again: "Your unbelief, Mr. Fort. How can I help it?"

The wolf moved forward, hunkered down as if to pounce, and at once became an army of rats that swarmed across the stage and into the orchestra pit and emerged in the aisle as the proprietor who had led me down here. "Does this help?" he asked of me.

I rose to my feet and began to frantically make my way over the seats toward what I believed to be the staircase I had descended earlier. My heart was pounding against my chest with such force I feared it would smash through my ribs and tissue.

The proprietor became several bats who quickly swooped down and around me, assaulting me with their wings. I fell to the floor and the bats collided in a flash of darkest shadow and became the proprietor again, only now he was much younger in appearance, taller, stronger.

Eternal.

"Look upon me and fear, Mr. Fort. For I am as real as you dread I am."

He reached down and grabbed onto my jacket with one hand, lifting me off the floor with unnerving ease so that my feet dangled above the aisle like some marionette left hanging on a peg.

I could not take my eyes from his blood-red gaze.

"My biographer, my creator, wishes for his cast to be given their proper curtain call, the one denied them so many years ago." He slammed me down into the nearest seat and held me there with one mighty hand on my shoulder.

"Nothing less than your most enthusiastic applause will ensure your safe exit from this place," snarled Count Dracula in my ear.

An iron grate in the floor near the foot of the stage

shifted with a nerve-wracking shriek and was cast aside by a hand that was more bone than flesh.

And the parade of the dead began.

How to describe what I saw? How to convey the pathetic, sad, depraved sight which my eyes beheld?

Their flesh—what remained of it—had the color and texture of spoiled meat. Worms and other such creatures of filth oozed in and out of the holes in their faces where once their eyes had resided. The stench of death was sickly sweet in the air. Some shambled, a few crawled, and one—a woman—had to be carried by another cast member because much of her lower torso was gone, leaving only dangling, tattered loops of decayed intestine which hung beneath her like a jellyfish's stingers.

I wept at the sight of them, but I applauded them; oh, how I applauded!

And I was not alone in my efforts.

Surrounding me, each of them as decayed and pathetic as the sad creatures who were assembling on the stage before us, were all the characters from Stoker's novel, all of them flesh and blood, all of them—thanks to the Count's actions—now equally un-dead: here was Mina Murray and Jonathan Harker; there was Dr. Seward and Lucy, Lord Godalming and Quincey, and every last character from the novel who had participated in Dracula's destruction, only now they were the destroyed ones . . . even the great Abraham Van Helsing. All un-dead and applauding those whose portrayals and belief had brought them into this world and given them life—albeit briefly.

I became aware of several women clothed in white encircling me as I continued to applaud and the cast to take their individual bows.

The brides of Dracula surrounded me, caressed me, touched me with their lips and hands. My temperature rose in depraved want for them, and I applauded all the harder for it.

"My cast," intoned Stoker from the stage, gesturing

to each member of his troupe. "My fine cast, my dear friends."

Dracula wiped something from one of his eyes. Looking at me, he smiled his awful, bloody grin and said, "I am moved, are you not the same?"

"I am," I said, quite dizzy.

The applause from the audience grew deafening. Dracula parted his arms and became a giant man-bat thing with slick flesh. He flew above stage and proceeded to land gracefully in the center of the players.

"Let my brides pleasure you, Mr. Fort," he bellowed above the noise in a voice part human and part beast, "and worry not, for they will not feed on you. You are our messenger now. Leave here, and tell the world, if you have the courage, that I am real, and that as long as men read my story, I shall never die. With the coming years and centuries, my story will be read by thousands, millions more, and each time the book is opened, each time a page is turned, I grow stronger and more eternal! Tell this to the world, sir, if you dare! For in the centuries to come my followers will grow, they will read of me, go forth, and multiply, and there will come a night when the entire earth will awaken and pull in the sweet damned breath of the un-dead, and then I will be as I should have been from the very beginning: the true Prince of Night, the king of my kind! Go, then, and tell them, if you dare."

One of his brides fell on her knees before me whilst another began to tear at my shirt.

The applause swelled as Dracula himself took a bow, and then I fell down into a dizzying pit of desire and darkness.

When I regained consciousness, I found myself outside the Lyceum Theatre, some good distance from where I was staying.

I cannot say for certain how I came to arrive safely

back at my rooms at Bedford Place, only that I did find my way back there and was at once taken by the arm and led to an office where I was given a stiff drink of whiskey while a constable was called to take my statement.

"Robbery and Assault" was the official explanation for my condition. I saw no reason to argue their conclusion.

The next day, no fewer than three bodies were discovered around London, the blood drained from their veins.

The next day, I discovered reports of several other deaths in Canada, the United States, and Germany.

I returned home soon after, and for the rest of my life continued to gather such stories of bloodless bodies.

I am now an old man and my time is short. It has taken me a lifetime to muster the courage to set this tale to paper. Whether or not you choose to believe this is a matter between you and your conscience. I can no longer say I neither believe nor disbelieve anything. Belief or unbelief, the dark forces of the Universe will have their way, regardless.

At my window last night I beheld the countenance of Mr. Bram Stoker, himself among the un-dead now; beside him was his creation, the Count, and in his eyes was a promise: *Soon.*

I fear I may not be alive come morning.

Not that I would have lived that much longer, anyway.

So I take my leave of you. Do with this narrative what you will. The night is nearly upon us.

An article in yesterday's *New Yorker* listed *Dracula* as one of the best-selling books of all time. To this date, it is estimated that somewhere around five million copies in twenty different languages have been sold.

So many readers. So many pages turned.

And he grows stronger with each word read.

There will come a night, he said.

I fear it may be sooner than we think.

I shall lay down my head for the last time now.

God go with you in all the damned places that you walk.

Soon, such places shall be all there are.

—Charles Fort, the Bronx, May 3, 1942

Renfield or, Dining at the Bughouse

BILL ZAGET

The Master comes, not on an ass, but riding the waves, sailing a schooner from Varna. Not dragging a cross, but hauling his native soil. The dark Transylvanian earth. This is the Master, in whose veins flows the blood of the ferocious and the lion-hearted, of Thor and Wodin, of Icelandic tribes with their Berserkers, the blood of the Szekelys, more potent than that of the ancient witches of Scythia, who mated with desert demons; the blood of Attila and the warlike fury of the Hun, who scorched the earth like living flame; He, who drove back the Magyar, the Lombard, the Bulgar, and the Turk; He the noble Voivode, Count Dracula, the Son of the Dragon, in The Land Beyond the Forest.

F-f-f-f-flap of wing . . . Breath of fire . . . Smouldering . . . The demon blood . . . Sea and foam . . . Sailing 'cross the Channel . . . Fifty boxes of earth . . . Sweet teeth . . . Berserker . . . Fallen out . . . Believe . . . Not one . . .
Whip the child
Whip the child

Whip the child!

Where . . . ?

A room . . . and a meal. Breakfast? Lunch? Dinner? The Last Supper? A feast on St. George's Eve, yes. And to do it justice: a bowl of *mamaliga,* then some *impletata,* washed down with Golden Mediasch, with its queer but cunning sting on the tongue. Or a flask of plummy slivowitz, fit for the Carpathian palate, yes. But not, not the Doctor's bland and lumpen excuse for nourishment. Where is the *maitre d'?!* Where is the *maitre . . . ?*

Master?
Master?

It's not, you know, is not whipped icing and shavings—the whip and the blade perhaps—but not all sorts of f-f-f-fruity toppings that appeals. I mean, I used to believe that chocolate was mankind's greatest invention. Right up there with fire and telephone. I no longer believe. It is a child's belief, and I am not one. Not one!

The simple joys have been replaced. Joy is not so simple, now that my sweet tooth has fallen out; and in its gummy place, I swear, a sharper one is growing. As is the craving for more exotic delights.

Ergo, I wait with longing, and in the meantime, dance and rave—extraordinaire—for the good Doctor Seward; but will not, will not touch his culinary offerings, for I have begun to find and forage for myself—as it must be.

They are everywhere, yet are often unseen. They can blot out the sky, yet can seem to disappear. They burrow beneath or hug the surface of the Earth or take wing, and away . . . ! From the Latin, *insectum,* meaning "cut into" they are small, as I have been and wish at times to be. They crawl, as I have done and have been made to do. And so many have wings and take flight, as I could not and cannot. Still, the consumption of lower orders, and this, I suppose, is dead centre; the eating of things, that some may prefer to mash with the nasty heel of a boot—what a waste! These creatures may be empty of thought, but are full of vital substance. The building blocks of Life. In some countries, it is believed we become in part what we ingest—imbued with the life of the fallen, and are stronger for it. P-P-power.

It's all a food chain, round and round. The bigger eats the smaller. And what goes around may come around, but the hunger blots out the thought. Thinking is a terrible thing. As terrible as feeling . . . anything. No, I must eat life, step by evolutionary step, in order to break the bonds and forge new links, that I may become *truly* big or truly anything, and blot out the sky or seem to disappear. . . .

They come to me. The Doctor cannot stop them. They have no bones, to make one choke—imagine that! You see, they carry theirs on their backs; an "exo-skeleton" it's called. It holds them together, this protective shell, not to mention giving them a certain crunchy *je ne sais quoi*. And they can move about in this jointed suit of armor, but they cannot grow. So it's shed at intervals in the process called "ecdysis." They molt and grow and molt and grow some more.

And so the Grand Experiment continues. First, with flies. They sniff my shit in the chamber pot and are drawn like, well . . . flies.

Phylum—Arthrapoda, Class—Insecta, Order—Diptera. . . .

The Tale of the Fly
First. It was the smell that first attracted it. The fly. And the stillness. The scent of a human female, of a male, and another, who was lying flat—no longer human, but very nearly so.

Decay is-z-z-z-z-z . . . dizzying, like rotting meat. Ahh . . .

The fly, the proverbial on-the-wall-type fly, took in the intimate scene with its feelers, sense hairs, and compound eyes, like huge bulging buds atop its head. Patches of light and shadow; a young boy, grub-human and curious, entered the room. The fly, also curious, flit and rode in on his head, smelled his shining hair, and licked the oils with its s-s-sucking mouth. The boy stopped and stared at the body, which lay on the bed.

"T-Timmy," the female clicked and hummed. Her oils had a similar taste. The taste of Mother.

The other male, not flat, but standing grim, the one the Mother called "Doc-tor," hissed at the boy, "Stay out of the room!"

The shaking air wafted waste. Flesh, losing freshness, the turning of oils, excited the fly-e-e-e-e-e. It lit upon the Almost-Man, who was not really asleep, but near death. He too tasted like the boy, in a subtle sort of way, this Father-Flesh.

"But Mummy, I, I . . ."

The Mother-Flesh shook her head and sighed. The Great Doctor-Human pointed, "Out!" The fly landed on his medicinal nail, then the wall, and finally the bedsheet, which quivered for a moment—a pale foot stuck out and gasped for air—and then was still. The fly settled on a stubby toe, set its proboscis down and lapped the stillness and the sweat, the darkness that was nestled there.

"Timmy!"

And the boy ran out. Oh, there'd be other times to savor his youthful juice. For now the No-Longer-Father-Flesh was a treat the fly could not resist. But living smells invaded the feast. The mosaic blur that was the Mother missed the fly, but barely, as it leapt and flew, attaching itself to the overhead light. It could sense the looks it was getting. The Doctor-look, stern and arrogant. The Mother-look, with heaving breath, trickling the ancient odor of superstition.

"I am but a fly," he buzzed. And then was still. "I"

was new. The death-sweat and the pain were new and surely belonged to the Dead. And yet he felt the Father no longer down below, but within his insect gizzard. It clung to his hairs and rimmed his eyes. Even his eyesight had somehow changed, although he wasn't exactly sure how.

Perhaps the Mother was to blame, with her woeful Mother-stare and the fear that souls can be stolen at the moment of death—all directed at this common fly and somehow made real. Or so the fly thought, with almost human craft.

Not even as a maggot had he felt such squirming novelty. The Father lay heavily on his wings, but he was able to make it out an open window. Soon his wondrous cargo no longer weighed him down. He felt so light and *of* light itself. Never had he flown so high. Could he fly to a place called Heaven? That was new too, this "Hea-ven," where he sensed could be found an Infinite Love and Infinite Wisdom and Infinite Sweetness, like the mixing of sugar and excrement, but sweeter still by far.

Open . . . gates . . . Heavy Father . . . Out! The gizzard . . . the flesh . . . Sucking . . . Dark . . . The Daddy-toe . . . Rotting meat . . . The chamber pot . . . Ecdysis . . . Decay . . . Ecdysis . . . Power . . . Dead centre . . . Chains . . .
Cut into
Cut into
Cut into
Out!

The Nasty Heel of a Boot.

I never even got to touch his toe. Little things can have power, too. The imploding heart . . . and he was gone. I was five and couldn't understand, and yet I knew that something had come crashing and would never fly again. My mother soon remarried; the tears had dried, I guess. And This Husband couldn't be, would never be . . . but now made real the striking of flesh and bone, rather than the birthing of flesh and blood.

Blood . . .

Fly Number 139. When I first began my Grand Experiment, I kept tally, of a sort, by notching the back of the door with a dinner knife after lights out. I now jot numbers down in a little book the Doctor has asked me to use. He insisted on a written entry, and not knowing what else to do, I laughed. He tried to confiscate my notching-tool and paid dearly for it. Oh, it was hardly a mortal wound. You're more likely to die from the food than a swipe from what was meant to cut into that crap. But he managed to bleed copiously—there on the floor. The taste was exquisite! He was appalled at the sight of me lapping on all fours the puddle of his deep red. To this day, I am limited in my cutlery to only using a spoon. Now, a spoon takes more effort, but makes a more artistic gouge.

But I have agreed to also make entries in his "little book." He thinks it gives a sense of order to my world. Certainly to his, but not to mine. Numbers, like order, are not real. Thus have I rendered them meaningless. Number 81 sits beside the number 4, 21 beneath 39, and on and on. Oh, he will ponder and search for meaning, and when he finally deciphers a pattern, he thinks I may yet be cured. But the only pattern, and what *is* real are my notches on the door over there. They don't signify any number, but an instance of pleasure in the consumption of life. I have configured a wondrous thing, a veritable work of Art . . . and Magic. With each mark The Master is drawn that much closer. And when the pattern is complete, He will be here for me. There is as much method in my madness as in the Doctor's. But Herr Doktor Seward, I look seaward for my salvation, ha! and I will never be *your* creature.

The cure is not in little books, but sailing here to Carfax. From out of His castle near the Borgo Pass, He comes where He is needed most. Soldier and alchemist, with a mighty brain, learning beyond compare, and a heart that knows no fear. I keep crude count, and oddly, but that Count Dracula may one night appear with that great lofty dome of His forehead, the aquiline nose, long sharp nails, extraordinary pallor, and vengeful red eyes that blaz-z-z-z-ze!

Order—Hymenoptera . . . yellow, black, and fuzzy . . . Apis . . . Apis. . . .

The Tale of the Bee

The usual riot of color—the redyellowbluegreen of it all—and the smell, the woozy, intoxicating scents that teased and drew and beckoned; and they were all still about, but strange. Dulled and blunted almost beyond recognition. And the sun—high in the bright blue air, or had been. Don't know where to go; but go. And the bee, knocked almost senseless to reach the world it had known, hit a barrier it couldn't really see. And it hurt. The hardness and the heat. Glass; the bee had known this thing before, but then there was always some eventual escape from its cool deception. Now the bee was surrounded by that memory, but with metal on top and punched with holes. Bits of blue air sneaked in— a healing breeze—and roused the bee from its stupor. Sort of. For now it seemed to be flying, and yet its wings were still. Focus was not a simple thing, but the bee soon realized a young human was carrying the jar in which it had been trapped. The boy pressed his own proboscis against the glass. A monstrous face.

Boys will be boys.

Through the holes in the lid he poked blades of grass and bits of clover. Lovely clover. Its tantalizing odor revived the bee even more—enough to see an older male approaching the boy. The man's body seemed to weave, although this could have been a distortion of the glass. And with a flashing thud, the jar flew out of the young boy's hand, landing in a soft clump of grass.

A few minutes passed before the bee could get its bearings. If the bee could've understood the human tongue, it would've heard the man, with slurring speech:

"Who're you laughing at, eh?" Slap! "Sneaking a peek at your Mum and me?! I'm on to you. You're no good." Slap! (Boys will be . . .) "Your Mum will give you away, and it'll serve you right. You're nothing and will always be. Fly-catching son-of-a-bitch!"

The Young One shakily challenged the Dominant Male. "I-It's a bee, and it's bee-eautiful."

Now, the bee could not follow this, and yet, and yet . . . Smack! And then the heady smell of blood. Beloved rose-deep-red trickling down the Monster-Boy's face.

"What do you know about beauty? Infant!"

And with the nasty toe of the boot, the Step-Father kicked the jar aloft. The glass-eyed planet panicked and flew by in flashes of light. The bee and all—shattered 'gainst a rock. On fire; and the bee was speared by a shard of glass.

Somehow . . . somehow, he found some humming spark and shook himself free. Bumbling and erratic, he weaved towards them through the air. He could no longer sense the sun's direction, and his aim was mostly gone. He didn't even know if he still had a stinger to do the job up proper. Blood-rose and clover bits would be the last to tempt his tender labium, but even that memory was thrown in shadow by the urge to inflict on another his pain and dying.

Boys will be boys, and bees will be; and with his last ounce he dove towards the moving smudges of light that were the Kick-Father and the Bleeding Son. Perhaps the bee would be able to pierce the Giant, the Killer of Beautiful Things and restore the world to its honeyed state. Nectar flows, and so does time. . . .

Slap! . . . The tender labium . . . Sucking sweet . . . Nothing . . . Nothing . . . Bee-eautiful . . . Boys will be . . . Poking . . . Blades of grass . . . Shards of glass . . . Distortion . . . Trickling laughter red . . . The heat . . . The hardness . . .
Smack!
The Killer
Senseless.
Surrounded by memory and the healing breezzzze . . .

The usual riot.

I started up. I stirred things up. I deserved what I got. And I was bad. I was eight years old! Whose truth is true?

He confused my mother with his charm—and harm; kept us in check, then left with all our goods. Worldly. The bigger eats the smaller in a chain that circles the Earth.

So with much fretful caring, my mother, poor and broken down, did send me away, after all. Whose truth . . . ? She could no longer provide. She could no longer find it within herself. She could no longer find herself. But, in time, I soon found *myself* in a home for waifs and wayward youths!

Home . . .

If only I could sleep through until He comes. The Doctor can give me chloral, the modern Morpheus, $C_2HCl_3OH_2O$. No! My Un-dead Master comes; I mustn't be . . . un-ready.

I will welcome and invite Him in. Beings of His ilk cannot come unless bidden at first to enter. And then nothing can stop Him from slipping through the crack beneath the door or through the bars on the window on moonlight rays. Elemental dust that settles into something long and dark with fiery eyes. Bright avenging beacon; He is my only hope.

He is of the night, yet He does not cast a shadow, as do-gooding humans do. Shadow will be dispelled. I want no shadows! Nor can He reflect himself in a looking glass. One sees only oneself.

Mirror and shadow; why are they such mysteries? Why do they hound us so? The blow from a fist or a flick of a switch renders them quite useless. A scientific explanation renders them merely tedious. A vampire abolishes. He cuts through invention and natural occurrence, straddles the dimensions, and toys with perception with a flick of a thorny nail. This is a *good* thing! He takes away control from "X" and gives to "Y" with a piercing kiss.

In the dark pitch of perfect blackness shadows do not exist, nor does reflection.

Why am I so weak? I need sustenance—with something more than just six legs. Hmmm . . .

*   *   *

Eight-legged, with claws and an attitude, Class—
Arachnida . . . Spinner of silken tales . . .

The Spider

Cool shadow and the damp pleased the spider. And
corners—perfect home for its woven artistry, and more.
There; the crumbling husks of a fly, and even a bee,
once so, but then paralyzed with poison, and now
sucked dry and bound up in steely strands of silk.

A quiet chattering drew attention. The spider knew
that sound. The chattering of adolescent teeth. The
young visitor yet again. His entrance was always sudden, loud, and violent. A dark silhouette with a rumbling voice would push the boy into the underworld of
the spider.

"And pray for forgiveness!"

The slam of a door. The momentary rising of dust.
A short bout of whimpering. And then the chatter.
And shivering. Bare white flesh—not much good for
hiding. And in the course of time that it took the spider
to drop along the thread of its dragline and cautiously
approach the naked form, back off, and climb up to a
ceiling beam, another silhouette had entered the basement storage room. He dropped a tin plate with a
clunk and nudged it towards the youth with his foot.

"Food for Fido." Or Spot or Rex. The boy seemed
to be called by a number of names. "No, you're a *flea*
on a dog named Fido." Mocking laughter, then he
was gone.

Now the spider had known the occasional flea. Not
bad, but not very filling. Just what sort of flea was this
pale chattering giant? Perhaps another dropping-down
was in order. But the slow creaking of the door and
the flickering flame of a candle held the spider back.
And a quiet voice:

"Timmy?"

The faithful flea-boy drew a breath. "Brother Tom?"

"Poor lad; what will we ever do with you?"

"I didn't mean to hurt anyone. It was only a scratch. Morgan called me names, and Brother Jim, he . . ."

"He took his side; I know. It pays to be popular, I suppose. You must be freezing." He briskly rubbed the boy's cold chest from behind.

Then silence. The spider stared at the flickering of the tallow shaft. Light had brought a play of shadows into its domain. This was all proving quite the spectacle.

The bearer of light and warmth enfolded the naked youth in his baggy robe. The boy tried to pull away, but claws—the spider envied such claws—pressed against the slim neck. The boy, he *tried* to pull away! A tongue darted into Timmy's startled eyes, licked the salty tears away. The spider was impressed. Then Brother Tom made the young boy's head seem to disappear in the woolen folds of his robe. No more chattering, but choking and gasping. Forceful arms and legs holding tight the struggle in. An elated shout . . . a muffled cry—quite the spectacle—ending in threatening tones:

"You mustn't tell. Ever. You were asking. I gave from the heart. The sin is yours. It could go very badly for you. I'd pray if I were you."

The spider dropped. The two already seemed half-paralyzed. Fear, and satiation. Tom held Tim in wrapping arms. It was as if they slept as the not-so-itsy-bitsy spewed out his thread from his spinneret. It was as if they dreamt him large. And so the silken threads became ropes of steel; cephalothorax and abdomen and legs with combs and claws now hugely spread. Inspired by their dreams, the spider sewed them shut. Wound airtight the eyes and nose and mouth. Too bad the boy had to be twined, but the spider couldn't tell where one ended and the other began. By midnight Brother Jim would find their mummified remains. And a dark and hungry god to feed, in the bowels of the home for waifs and wayward, wayward . . . !

Sewn shut . . . the naked shadows . . . prey for
forgiveness . . . the darting tongue . . . suck dry . . .
the crumbling . . . flea
Flee
Flee
Flee!

The perfect home.

It was a consummation neither devout nor to be
wished. Things got more complex after that, and not a
little absurd. He once told me to bite his tongue. I did
it once. He liked it. But not too hard. It was sorely
tempting to pierce straight through. But misbehavior
would lead to being dunked in a bath of icy water and
left naked in the basement, shivering for hours. Some
boys were tied up and hidden behind a screen for being
too marked up for show. Bed wetters, stripped half-
naked down below, had to face a wall and bang their
heads and feet against the brick 'til they were swollen
and dripping blood.

Blood.

It was not the slapping hands and fists that was the
worst, but creeping . . . creeping hands that slid like
slugs on a trail of slime. And places touched that
should not have been. The Brothers swarmed like a
plague of locusts. Gregarious, they spoiled with pennies
and sweets, before despoiling their youthful charges.
Us.

Things were done that should not have been! I cannot
describe the pain of, of . . . entry. Perhaps if there had

been love . . . But the bigger eats the smaller, and power
is the game. I had to bury my underclothes, soiled and
soaked with blood, in the playground after lights out.

And when, with time, I no longer felt the physical
pain of, of . . . I knew that I was truly lost.

I want back the blood I shed! The years that were
taken away from me. If it takes a thousand years, I
swear . . . !

When The Master, Count Dracula comes, He will
bring life everlasting. And then, how they all will
quake! Wild justice will tame all those lily hearts, hiding stamen that stab, that *have* stabbed. No more. God
is no shield. But a mask. Oh, let their souls try to
upward go; I care not. It's blood I crave and the flesh
and the deep dark earth. My Vampire-Lord doesn't
deal with souls; He spits them out. Like seed. They
sprout, rooted to *this* world, not the next. They will not
join Sweet Jesus, though they will try and reach. But
the heat of the sun turns cold and hollow. Winter cuts
them down to size. And We will laugh.

Ha.

The Doctor plagues me about souls. Perhaps *he*
should've been a man of the cloth. He wants me to
feel guilt for devouring all those little buggers. But I
have not eaten insect *souls*. Show me, Dr. Seward,
where? I want **none**. I have no use. It's Life I want.
And will have. **Perhaps** flies are poor things, after all.
And bees and spiders; well, blow them all! I'll move
up the evolutionary scale. Scale the heights. From birds
and rats and rats and more rats still, to cats and the
higher orders yet to come. Horse and ape, and especially that jewel in the crown of Creation—Man. The
ones that run the operations, pull the strings and make
the rules and make us pay, while breaking those
selfsame rules! Homo sapiens—God, how it rolls off

the tongue! And if there be angels, why, I'll pluck their wings and eat them, too. Lip-smacking good!

But each bite is a link in a chain, and I must start somewhere. Yes . . . The little bird in the bush in a garden; this is Renfield's tale: the story of a boy impossibly old beyond his years, who was hurt and needs to heal. A ward of the state, messed with and betrayed. He left the home at seventeen, but not for long. In and out and in again for years. Jobs that didn't last. He was given to inexplicable crying jags and sleepless nights and more than the occasional drink.

During one of his years in the Real World, the orphanage had made a deal with the government and was reclassified as house for the mentally disturbed. Thereby did their subsidy rise ninety pennies per youth per day. The boys were all still there, but now were "not all there." A small, wayward joke. They almost had *me* convinced. I am not mad. Somehow.

So Timmy came back to the fold. Hardly prodigal—just back. He was now old enough, you see; he was left alone. Not really an inmate—just "in." He tended their garden and swept their halls. Became the handy-man. He closed his eyes and ears. . . .

'Til one day, years later, a new boy entered the picture—not unlike Timmy, when *he* first came through those large oak doors. He befriended that new boy. Befrien-ded . . . Look, he needed something—guidance; I don't know. I told myself I was just protecting him from the others. Be his dark beacon and save him from the blinding light of, of Brotherhood. I'm not worthy. If I could've been a father to this child and thereby gained my own . . . But that purity just wasn't in me. Oh, I did not creep; I only wished to reassure. The healing touch. But I touched places I should not have been! He pulled back and so did I, but the moments between—it was a lifetime—mine and his. Where did one end and the other begin? Oh God . . . !

*   *   *

God . . .

I have called this my home for most of my life. I have been murdered by inches. My poor crushed brain knows things, but can't seem to, to . . . Nowhere to go; but go!

I too am lugging my native soil, sleeping deep while the sun has shone. Dreaming . . . Nosferatu . . . come. The vision has somehow turned. I don't want to be powerful. Just at peace.

Vlad, Vlad, Impaler Vlad. Can I dump the earth and sink the ship before he reaches port? I must not deceive myself; he has always been here. He is my father and my mother, the Brothers, and the pain. The Doctor of my youth and my Doctor's little book. All the bits of life consumed, the laughter and the tears. He's the whole bloody ball of wax, rolling from my day of birth to . . . St. George's Eve, when, it is said, all the buried treasures are at last revealed, even while all evil things hold sway.

At midnight, the Dragon and the Saint are one. Lance and claw, shield and wing, and scales . . . of justice wildly pitch. Where does one end . . . ? We cross ourselves and lose our way in the smoking breath and rising dust of hooves. We are teetering by the hissing gorge, and the rough and tumble fall from Grace may actually be a soaring up. But I seem to be suspended on a thread, neither here nor ever there. I'm squirming in a pupal state, pressing 'gainst the membrane, poking feelers out. Yes, cocoons *can* rip apart, as chains can break away. And doors, yes doors, can surely open!

I am a veritable work of Art. I am Magic.

That is, one day, I hope I can

believe . . .

About the Authors

Julie Barrett is the author of *Quantum Leap A–Z* and several short stories. She also writes ad copy and designs websites. Julie lives in Plano, Texas, with her husband and son. They all enjoy watching the cats chase a very focused beam of red light.

Nigel Bennett won the prestigious Gemini Award for his role as the vampire patriarch LaCroix on the series *Forever Knight*. British-born Bennett directs as well as writes and has appeared in many stage, television, and film productions, including *The Rocky Horror Picture Show, Hamlet, Psi Factor, Legends of the Fall, Murder at 1600,* and *Lexx.* His website is www.blackhat station.com.

Elaine Bergstrom is the author of several novels, including *Blood to Blood; The Dracula Story Continues, Mina,* and *The Door through Washington Square.* She lives in Milwaukee, Wisconsin.

K. B. Bogen has a head for technology, a knack for

humor, and a taste for the macabre. A native Texan, she holds a Bachelor of Science degree in Computer Science and Engineering from UT Arlington. Her favorite form of communication is humor; she prefers to make people laugh rather than cry, though she is not above causing the occasional shiver in her audience. Part-time party decorator, and full-time wife and mother, she plays domestic when she has to and reads forensic anthropology textbooks for fun.

Gary A. Braunbeck is the author of the acclaimed collection *Things Left Behind,* as well as the forthcoming collection *Escaping Purgatory* (in collaboration with Alan M. Clark) and the CD-Rom *Sorties, Cathexes, and Human Remains.* His first solo novel, *The Indifference of Heaven,* was recently released by Obsidian Books, as was his Dark Matter novel, *In Hollow Houses.* He lives in Columbus, Ohio, and has, to date, sold nearly 200 short stories. His fiction, to quote *Publisher's Weekly,* "stirs the mind as it chills the marrow."

Roxanne Longstreet Conrad is the author of several novels, including: *Stormriders, The Undead, Red Angel, Cold Kiss, Slow Burn* (as Roxanne Longstreet), *Copper Moon, Bridge of Shadows* (as Roxanne Conrad), and *Exile, Texas.* Her short story "Faith Like Wine" appeared in the anthology *Time of the Vampires.* She lives with her husband, award-winning artist Cat Conrad, in Arlington, Texas.

While a tech writer, Gene DeWeese produced everything from cleaning instructions for U.S. Air Force computer ball bearings to NASA space navigation texts. Since Robert Coulson recruited him to help out on a *Man from U.N.C.L.E.* novel thirty-odd years ago, he's also produced thirty-odd books, including *The Wanting Factor, Something Answered,* and *Adventures of a Two-Minute Werewolf.* Another book, on doll-making, explains how to make dried-apple shrunken heads. He lives in Milwaukee with his wife Beverly and two one-eyed cats, Toughie and Suzilla, and two "normal" ones, Octavia and Roscoe.

P. N. "Pat" Elrod has written over sixteen novels, including the ongoing *Vampire Files* series for Ace; the *I, Strahd* novels for TSR and Quincey Morris, Vampire Dracula adventure books for Baen. She has coedited two anthologies with Martin H. Greenberg and is working on more toothy titles in the mystery and fantasy genres, including a third Richard Dun novel with Nigel Bennett.

Amy Gruss, graduate of SMU (English/Creative Writing), is a prize-winning poet and a professional scriptwriter, who has been known to teach everything from Renaissance dance to water aerobics and Olympic-grade belching. Working with Tempest Productions as a writer, narrator, and production assistant for short documentary films, she fills the last three months of every year with song, as the musical director of the Omni Carolers. "Beast" is her first professional fiction publication.

Tanya Huff lives and writes in rural Ontario with her partner, four cats, and an unintentional chihuahua. After more than sixteen fantasies, she's written her first space opera, *Valor's Choice* (DAW). In her spare time she gardens and complains about the weather.

Award-winning author Nancy Kilpatrick has published fourteen novels, more than 125 short stories, and has edited seven anthologies. Her latest works include the collections *The Vampire Stories of Nancy Kilpatrick* (Mosaic Press) and *Cold Contact* (Dark Tales Publishing); the anthology *Graven Images* coedited with Thomas Roche (Ace Books); *Bloodlover,* the fourth novel in her popular vampire series "Power of the Blood" (Baskerville Books). Currently she is working on several pieces of short fiction, a new novel, and is about to begin editing another anthology.

Catt Kingsgrave-Ernstein lives in Denton, Texas, where, in the company of her husband, four cats, and a surly hedgehog, she has been writing and publishing fantasy, horror, and science fiction stories in small presses across the United States and Canada since 1989. Spliced into the cracks between performing in her Celtic band, Ravens, forays in community and street theater, and seven years of running a professional fantasy art studio, her writing career waited to fully blossom until 1996, and the release of *Time of the Vampires*. "Beast" is her first collaborative work in publication.

Jody Lynn Nye lists her main career activity as "spoiling cats." She lives northwest of Chicago with two of the above and her husband, author and packager Bill Fawcett. She has published twenty-five books, including five contemporary fantasies; four SF novels; four novels in collaboration with Anne McCaffrey, including *The Ship Who Won;* a humorous anthology about mothers, *Don't Forget Your Spacesuit, Dear!*; and over sixty short stories. Her latest books are *License Invoked* (Baen Books), co-written with Robert Asprin; and *Advanced Mythology* (Meisha Merlin Publishing), fourth in the Mythology 101 series.

Judith Proctor says, "My interest in writing grew out of an old British science fiction show—*Blake's 7*. My interest in theatre grew from my appreciation of the lead actor—Gareth Thomas. (My knowledge of Shakespeare has now progressed to the extent where my thirteen-year-old son can impress his English teacher by explaining bits of *A Midsummer Night's Dream* that she didn't know about.) Writing this story gave me a good excuse to read the Ellen Terry/George Bernard Shaw correspondence, which I'd been meaning to do for years. I also love folk music and play the concertina." She is also happily married with two children and lives in Dorset, England.

Fred Saberhagen is best known for his Berserker® series, about self-replicating robots that seek to end all organic life. The latest novel in the series is *Shiva in Steel*. He has also written in such diverse worlds as high fantasy, chronicled in his Swords series, and Gothic horror, in his novels about Dracula. His short fiction has been published in classic science fiction magazines, such as *If, Galaxy,* and *Amazing,* as well as *Omni, Analog, The Magazine of Fantasy and Science Fiction,* and *Isaac Asimov's Science Fiction Magazine.* He lives with his wife in Albuquerque, New Mexico.

Not long ago Brad Sinor ran into someone who he hadn't seen for several years. The friend asked if Brad was still writing. Brad's wife, Sue, said, "There's still a pulse. So he's still writing." His short fiction has appeared in the *Merovingen Nights* series, *Time of the Vampires, On Crusade: More Tales of the Knights Templar, Lord of the Fantastic, Horrors: 365 Scary Stories, Merlin,* and *Such a Pretty Face.*

Chelsea Quinn Yarbro is the author of more than sixty books, among which are the Saint Germain cycle of vampire novels.

Born in Detroit, raised in Montreal, and educated there and in London, Bill Zaget is also an actor (as Zag Dorison), playwright, director, and performance poet. "Renfield or, Dining at the Bughouse" is adapted from his one-man show of the same title, and is his first foray into short fiction. He presently resides in Toronto.

Copyrights